NEW WORLDS 10

is a collection of stories, illustrations, and criticisms from the world of science fiction. Talented newcomers and well-known established authors are published side by side in this exciting and fascinating forum for the s.f. media.

Edited by HILARY BAILEY

Also in the NEW WORLDS series
NEW WORLDS 9
and published by Corgi Books

New Worlds 10

Editor: Hilary Bailey

Art Editor: Richard Glyn Jones

Literary Editor: M. John Harrison

CORGI BOOKS

A DIVISION OF TRANSWORLD PUBLISHERS LTD

NEW WORLDS TEN
A CORGI BOOK 0 552 10182 6

First publication in Great Britain

PRINTING HISTORY
Corgi edition published 1976

This book is set in 10pt Intertype Times

Corgi Books are published by Transworld Publishers Ltd.,
Century House, 61–63 Uxbridge Road,
Ealing, London, W.5.
Made and printed in Great Britain by
Hunt Barnard Printing Ltd., Aylesbury, Bucks.

CONTENTS

New Worlds 10

CAWTHORN·75

CONSTANT FIRE

A Tale of the Dancers at the End of Time

by MICHAEL MOORCOCK

Kindle me to constant fire,
Lest the nail be but a nail!
Give me wings of great desire,
Lest I look within, and fail!

... Red of heat to white of heat,
Roll we to the Godhead's feet!
Beat, beat! white of heat,
Red of heat, beat, beat!

– George Meredith
The Song of Theodolinda

1

In Which Your Auditor Gives Credit To His Sources

THE INCIDENTS INVOLVING Mr Jherek Carnelian and Mrs Amelia Underwood, their adventures in Time, the machinations of, among others, the Lord of Canaria, are already familiar to those of us who follow avidly any fragment of gossip coming back from the End of Time. We know, too, why it is impossible to learn further details of how life progresses there since the inception of Lord Jagged's grand (and some think pointless) scheme, details of which were published in the three volumes jointly entitled 'The Dancers At The End Of Time'. Time travellers, of course, still visit the periods immediately preceding the inception of the scheme: They bring us back those scraps of scandal, speculation, probable fact and likely lies which form the bases for the admittedly fanciful reconstructions I choose to call my 'legends from the future' – stories which doubtless would cause much amusement if those I write about were ever to read them (happily there is no evidence that the tales will survive our present century, let alone the next couple of million years!).

If this particular tale seems more outrageous and less likely than any of the others, it is because I was gullible enough to believe the sketch of it I had from an acquaintance who does not normally journey so far into the future. A colleague of Miss Una Persson in the Guild of Temporal Adventurers, he does not wish me to reveal his name and this, happily, allows me to be rather more frank about him than would have been possible. His stories are always interesting but consistently highly-coloured; his exploits have been bizarre and his claims incredible: if he is to be believed he has been present at a good many of the best known key events in history, including the crucifixion of Christ, and has often played a major rôle. From his base in West London (20th century, Sectors 3 and 4) he has ranged what he terms the 'chronoflow', visiting periods of the past and future of this Earth as well as those of *other* Earths which, he would have us accept, co-exist with ours in a complex system of intersecting planes making up something called the 'multiverse'. Of all the temporal adventurers I have known, he is the most ready to describe his exploits to anyone who will listen. Presumably he is not subject to the Morphail Effect mainly because few but the simple-minded, and those whose logical faculties have been ruined by drink, drugs or other forms of dissipation, will take him seriously. His own explanation is that he is not affected by such details; he describes himself as 'a Chronic Outlaw' – and that self-view should give the reader some insight into his character. You might think he charmed me into believing the tale he told me of Miss Mavis Ming and Mr Emmanuel Bloom, and yet there is something about the essence of the story that inclined me to believe it for all that it is, in many ways, one of the most incredible I have yet to hear and cannot in any way be verified (certainly so far as the final chapters are concerned).

As usual, the basic events described are as I had them from my source. The 'fleshing out' of the narrative, the interpretations where they occur, many of the details of conversations, and so on, must be blamed entirely on your auditor.

In a previous story I have already recounted something of that peculiar relationship existing between Miss Ming and Doctor Volospion – the unbearable bore and that ostentatious misanthrope. Why Volospion continued to take perverse pleasure in the woman's miserable company, why she allowed him to insult her in the most profound of ways – she who spent the greater part of her days in avoiding any sort of pain – we cannot tell. Suffice to say that relationships of this sort exist in our own society and are equally puzzling. Perhaps he found confirmation of all his misanthropism in her; perhaps she preferred this intense, if unpleasant, attention to no attention at all. She confirmed his view of life, while he confirmed her very existence.

2

In Which Miss Ming Experiences A Familiar Discomfort

THE PECULIAR EFFECT of one sun rising just as another sets, causing shadows to waver, making objects appear to shift shape and position, went more or less entirely unobserved by the great crowd of people who stood, enjoying a party, in the foothills of a rather poorly finished range of mountains erected some little time ago by Werther de Goethe during one of his periodic phases of attempting to recreate the landscapes, faithful to the last detail, of Holman Hunt, an ancient painter he had discovered in one of the rotting cities. Werther had not been the first to make such an attempt, but he held to the creed that an artist should, so far as his powers allowed, put up everything exactly as he saw it in the painting. He volubly denied the criticisms of those who found such literal work bereft of what they regarded as true artistic inspiration. His theories of fidelity to art had enjoyed a short-lived vogue (for a time the Duke of Queens had been an earnest acolyte) but his fellows had soon tired of such narrow disciplines; Werther alone refused to renounce them.

One of the suns eventually vanished while the other rose

rapidly, reached zenith, and stopped. Only three of the guests had paused to observe the phenomenon. One of these was Miss Mavis Ming.

'Go on, Li Pao,' she prompted (she was extremely bored), 'you were saying something about Doctor Volospion.'

Li Pao was embarrassed. 'No, no – I spoke of no one specifically. I merely observed that only the weak hate weakness; only the wounded condemn the pain of others.' He wiped a stain of juice from his severe denim blouse and turned his back on the entertainment provided by Abu Thaleb, Commissar of Bengal, whose party this was.

Mavis did her best to concentrate on the conversation, but she had to admit she was a little piqued. Before the former chairman of the 27th century People's Republic had arrived and turned the subject to politics, she had been having a very interesting chat with Ron Ron Ron who was, like herself and Li Pao, an expatriot (from the 140th century, in his case).

Ron Ron Ron shrugged his squared-off shoulders; an expression of hauteur formed on his perfectly oval face. 'By the same argument, Li Pao, you would imply that a strong person who exercised that strength is, in fact, revealing a weakness in his character. Indirectly, therefore, you would condemn my efforts as leader of the Symmetrical Fundamentalist Movement when we tried to seize power from a decadent government during the Anarchist Beekeeper period. Certainly we were strong enough. If the planet had not, in the meantime, been utilised as a strike-base by some superior alien military force (whose name we never did learn), who killed virtually all opposition and enslaved the remaining third of the human race during the duration of its occupation – not much more than twenty years, admittedly – before they vanished again, either because our part of the galaxy was no longer of strategic importance or because their enemies had defeated them, who knows what we could not have achieved. As it was Earth was left in a state of semi-barbarism which had no need, I suppose, for the refinements either of Autonomous Hiveism or Symmetrical Fundamentalism, but given a chance I could have – still, I digress . . . As it was, because of my efforts to parley with the aliens, my motives were misinterpreted and I was forced to use the experimental time-craft and flee here. However, my point is this . . . '

Miss Ming murmured: 'Oh, you men and your politics. I . . . ' (But she had not been forceful enough. Ron Ron Ron's (or Ron's Ron's Ron's, as he would have preferred us to write) voice droned on. The only thing the two men had in common, really, was a past taste for political activity and a present tendency to criticise the shortcomings of their fellows here at the End of Time. She had been enjoying her own chinwag with Ron Ron Ron, too, and she suspected that he had relished it better than all this stuff about politics. But she knew what it was like with some people; it was as if a string was pulled in them and they couldn't stop themselves. A lot of people back home in the 21st century, in Iowa, had been like that.

She had been telling Ron Ron Ron about the house-plants she had kept in her apartment before her own foray into the future had trapped her here. He had been interested, she could see, because he had scarcely uttered a word while she had recounted the trouble she had had with a Swiss Cheese Plant whose leaves were not separating properly. Then Li Pao had butted in! People could be very rude sometimes. It was her own fault, she knew, for not being more aggressive, not being as rude as they were. She let people walk all over her. Still, she did her best to keep her end up. There came a pause in the monologue. She chipped in brightly:

'Say what you like about my ex, Donny Stevens – the heel – but was he *strong*! Betty – you know, that's the friend I told you about before – *more* than a friend, really . . . ' she winked, ' . . . she used to say that he was prouder of his pectorals than he was of his prick.' She laughed.

The two men looked at her in silence.

Li Pao sucked at his lower lip.

It now seemed up to her to keep the thing going. 'And that was saying a lot, where Donny was concerned,' she added.

'Really?' said Ron Ron Ron in a peculiar tone.

The silence remained. Dutifully she tried to fill it. She put a hand on Ron Ron Ron's tubular sleeve. 'I shouldn't tell you this, what with my convictions and everything – I was polarised in '65, became an all-woman woman, if you get me, after my divorce, but I miss that bastard of a bull sometimes. What this world needs, if you ask me, is a few more real men. You know? Real men. The girls round here have got more balls than the guys. One real man and, boy, you'd find my tastes changing just like that . . . ' She tried, unsuccessfully, to snap her fingers. 'Anyway, it's the same with Swiss Cheese plants – they're strong. Any conditions suit them and they'll strangle anything that gets in their way. They use the big ones to fell trees in Paraquay. But when it comes to getting the leaves to separate, well, all you can say is they're buggers to train. Like strong men, I suppose. In the end you have to take 'em or leave 'em as they come.' She laughed, waiting for their responding laughter, which did not materialise. 'I stayed with my house-plants, but I left that stud to play in his own stable. And how he'd been playing. Betty said if I tried to count the number of mares he'd serviced while I thought he was stuck late at the lab I'd need a computer! *Two* computers!' She had definitely injected a bit of wit into the conversation, but obviously neither had much of a sense of humour. Li Pao was staring at his feet. Ron Ron Ron had a silly fixed grin on his face and was just grunting at her. She soldiered on. 'Did I tell you about the Busy Lizzie that turned out to be Poison Ivy? We were out in the country one day, this was before my divorce – it must have been just after we got married – either '60 or '61 – no, it must have been '61 because it was spring – probably May . . . '

'Look!' Li Pao's voice was so loud that it startled her. 'There's Doctor Volospion signalling to you Miss Ming. Over there!'

She smiled indulgently. 'Oh, let him wait. Just because he's my host doesn't mean I have to be at his beck and call the whole time.' She was actually quite glad that Doctor Volospion had turned up, but it wouldn't do to let Li Pao and Ron Ron Ron think she was abandoning them because she found their company a bit dull.

'Please,' said Ron Ron Ron, taking a small, pink hand from a perfectly square pocket. 'You mustn't let us, Miss Ming, monopolise your time.'

'Oh, well . . . ' She was relieved. 'I'll see you later, perhaps. Byee.' She gave them a cute wink and waggled her fingers at them, but as she turned to seek out Doctor Volospion it seemed that he had disappeared. She set off in the general direction indicated by Li Pao, making her way between guests and wandering elephants who were here in more or less equal numbers.

The elephants, although the most numerous, were not the largest beasts providing the party's entertainment; its chief feature was the seven monstrous animals who sat on green-brown haunches and raised their heavy heads to heaven, singing in deep, melancholy voices. These were the pride of Abu Thaleb's collection, perfect reproductions of the singing gargantua of Justine IV, a planet long since vanished in the general dissipation of the galaxy. Abu Thaleb's enthusiasm for elephants and the elephantine was so great that he had changed his name to Commissar of Bengal solely because one of that legendary dignitary's other titles had been Lord of All Elephants. The gargantua were more in the nature of huge baboons, their heads resembling those of long-extinct Airedale terriers, and were so large that the guests standing close to them could not see them as a whole. As a result, so high were their shaggy heads above the party that the beautiful music of their voices was barely audible. Elsewhere the commissar's guests ate from trays carried on the packs of baby mammoths, or leaned against the leathery hides of hippopotomi who kneeled here and there about the grounds of Abu Thaleb's vast palace, itself fashioned in the shape of two marble elephants standing forehead to forehead, their trunks entwined.

Mavis felt a trifle desolate as she wandered through the cheerful crowd; almost everyone she knew seemed to turn aside just as she was about to greet them and Doctor Volospion was nowhere to be seen. She had begun to find the party rather tedious when Sweet Orb Mace, in flounces and folds of different shades of grey, presented himself before her, smiling and languid.

'What a supehb fwock, Miss Ming. So fwothy! So yellah!'

The short-skirted yellow dress, with its several petticoats, its baby-blue trimmings (to match her eyes, her best feature), was certainly the sexiest thing she had worn for a long while and she was not surprised by the compliment. She gave one of her little-girl giggles and pirouetted for him. 'I thought it was high time I felt feminine again. Do you like the bow?' The big blue bow in her honey-blonde hair was trimmed with yellow and matched the smaller bows on her yellow shoes.

'Wondahful!' pronounced the dandy. 'Without compahe!'

She felt much better all of a sudden. She blew him a kiss and fluttered her lashes. She knew that she had been cunning in wearing a full skirt to make her waist look a little slimmer. She was the first to admit that she wasn't the thinnest girl in the world, but she wasn't about to emphasise the fact! She warmed to Sweet Orb Mace, who could sometimes be such good company (whether as a man or a woman, for his moods varied from day to day), and took his arm. 'You do know how to flatter a girl,' she whispered. 'I suppose you, of all people, *should* know.'

Amiably, Sweet Orb Mace strolled in harness while Mavis told him about the polka-dot elephant she had had when she was seven. She had kept it for years until it had been run over by a truck, she said, when Donny Stevens had thrown it through the apartment window into the street, during one of their rows. But although Sweet Orb Mace nodded and murmured little exclamations, he scarcely seemed to have heard the anecdote. If he had a drawback as a companion, she thought, it was his vagueness; his attention wavered so.

'He accused *me* of being childish. He had the mental age of a dirty-minded eleven-year-old! But there you go. I got more love from that elephant than I ever got from him. It's always the people who try to be nice who come in for it, isn't it? He blamed me for everything. Little Mavis always gets the blame – ever since I *was* a kid. Everybody's whipping boy, that's Mavis. My father . . . If you don't stand up for yourself, someone'll step on you. The things I've done for people in the past. And have them turn round and say the cruellest things. That woman – Dafnish – *well* . . . Doctor Volospion said I'd been too easy-going with her. I looked after that kid as if it was my own. It makes you want to give up sometimes. But you've got to keep on trying, haven't you? Some of us are fated to suffer . . . '

Sweet Orb Mace paused beside the gently tapping toe of one of the gargantua. He stared gravely up, unable to see the head of the beast. 'Oh, cehtainly,' he agreed. 'Pwetty tune, don't you think?'

She lifted an ear, but shrugged. 'Too much like a dirge for my taste. I like something catchy.' She sighed. 'This is a very boring party.'

'This pwofusion of pachyderms! Bohwing? Oh, no. Still, evewyone knows how easily impwessed I am. But wheah is Awgonheaht's contwibution? He was wumouhed to be supplying the main feast.'

'I didn't know that.' Her boredom seemed to produce a slight stirring in the region of her pelvis. She looked speculatively at her posturing escort. 'I might go home if things don't perk up. You don't feel like coming with me, do you? I'm still staying at Doctor Volospion's.' She regretted her choice of phrase. She should try to sound more positive, she knew. She had started to get depressed even before Sweet Orb Mace produced his elegant excuse, something to do with having promised to meet O'Kala Incarnadine here.

' . . . and theah he is!' he carolled. 'If you will excuse me . . . '

'No sweat,' she murmured, watching Sweet Orb Mace rise a few feet into the air and drift toward O'Kala Incarnadine, who had come as a rhinoceros. The way she was beginning to feel, even O'Kala Incarnadine looked attractive. Luckily she had just caught sight of Doctor Volospion, who had first found her when she had arrived at the End of Time, had claimed her for his menagerie and now allowed her full run of his house, though she did not fit into his menagerie, which was religious in emphasis, consisting of nuns, prophets, gods, demons and so forth. He was hailing the Commissar of Bengal, whose howdah-shaped golden air car was drifting back to the ground (apparently he had been feeding his gigantic pets).

'Coo-ee,' cried Mavis as she approached, but he had not heard her. He was already in conversation with Abu Thaleb. 'Doctor!'

Now the sardonic, saturnine features turned towards her. The sleek black head moved in a kind of bow and the corners of the thin, red mouth lifted.

She was panting as she reached them. 'It's only little me!'

'Miss Ming! Scheherazade come amongst us again!' The deep-voiced dusky commissar was a frequent visitor at Doctor Volospion's. 'You enjoy the entertainment?'

'It's a great party if you like elephants,' she said. But the joke had misfired; he was frowning, so she added eagerly: 'I love elephants. When I was a little girl I used to go for rides at the zoo whenever I could. My daddy had to take me every birthday, not matter what . . . '

'I must join in the compliments,' said Doctor Volospion, casting a glinting eye from her toes to her bow. 'You outshine us all. We are mere flickering candles to your super-nova!'

As usual, though she dimly suspected him of satire, his

flattery made her feel almost euphoric, like a fondled cat. She would have purred if she could. She caught herself smiling, when she had meant to take his remarks coolly, with the dignity she always tried to show in his company. She tried to think of a witticism that would please him, but already he was talking to Abu Thaleb again, his thin arms hardly able to move the black and gold brocade of the heavy gown he wore. 'You bring us a world of gentle monsters, exquisite commissar. Gross of frame, mild in manner, delicate of spirit, your paradoxical pachyderms.'

'They are very practical beasts, Doctor Volospion.' Abu Thaleb spoke defensively, as if he, too, suspected irony. She thought it odd how often people responded in this way to Doctor Volospion's remarks which were almost always, on the surface at least, bland enough. He could make you feel really foolish sometimes. It was probably not his fault. He had an unfortunate tone; he seemed to mock everything. He was really quite shy, like herself, she was sure.

'Oh, indeed!' Doctor Volospion eyed a passing calf which had paused and was tentatively extending its trunk to accept a piece of fruit from the commissar's open palm. 'Servants of Man since the Beginning of Time. Worshipped as gods in many eras and climes. Ganesh . . . '

Abu Thaleb had lost his reservations. 'I have recreated examples of every known species – the English, the Bulgarian, the Chinese, and, of course, the Indian – but my favourites are the Swiss Alpine elephants – there! notice the oddly shaped hooves – the famous White Elephants of Sitting Bull, used in the Liberation of Chicago in the 50th century.'

'Are you absolutely certain of that, Commissar?' she asked. She had an idea she had heard a similar story in her own time, well before the 50th century. She was an historian, after all. 'You're not thinking of Carthage . . . ?' Then she became confused, afraid that she might have offended him. 'I'm sorry. You know what an ignoramus I am . . . '

'I am absolutely certain, my dear,' said Abu Thaleb kindly. 'I had most of it from an old tape which someone found for me in one of the cities. The translation might not have been perfect, but . . . '

Doctor Volospion broke in. 'What romantic times those must have been! Your own stories, Miss Ming, are redolent with the atmosphere of our glorious and vanished past!' He looked at Abu Thaleb as he spoke. Abu Thaleb seemed uncomfortable.

She laughed. 'Well, it wasn't all fun, you know.' The thing she liked about Doctor Volospion was the way he always let her talk. Say what you like about him, he was a gentleman. 'In a lot of ways it was hell, though I must say there were satisfactions I never realised I'd miss till now. Sex, for instance.'

'You mean sexual pleasure?' asked the Commissar of Bengal, drawing a banana from his quilted sleeve and beginning to unpeel it.

She was taken aback for a moment by this gesture. Then: 'I certainly do mean that! Nobody round here ever seems to be interested. I mean really interested. If that's what's meant by an ancient race, give me what you call the Dawn Ages – my time – any day of the week!' She was in danger of becoming intense, so she tried to lighten the effect by breaking into a musical laugh.

When her laugh had died away, Doctor Volospion fingered his left eyelid. 'Oh, that cannot be true, Miss Ming. My Lady Charlotina, O'Kala Incarnadine, Gaf the Horse in Tears, Mistress Christia and many others concern themselves with little else.' He made as if to search the party for those he mentioned. 'Jherek Carnelian . . .'

'They play at it. They're not really *motivated* by it. It's hard to explain. Anyway, I don't think any of those are my types, actually.'

Doctor Volospion was staring behind her, studying something as he continued. 'I seem to recall you were quite struck by My Lady Charlotina at one time. And then there was that other woman, recently. The time-traveller, whom I rather took to. *You* were in love, you said.'

'I'd rather you didn't mention . . . ' Was he deliberately cruel?

'Of course,' turning so that he looked across her other shoulder. 'A tragedy.'

She did not like to remember how badly she had been let down by Dafnish Armatuce and her son Snuffles. If Doctor Volospion hadn't consoled her then, she didn't know what she would have done, but she wished he wouldn't bring it up. She sometimes suspected him of enjoying her misery. People could be baffling. She wasn't perfect, she knew, but she did try her best to be tactful, to look on the bright side, to help others. Betty had told her that she gave too much of herself away. Betty had said that she ought to think more of her own interests. She wasn't selfish enough, that was what it was. People must think her a terrible fool – when they thought of her at all!

'Well,' she began with a sniff, craning to look back. She saw that Li Pao was nearby, bowing briefly to Doctor Volospion and making as if to pass on, for he was apparently in some haste, but Doctor Volospion smilingly called him over.

'I was complimenting our host on his collection,' he explained to the prim-lipped oriental.

'To be sure,' agreed Li Pao. 'It is pleasant to see the beasts working, if only for the delight of these drones.'

Doctor Volospion's smile broadened. 'Ah, Li Pao, as usual you refuse amusement! Still, that's your recreation, I suppose, or you would not attend so many parties.'

'I come, Doctor Volospion, on principle. Occasionally there is one who will listen to me for a few moments. My conscience drives me here. One day perhaps I'll begin to convince you of the value of moral struggle.'

'You do not need to convince me of its value, to the 27th century. But here we are at the End of Time. Our future is uncertain, to say the least. Will industry put a stop to the dissolution of the universe, Li Pao? I think not.'

'Then you fear the end?' said the Chinese.

'Fear? What is that?' Volospion affected a yawn.

'Oh, it's rare enough here, but I think you reveal a touch of it.'

'Fear!' Doctor Volospion's nostrils developed a contemptuous flare. 'A baseless observation. An accusation without . . . '

'I do not accuse, Doctor Volospion. Fear, where real danger threatens, is a sane enough response, a healthy one. It is insane to ignore the knife which strikes for the heart.'

'Then you must judge me insane, Li Pao.'

'No. You are afraid. Your denials display it, your posture pronounces it!' Li Pao spoke softly and his gaze was steady.

Doctor Volospion moved a shoulder. 'Such instincts have atrophied at the End of Time, Li Pao. You transfer your own feelings on to me, I think.'

Li Pao smiled. 'I am not deceived, Doctor Volospion. What are you? Time-traveller or space-traveller? You are no more born of this age than am I, or Miss Ming here. You say you do not fear, yet you hate well enough, that's plain. Your hatred of Lord Jagged, for instance. And you exhibit jealousies and vanities that are known, say to the Duke of Queens. It is why I know there is point in my talking to you. I praise these emotions, in their place –'

'Praise?' Doctor Volospion raised his hands, palms outward, to bring a pause. His voice was almost a whisper. It threatened. 'Strange flattery, indeed!'

Mavis thought Li Pao had gone too far. Why was he so bent on baiting Doctor Volospion?

'Really,' she said, with nothing in mind save to break the tension, 'I wonder what – Oh, look there. It's Argonheart Po, isn't it? Who said he was providing the food?'

Li Pao and Doctor Volospion both ignored her. Only Abu Thaleb recognised the reason for her efforts. He gave a little sympathetic shrug.

'Not flattery, but truth,' continued Li Pao relentlessly. 'There is hope for those who fear.'

'What? The end looms – the inevitable beckons. Death comes stalking over the horizon. Mortality returns to the Earth after an absence of millenia. And you speak of hope.' Doctor Volospion's laugh was harsh. 'This age is called the End of Time for good reason, Li Pao.'

'But if a few of us were to consider . . . '

'Forgive me, Li Pao, but you bore me. I have had my fill of bores today.'

'You boys should really stop squabbling like this.' Determinedly, Mavis adopted her matronly role. 'Silly, gloomy talk. You're making me feel quite depressed. What possible good can it do for anyone. Let's have a bit more cheerfulness, eh? Did I ever tell you about the time when I was about fourteen when we got caught in the church by the Reverend White . . . '

Doctor Volospion's temper was not improved. She had made another misjudgement, as she realised with horror when her host rounded on her.

'The role of diplomat, Miss Ming, does not greatly suit you.'

'Doctor Volospion – oh, dear . . . '

The exaggeration of his irony banished all wit; instead it gave his voice the menace of a lead-weighted cosh. She took a backward step, feeling a thrill of fright.

'How would you suggest we settle our dispute, Miss

Ming? With swords, like Lord Shark and the Duke of Queens? With pistols? Reverb-guns? Flame-lances?'

Her throat was dry. 'I didn't mean . . . '

'Well, my portly referee, speak up!' His long chin pointed at her throat. Her stomach churned. She knew that she was blushing with humiliation; she dare not look at the other faces. Tears threatened to pour. 'I was only trying to help. You were so angry, both of you . . . '

'Angry? You are witless, madam. Could you not see that we jested?'

There was no evidence. Li Pao's lips were pursed, his cheeks were pale. Doctor Volospion's eyes were hard and fiery. A terrible fascination fixed her in position now – her urge to flee was balanced by her compulsion to stay, to fan these flames, to produce a holocaust that would consume her, and she found her voice crying: 'Not a very funny joke, I must say, calling someone fat and stupid. Make up your mind, Doctor Volospion. Only a minute or two ago you said how nice I looked. Don't pick on little Mavis, just because you're losing your argument!' She cast about for allies, but all eyes were averted, save Volospion's, and those pierced.

'I should be more than grateful, Miss Ming, if you would be silent. For once in your life, you might reflect on your own singular lack of sensitivity, of your inability to interpret the slightest nuance of social intercourse save in your own crude terms. A psychic cripple, Miss Ming, has no business swimming in the fast-running rivers of philosophical discussion.'

She experienced only his tone, his vicious stance. 'You *are* in a bad mood today . . . ' she began, and then words gave way to her strangled, half-checked sobs.

'Come now, Volospion,' murmured Li Pao.

Abu Thaleb spoke conversationally, leaning forward to stare at her face, his huge, feathered turban nodding. 'Are those tears? I had heard of elephants weeping – or was it giraffes – but never thought I would have the chance to witness . . . '

His tone, in turn, produced a partial recovery. She rounded on him. 'Oh, be quiet. You and your stupid elephants.'

'So this is politeness, is it?' continued Volospion coolly.

'I fear we have yet to grasp the essence of your social customs, madam.'

She trembled. She knew remorse. 'Oh, I'm sorry, commissar. I'm so sorry. I'm sorry, Doctor Volospion. I didn't mean to . . . I was only trying to help . . . Why does it always have to be me . . . ?'

Doctor Volospion had placed a hand on her arm. 'Perhaps I had best escort you home.' He was magnanimous. She wanted to be comforted, to be embraced, but the proximinity of his thin body reminded her of the only words she had understood. He was right. She was fat; she was unattractive. She pulled away from him.

'I'm fine now. I just didn't want to see anyone quarrelling.' She sniffed. 'I'll go . . . '

His hand still steadied her, but he was looking beyond her. 'Ah, look! Here's your friend, the cook.'

She glanced round. It was Argonheart Po, in smock and cap of dark brown and scarlet, so corpulent as to make her feel immediately thinner. She smiled as he advanced with monumental dignity, to greet them with a brief bow and to address Abu Thaleb.

'I have come to apologise, epicurean commissar, for the lateness of my contribution. There is an integral fault in my recipe, I regret, which I am loathe to disguise by any artifice . . . '

The Commissar of Bengal waved a white-gloved hand. 'You are too modest, Master of Chefs – too much a perfectionist. I am certain that nobody would notice . . . '

Argonheart Po acknowledged the compliment with a smile. 'But *I* would know. The cry of the artist, I fear, down the ages. I hope that things will right themselves before long. If not, I shall bring you those confections which have been successful, and will abandon the rest. I came in the hope of gaining an opinion. Someone who will return with me and sample my creations, not so much for their flavour as for their consistency . . .'

'Miss Ming!' said Doctor Volospion. 'Here is your chance to be of service.'

'Well . . . ' she began. 'As everyone knows, I'm no gourmet . . . '

'You do not have to be,' Argonheart told her. 'You will do excellently, Miss Ming. If you can spare a little time.'

Her spirits were recovering rapidly, although she remained

wary of Doctor Volospion. She stepped forward and linked her arm in Argonheart Po's. 'Delighted.'

They made their adieux. She congratulated herself that the air had been nicely cleared and that she could now escape with honour, allowing everyone's tempers to settle before she rejoined the party.

3

In Which Mr Emmanuel Bloom Returns To Claim His Kingdom

ARGONHEART PO DIPPED his fingers into his rainbow plesiosaurus (sixty distinct flavours of gelatine) and withdrew it as the beast turned its long neck round to investigate, mildly, the source of the irritation. The master chef put hand to mouth, sucked and sighed. 'Excellent taste. What a shame . . . ' His creature, lumbering on massive legs that were still somewhat wobbly, having failed to set at the same time as the rest of its bulk, moved to rejoin the herd grazing some distance away on the especially prepared trees of pastry and angelica he had designed to occupy them until it was time to drive them to the party which was only a mile or two off (the gargantua were plainly visible on the horizon). 'You agree, then, Miss Ming? The legs lack coherence.' He licked disappointed lips.

'Isn't there something you could add?' she suggested. 'Those legs were meant for the sea, you know . . . '

'Oh, indeed. A twist of a power ring and all would be well, but I should continue to be haunted by the mystery. Was the temperature wrong, for instance? Or does the weight of the beast alter the atomic structure of the gelatine? There is no time to begin again. I must cull the herd of the failures and present only a partial spectacle.'

'Abu Thaleb will still be pleased, I'm sure.'

'I hope so.' He voiced a huge and sultry sight.

'It's nice to be out of the hurly burly for a bit,' she told him, her mind moving on to other topics. She smiled at him. 'Out here alone with a real man, with someone who *does* something. I've always wanted . . . ' She hesitated as he jumped, his hands flailing, to taste a passing pteradactyl. He missed it by several inches, staggered and fell to one knee.

'Cunning beasts, those,' he said as he picked himself up. 'My fault. I should have made them easier to catch. Too much sherry and not enough blancmange.'

'My husband, Donny Stevens, was a real man, for all his faults,' she said, advancing. 'I never thought I'd miss the bastard. You remind me of him a little.'

Argonheart Po's only weakness was for metaphysical speculation. Miss Ming had captured his attention. Turning from his investigation of the half-melted remains of a completely unsuccessful stegosaurus, he said with interest: 'You believe everyone else imaginary, then? But why should I be real when the others are not? Why should *you* be real. Reality, after all, can be the syllabub that melts upon the tongue, leaving not even a flavour of memory . . .'

'I meant that Donny was a manly man. Stupid and vain, of course. But that's probably all part of it. I like you Argonheart. Have you ever thought . . . ?'

But the chef's attention was wavering again as he bent to scoop up a little iguanadon and hold it out for her inspection. With a frustrated sigh, she licked the beast's quivering neck. 'Too much lime for my taste.' She gave a theatrical shudder and laughed. 'Far too bitter, Argonheart, dear.'

'But the texture . . . ?' The iguanadon struggled, squawking rather like a chicken, and was released. It ran, glistening, semi-transparent, green and orange, in a crazy path towards the nearby cola lake.

'Perfect,' she said. 'Firm and juicy.'

'The smaller ones are by far the most successful, but that will scarcely satisfy Abu Thaleb. I meant the monsters for him. The little beasts were only to set them off. I've tried to produce too much and too many. I can see that now.' His fat brow wrinkled.

'You haven't been listening, Argonheart dear,' she said.

Reluctantly he withdrew from his contemplations. 'You were discussing men.'

She patted at the yellow flounces of her frock. 'Or their absence?' She giggled. 'I could do with one . . . '

He had picked up a ladle in his plump, gloved hand. She followed him as he approached his lake, bent on a final taste. 'Couldn't you make something – someone, I mean – to suit you? Doctor Volospion would help.'

She felt a moment's pain. 'There's no need, dear, to throw that particular episode in my face.'

'Um.' He stooped, dipped his ladle, drew it to his red lips, sampled self-critically and shook his head. 'The conception was too grandiose. Given another day it could put everything to rights, but poor Abu Thaleb expects . . . Ah, well.'

'Forget about all that for a moment.' Lust was mounting in her. She slipped a hand along his massive thigh. 'Make love to me, Argonheart. I've been so unhappy.'

He rubbed his round chins. 'Oh.'

'You can spare a few minutes, surely.'

'Well, I certainly cannot improve anything. Perhaps . . . Yes.'

She pulled him towards a pile of discarded dark brown straw. 'Here's a good place.' She sank into it, tugging at his hand.

'What?' he murmured. 'In the vermicelli?'

It was already beginning to stick to her, but she no longer cared. 'Why not? Why not? Oh, Argonheart!'

It was at the point where she had helped him to drag the tight scarlet smock up to his navel whilst wriggling her own blue lace knickers to just below her knees that they heard a shriek that filled the sky and saw the crimson spaceship falling through the dark blue heavens in an aura of multi-coloured flame.

'Golly!' said Mavis.

Argonheart was already rolling over in the vermicelli, pulling his smock back into position. He stood up. Shreds of half-melted confectionery dropped from his legs.

'Oh, fuck!' she said, the heat in her groin already dissipating. She drew up her underwear. 'What a moment to pick!'

It was a spaceship from some mythical antiquity, all fins and flutes and glittering bubbles, tapering at the nose, bulbous at the base, where its rockets roared. It slowed as they watched, falling with a peculiar swaying motion, as if its engines malfunctioned, the vents first on one side and then on the other sputtering, gouting, sputtering again until, just before the ship reached the ground, the rockets flared in unison, bouncing the machine like a ball on a water jet, gradually subsiding until it had settled to earth. Flame still roiled around the hull, sensuous: it caressed the scarlet metal. The surrounding terrain sent up heavy black smoke, crackling as if to protest; the smoke curled close to the ground, moving towards the ship: eels attracted to wreckage.

She was in no temper to admire the machine; a little love-making would have improved her spirits no end and taken away the nasty taste of Doctor Volospion's outburst. It wasn't, she thought, as if she got the chance every day, and she would have liked to have known if a man, even Argonheart, could still satisfy her. She pouted, brushing at the nasty sticky stuff clinging to her petticoats, too furious to speak.

Argonheart helped her from the pile and, perhaps moved by unconscious chivalry, pecked her upon the cheek. The smell of burning filled the air. 'I've never found that odour attractive,' he said.

The heat from the ship was heavy on her skin. Argonheart made to move away but then gave a cry of horror. 'Look what it has done! Oh, it's too bad!'

She looked. She saw nothing. 'What?'

'It has melted half my dinosaurs. That is what made the smoke!'

Argonheart began to roll rapidly in the direction of the ship, Mavis forgotten. 'Hey!' she cried. 'What if there's danger?' There was nothing for it but to follow him.

'Murderer!' Argonheart was crying. 'Philistine!' He shook his fist at the ship then fell to his knees in the glutinous mess. 'Oh my monsters! My jellies!'

She had been abandoned while he mourned his ruined creations. Her attention focused upon the ship, curiosity conquering caution. She had seen alien spacecraft before, but this, though old-fashioned, had a distinctly human look to it. Now she studied it closely, she thought, it had quite a romantic appearance. It was the sort of ship that her fictional girlhood heroes had possessed. Perhaps at long last her prayers were to be answered and her handsome space-knight had arrived to carry her off to the planet of Paradise V. But there again, she thought, the ship could as easily carry a villain, some pirate captain and his cut-throat crew. Her two favourite ancient authors had been J. R. R. Tolkein and A. A. Milne and now, as she anticipated the occupants of the ship, he was torn between poles represented in her fantasies by the evil, fascinating Souron and Winnie the Pooh. Would the visitors be fierce, she wondered, or cuddly? Better still, they might be fierce *and* cuddly.

She retrieved herself from sentiment (it was not always socially acceptable, she had learned) by a return to her alternative vein of cynicism. 'Well,' she said aloud, 'at least it might be someone to relieve the awful boredom of this bloody planet.'

Her baffled and grieving escort turned, bowed from the blackened fragments of his culinary dreams to stare wistfully after his surviving stegosauri and tyranadons which, startled by the ship, were in rapid and uncertain flight in all directions. His little shrug went virtually unnoticed by her.

'It is fate,' said Argonheart Po. 'At least I am no longer in a dilemma. The decision had been taken for me.'

There came a grinding noise from the ship. A circular section in the hull was turning. The airlock was opening. It swung back and, for a second, flames seemed to pour from within the ship so that Mavis wondered if the occupants were to be human after all. From the darkness revealed tiny flashes of light continued to appear, reminiscent of fireflies.

An engine murmured and a ramp began to slide from the airlock to the ground while now she could hear a muffled, querulous voicing speaking a language that was faintly familiar to her and might well have been her own original tongue, before she had taken a translation pill to make the language of this world intelligible. She brightened. The only thing she didn't like was the high-pitched note of the voice. It tended to trill, like birdsong, and although not unpleasant was not what she would have called manly. Still, the pitch could always be affected by a change in the atmosphere.

Her hopes, however, had been completely without foundation. At last the traveller emerged. He, too, was somewhat birdlike. There was a wild crest of bright auburn hair, a sharp nose, vivid, almost bulging blue eyes, a head which craned forward on an elongated neck; a tiny body that moved in rapid, poorly-co-ordinated jerks and twitches, arms held stiffly at the sides like wings. After peering curiously this way and that, the eyes fixed on Mavis and Argonheart Po. He blinked imperiously at them and trilled a few words.

'You have ruined the Commissar of Bengal's dinner, sir,' said Argonheart Po. 'You have reduced a carefully planned feast to a rabble of side-dishes.'

'Fallerunnerstanja,' said the visitor from space. He had been in shirtsleeves. Now, as he spoke, he donned a black frock coat from a period a couple of hundred years before Mavis Ming's own. The coat, she noted, was not even very clean.

Argonheart recalled his usual good manners and said with some effort: 'Welcome to the End of Time.'

The space-traveller frowned and consulted an instrument he held in his right hand. He tapped it, shook it, held it to his ear.

'Well,' said Mavis with a sniff, 'he isn't much, is he?'

As if in response to her criticism the creature waved both his arms in a sort of windmilling motion and, with movements reminiscent of a marionette, retreated back into his ship.

'Did we frighten him, do you think?' asked Argonheart Po.

'Quite likely. What a weedy little creep.'

'Humanoid, though,' said Argonheart. 'It makes a change from all those others.'

'Not much of one?'

A familiar voice sounded from above. They looked up.

'Aha!' said Abu Thaleb. His face, with its beard carefully curled and divided into two parts, set with pearls and rubies, after the original, peered over the edge of his howdah. 'I thought so. See, Volospion, I was right.'

Mavis's heart sank when she realised Doctor Volospion was also in the air car. She had hoped not to see him for a while, until they both felt better, but she managed to smile.

'Yes, indeed,' came Volospion's voice. 'A spaceship.' The howdah landed. Within it was lined with dark green and blue plush. Doctor Volospion lay amongst cushions, still in black and gold, making no attempt to move. He scarcely acknowledged Miss Ming's presence as he said to Argonheart: 'Forgive the intrusion, great Prince of Pies, but the Commissar of Bengal is bent on satisfying his curiosity.'

'That ship,' said Argonheart almost sullenly, 'destroyed most of the dinner I had prepared for you, Abu Thaleb.'

The commissar climbed from the howdah to clap the chef upon the back. 'Another time, dear Argonheart, I hope. What a lovely little ship, though. I had yearnings to embellish my menagerie, but I do not think . . .'

Doctor Volospion called from his cushions: 'Your menagerie is already a marvel, Belle of Bengal. The most refined collection in the world. Splendid, specialised, so much more sophisticated than the scrambled shelter of species scraped together by certain so-called connoisseurs whose zoos surpass yours only in size but never in superiority of sensitive selection.'

Mavis was confused. Doctor Volospion seemed to be speaking for her amusement. He winked at her. Perhaps it was to show that he had completely forgiven her the outburst. In turn she, of course, forgave him anything nasty he might have said. She grinned. He was having a joke, she realised, at old Abu Thaleb's expense. She loved it when he let her in on jokes like this. She could hardly keep from giggling. He continued:

'In taste, salutory Commissar, you are assured of supremacy, until our planet passes at last into the limbo of silence and non-existence which must soon, we are told, be its fate.'

She held her breath, glad the Abu Thaleb's back was to her. She knew he would laugh aloud if he turned at that moment.

'Oh, really, Volospion,' said the commissar good-naturedly, 'you are capable of subtler mockery than this!'

Mavis wondered what he would do, now that Abu Thaleb realised the truth, but Doctor Volospion was not diverted.

'You have seen the visitors, Miss Ming?'

'Briefly,' she said. 'Actually, there's only one.'

'Is he in any way – um – elephantoid?'

She allowed herself to giggle now. 'Not a trace of a trunk, I'm afraid. Not even a touch of a tusk. He couldn't be less like a jumbo, although his nose is a bit long, I suppose. He's more like one of those little birds, Abu Thaleb, who pick stuff out of elephant's teeth.'

Abu Thaleb turned and regarded her with mysterious gravity. 'Teeth?'

She giggled again. 'Don't they have teeth, then?'

Argonheart Po seemed much embarrassed. His glance at Doctor Volospion was almost disapproving. 'I'll wish you all farewell,' he said. 'There is nothing I can save. Not now.'

'Are we to be denied even a state of your palatable treasure, Argonheart?' asked Doctor Volospion in much the same voice he had used to speak of Abu Thaleb.

Argonheart Po shook his head. 'I think so.'

'Ah, mighty Lord of the Larder, how haughty you can sometimes be!' Just a morsel of mastodon ...'

'I made no mastodons.' The chief was striding away.

'Obsessives can be very boorish sometimes,' said Doctor Volospion. 'How were his dishes, by the by, Miss Ming? You tasted them, eh?'

She found herself adopting something of a worldly air for his approval. She gave a light, amused laugh. 'Oh, a bit over-flavoured, really.'

His thin tongue ran the line of his lips. 'Too strong, the taste?'

'He's not as good as they say he is, if you ask me. All this flash stuff.'

'But Argonheart is the greatest culinary genius in the history of the world!' Abu Thaleb was offended. 'And so good-hearted. The time he must have spent preparing the feast for today! His presents are famous. Not long since he made me a savoury mammoth that was the most delicious thing I have ever eaten. An arrangement of flavours defeating description, and yet possessing a unity of taste that was inevitable!'

'Perhaps you confused the subject matter with the art, admirable Abu,' slyly suggested Volospion.

Mavis was not to be outdone. Secure in the approval of her host, inspired by his wit, she put in: 'One man's elephant steak, after all, is another man's bicarbonate of soda!'

Abu Thaleb stared at her in frank bewilderment. Doctor Volospion had understood, however. His smile was secretive, and more for himself than for her.

'Well,' said the Commissar of Bengal weakly, 'I for one am always astonished by his invention.'

'Well, he can be very clever.' She relented, conscious once more of that tense sort of silence that sometimes followed her funniest observations (she could be too subtle and obscure, she was the first to admit). 'He's very nice. He's always made me feel very much at home . . .'

'My dear Miss Ming, you are being too kind again!' Doctor Volospion raised a long hand, the fingers curled forward so that it almost resembled a claw. 'Do not let this clever commissar confuse you into compromising your opinions. Be true to your own convictions. If you find Argonheart's work unsatisfactory, not up to the demands of your palate, then say so.'

'Volospion, you mock us both too much,' protested Abu Thaleb. 'Leave Miss Ming alone, at least.'

'I?' said Doctor Volospion, in apparent astonishment. 'Mock? You do me too much credit, my friend!'

Mavis laughed amiably. 'You never know if he's joking or serious, do you, commissar?'

'Well, Miss Ming, if you are not discomforted,' began Abu Thaleb, and then he was interrupted by Volospion, who pointed at the ship.

'Aha – our guest emerges!'

The tiny red-headed stiff-armed puppet stood once more at the top of the ramp. He had changes his clothes. He had on a suit of crumpled black velvet, a shirt whose stiff, high collar rose as if to support his chin, whose cuffs covered his clenched hands to the knuckles; and tiny, shining pumps on his feet. An altogether ridiculous figure, she thought, and might have whispered as much to Doctor Volospion had it not been for the compelling authority in his bulging blue eyes.

'Not from space at all,' complained the commissar. 'He's a time-traveller. His clothes . . . '

'Oh, no. We saw him . . . '

She would have continued had not the newcomer struck a pose, arms stiffly extended, little mouth smiling, and begun to speak in fluting tones that were completely comprehensible to them all.

'Greetings, representatives of the people of Earth. The Hero of your greatest legends, returns to you! You have yearned for me. Doubtless you have prayed for me. Well, I am here at long last!'

Abu Thaleb cleared his throat. 'I fear you have the advantage, sir . . . '

'We missed the name,' added Doctor Volospion.

'You do not recognise me?'

'Not instantly . . . '

The visitor looked down at his own body. 'Ah, well, it's possible. I have changed my physical appearance so many times I have forgotten how I looked then. The body has probably diminished quite a lot. Once, as I recall, I was as fat as your friend – the one who was here when I first emerged – and tall, I think, too. But I leant toward economy, and altered, irreversibly, my physique. This form was modelled after a hero of my own whose name and achievements I forget.'

'Your name, sir?' Abu Thaleb reminded the traveller.

'I am the Phoenix! I am the Sun's Eagle, the Sun's Revenge. I am the claws, come to take back the heart you stole from the centre of that great furnace that is my Lord and my Slave. Magus, clown and prophet, I – Master of the World! Witness!' Flames shot from his finger-tips. Flames danced in his hair. 'Clownly, kingly, priestly eater and disgorger of fire! Ha!' He laughed and gestured and balls of flame surrounded him. 'I have no ambiguities, no ambitions – I *am* all things! Man and woman, god and beast, child and ancient – all are compatible and all co-exist in me. I am Mankind. I am the Multiverse! I am Life and Death and Limbo, too. I am Peace, Strife and Equilibrium. I am Damnation and Salvation. I am all that exists – and I am *you*!'

He threw back his little head and began to laugh while the three people stared at him in silent astonishment. He walked part way down the ramp and now he sang:

> 'For I am God – and Satan, too!
> Phoenix, Faust and Fool!
> My Madness is Divine, and Cool my Sense:
> I am your Doom, your Providence!'

'We are still, I think, at a loss . . . ' murmured Doctor Volospion. But the man's eyes had fixed, as if for the first time, on Mavis. She thought the stare fishy. She did not welcome it.

'Ah, what a splendid woman.' He moved still further down the ramp. 'Oh, Madonna of Lust, my Tigress, my Temptation. Never have I seen such beauty, it is ultimate Feminity.'

'If you're taking the piss, chum,' said Miss Ming through dry lips, and she began to edge away.

He did not follow, but his eyes fixed her. 'Oh! I'll bring great wings to beat upon your breast. Tearing talons sharp your talents shall grasp! Claws of blood and sinew sharp shall catch the silver strings of your cool harp! Ha! I'll have you, madam, never fear! Oh! I'll bring your blood to the surface of your skin! Ai! It shall pulse there – in service to my sin! You shall be mine, madam. You shall be mine! This is worth all those many millenia when I was denied any form of consolation, any sort of human company. I have crossed galaxies and dimensions to find and reward you. Now I know my twofold mission. To save the world and win this woman!'

'You're pretty confident,' she said in her coollest voice, 'for a silly little sexless squirt.'

He ignored or, or else had not heard her, his attention drawn back to Doctor Volospion. 'You asked my name. Now do you recognise me?'

'Not specifically . . .'

Bang! A stream of flame had shot from the man's hand and destroyed one of Werther's unfinished mountains. 'There! Is that enough to tell you?'

Abu Thaleb demurred. 'That was one of a set of mountains manufactured by someone who was hoping . . .'

'Manufactured? You make these pathetic landscapes? They look like fakes, at that. Pah! Paint! I use all that is real for *my* canvases. Fire, water, earth and air – and human souls. I am the Controller of your Destinies! Re-born, I come amongst you to give you New Life. I offer the Universe. Follow me!'

The Commissar of Bengal passed a hand over the gleaming corkscrew curls of his blue-black beard, he tugged at the red Star of India decorating his left ear-lobe; he fingered a feather of his turban. 'By Allah, sir, I'm confounded. Follow you? Not a word, I fear. Not a syllable.'

'What? You must know me by one of my names, at least! I am your Messiah, the Prophet of the Sun. I am Emmanuel Bloom!'

'The name is not familiar,' said Doctor Volospion in bland amusement. 'You are originally from this planet, it seems. But when did you leave? Perhaps we are further in your future than you realise . . .'

'Pah!' Emmanuel Bloom jerked his hand and fire began to roar upon Argonheart Po's cola lake. 'I am Power. I am the forgotten Spirit of Mankind. I am Possibility.'

'Quite so. But I think you underestimate the degree of our sophistication.' Doctor Volospion turned a sapphire ring on his left finger. Clouds formed over the lake. It began to rain. The fire went out. 'A demonstration,' he added quickly, noting Bloom's expression, 'nothing more.'

'I am not here to match conjuring tricks with you, my jackal-eyed friend!' The little man swept his arms above his head and black clouds filled the sky; thunder boomed; lightning crashed. 'I am Salvation. Oh, call me Satan – for I am cast down from Heaven. The teeming worlds of the multiverse have been my domicile till now – but here I am, come back to you, at last. You do not know me now – but you shall know me soon. I am He for whom you have waited. I am the Sun Eagle. Ah, soon shall this old world blossom with my fire. For I shall be triumphant, terrible, intolerant Master of your Globe. This is my birthright, my duty, my desire. I claim the World. I claim you all as my subjects. I shall instruct you in the glories of the Spirit. You sleep now. You have forgotten how to fly on the wild winds that blow from Heaven and from Hell. The cold wind blowing now is the Wind of Limbo – it flattens you, deadens you, and you bow passively before it, because you know no other wind. I am the wind. I am the air and the fire to resurrect your Spirit. You two shall be my first disciples. You, woman, shall be my glorious consort.'

Mavis gave a little shudder. She couldn't think of anything much worse than shacking up with this bombastic little jerk. She shared a glance with Doctor Volospion. She said icily: 'Are you sure you have the right planet, Mr Bloom?'

He turned grave, intense eyes upon her. 'Beautiful and proud you may be, woman, yet you shall bend to me when the time comes. You shall not react with mawkish cynicism to me! Your true soul is buried now. But I shall reveal it to you. I am Life – you are Death. At this moment everything is Death that is not me!'

Mavis felt a certain pity for Mr Bloom. Plainly he had been so long in space that he had gone completely mad. At the same time she found his lunatic fanaticism frightening and repellent. She became anxious to leave. 'He's well over the top,' she whispered to Doctor Volospion. 'Can we go now, doctor? He might do something dangerous.'

But Doctor Volospion was dismissive of her anxieties. 'Nonsense, my dear Miss Ming. It has been ages since we had such an entertaining guest. I am eager to hear his views. You know my interest in ancient religions – well, here we have a genuine prophet, a preacher who shows Li Pao up for the parsimonious hair-splitter that he is. If we are to be berated for our sins, let it be with threats of blood and fire.'

'You think he's genuine?'

'Your meaning is misty.'

She accepted his decision to remain, though she could not help thinking it was all right for him. The madman had more or less announced his firm decision to rape her at the earliest opportunity. It would be like being raped by a pigeon, she thought. She smiled at her own wit.

'In turn, sir,' said Doctor Volospion, bowing low to Mr Bloom, 'may I introduce myself and my friends. This lovely lady, whose beauty has quite rightly made such an impression on you, is Miss Mavis Ming. This gentleman is Abu Thaleb, Commissar of Bengal and I, your humble servant, am called Doctor Volospion. I should be honoured if you would agree to be my guest, at least for a little while, until a suitable domicile may be built to house your illustrious presence.'

The lunatic responded well to this humouring. He put his little head on one side as he considered the offer. 'I am not sure . . .'

'Miss Ming would be pleased, too,' continued Doctor Volospion persuasively. 'She is also a guest at my palace.'

'Oh?' Thoughtfully, Mr Bloom licked his lips.

It was a bit much, thought Mavis, for Doctor Volospion to use *her* as a lure. Well, she would avoid the new guest as much as possible.

'My ship . . . ?' mused Mr Bloom.

'We can arrange for that, too, to be transported with us.'

'No. It can stay here. I have no use for it at present. It is safe enough. I have inhabited it for several centuries, perhaps longer. It would make a change to live in a palace, at least for a while.'

'Then you accept, sir?'

'You understand my mission now? To re-fire the Earth, as its leader and its hero. To restore Love and Madness and Idealism to this barren planet! To infuse your blood with the stuff that makes it race, that makes the heart beat and the head swim! You have no heroes any longer – and such paltry villains!'

'You have only met us three, so far,' said Abu Thaleb mildly.

'Three's enough to tell. Your society is revealed in your language, your gestures, your costumes, your landscapes. How you must have longed for me to return! Secretly, of course. You still do not realise it. But that realisation shall dawn anon, be sure of that! But can I bear to leave my ship behind, my much-named ship, the *Golden Hind* – or *Firedrake*, call her, or *Virgin Flame* – *Pi-meson* or the *Magdelaine* – sailing out of Carthage, Tyre, Old Bristol or Bombay: Captain, Emmanuel Bloom, late of Jerusalem, founder of the Mayan Empire, builder of pyramids, called Ra or Raleigh, dependant on your taste – Kublai Khan or Prester John, Baldur, Mithras, Zoroaster – the Sun's Fool, for I bring you Flame in which to drown! I am blooming Bloom, blunderer through the million planes – the Fireclown! Aha! Now you know me!' He strutted to the bottom of the ramp and, with hands on hips, stood staring up at Doctor Volospion. 'Eh?'

'Perhaps you could enlighten us over a meal,' said Doctor Volospion. 'I am still a mite confused. Your penchant for metaphor . . . '

The Fireclown clapped a tiny hand upon Volospion's brocaded back. 'One metaphor is worth a million of your euphemisms, Doctor Volospion. I'll be your guest for a while, for it's my duty to broaden your mind. You'll join us, Mavis Ming?' The huge blue eyes flashed suddenly with an intelligence, a humour, which shocked her, but she managed to maintain her composure.

In imitation of Doctor Volospion's irony, she curtsied. 'Oh, I'm flattered,' she said. 'I've never had dinner with a Messiah before.'

Abu Thaleb made his excuses.

4

In The Museum And The Menagerie Of Forgotten Faiths

'THE SECRET OF Eternal Life, Doctor Volospion, is enthusiasm, nothing more or less. To relish everything to the full – for its own sake – that's the answer. Away with your charms and potions, your Shangri Las, your Planets of Youth, of frozen cells and brain transfers – many's the entity I've seen last little more than a thousand years before boredom shrivels up his soul and kills him. Oh, his body may live. But one way or another, boredom kills him!'

Emmanuel Bloom's little body jerked from head to foot, as if to emphasise his statements, as Doctor Volospion led him down the long, unnecessarily dark passage towards his palace's basements and dungeons. They had eaten well, but Mavis's meal had been spoiled by this pipsqueak's attentions, by his megalomaniacal monologues. She was glad that they now toured the palace. She could not understand why a man of Doctor Volospion's intelligence should put up with this bore for more than a moment. She remained unmoved by Bloom's occasional extravagant praises. She suspected that he might be enjoying a joke at her expense; but then her morale hadn't been any too high since the party. She dragged behind the pair as they descended.

'Your references seem very old-fashioned to me, Mr Bloom. We have eternal life . . . ' Volospion shrugged.

'And your souls gutter like dying candles. This whole planet reeks of inertia. I am here to bring you Ideals.'

'I am sure you will be interested in my collection, my dear Mr Bloom. Mementoes of a million creeds. Many missionaries have come this way. Most have made attempts to – um – save us. You are more original, I would admit. However . . . ' He opened an iron-bound door. There was something in the gesture which made Mavis suspect that Doctor Volospion planned more than a mere tour of his treasures. ' . . . you would allow that your arguments are scarcely subtle. They allow for no nuance!'

The Fireclown strutted, stiff-limbed as ever, into the high vaulted hall, sniffing at the warm, heavy air. 'A pox on nuance! Seize the substance, beak and claws, and leave the chitterlings for the carrion that follow. Let crows and storks squabble over the scraps, these subtleties – the eagle takes the main carcass, as much or as little as he needs! What's this?'

'My collection of devotional objects, culled from all ages, from all the planets of the universe. Only the best have been preserved. I have discarded or destroyed the rest. Here is a history of folly!' He paused beside a scrap of skin to which clung a few faded feathers; he plucked it from its plinth. 'There. What is that?'

'The remains of a fowl. A chicken, perhaps.'

Miss Ming wrinkled her nose and backed away from the pair. She had never liked this part of the palace. It was creepy.

Doctor Volospion permitted himself a dark smile. 'It is all that remains of Yawk, Saviour of Shakah, founder of a religion which spread through fourteen star-systems and eighty planets and lasted some seven thousand years until it became the subject of a jehad. I had this from the last living being to retain his faith in Yawk. He regarded himself as the holy guardian of the relic, carried it across countless light-years, preaching the gospel of Yawk (and a fine, poetic tale it is), until he reached Earth.'

'And then?' Bloom reverently replaced the piece of skin.

'He is now a guest of mine. You will meet him later.'

Mavis chuckled inwardly. At last she had guessed what the doctor had in mind. He intended to add this lunatic to his collection.

'Aha,' murmured the Fireclown. 'And what would this be?' He moved on through the hall, pausing beside a cabinet containing an oddly wrought artefact made of something resembling green marble.

'A weapon,' said Volospion. 'The very gun which slew Marchbanks, the Martyr of Mars, during the revival, in the twenty-fifth century (A.D., of course), of the famous Kangaroo Cult which had swept the solar system about a hundred years previously, before it was superseded by some atheistic political doctrine. You know how one is prone to follow the other. Nothing, Mr Bloom, changes very much either in the fundamentals or the rhetoric of religions and political creeds. I hope I am not depressing you?'

Bloom snorted. 'How could you? None of these others has experienced what I have experienced. None has had the knowledge I have gained and, admittedly, half-forgotten. Do not confuse me with these, Doctor Volospion. It could mean your undoing.'

'You threaten?'

'What?' The little man ran his fingers through the tangles of his auburn hair. 'Eh? Threaten? Don't be foolish. A friendly word of advice, that's all. Now, then – what other pathetic monuments to the nobility of the human spirit have you locked up here?'

'What would you see? A wheel from Krishna's chariot? A tooth said to belong to the Buddha? A fragment of the true cross? The Holy Grail? Mohammed's sword? Bunter's bottle? Look in that case – you'll find them. And over here – ' a sweep of the black and gold arm – 'the finger-bones of Karl Marx, the knee-cap of Mao Tse-tung, a mummified testicle belonging to Heffner, the skeleton of Maluk Khan, the tongue of Suhulu . . . and those only from Earth's Dawn Age. There are many more. Rags and bones, Mr

Bloom. All that is left of a million mighty causes. All that, at core, these causes ever were!'

Mavis shivered again. The museum depressed her and the talk only made her feel worse. She hated anything like this. It was ghoulish to collect such things. She did not wish to criticise her host, but she had never been able to understand why he indulged this peculiar side of his nature. It was research material, of course, and Doctor Volospion's hobby was this particular aspect of the galaxy's past, but she could no more reconcile herself to its existence than she had been able to reconcile herself to Donny's cold-blooded killing of those sweet little rabbits and monkeys at the lab. She'd simply refused to let him or anyone else talk about it in her presence. She wished now that she had not agreed to accompany the two men here, but Doctor Volospion had been so insistent.

'No,' said Bloom, 'these were merely the instruments used to focus faith. Witness their variety. Anything would do as a lens to harness the soul's fire. Nothing here means anything without the presence of the beings who believed in their validity. Whether that piece of worm-eaten wood really did come from Christ's cross or not is immaterial. As a symbol . . .'

'You question the authenticity of my prizes?'

'It is not important . . .'

'It is to me, Mr Bloom. I will have nothing in my museum which is not authentic.'

'So you have a faith of your own, after all,' said Bloom, his small lips forming something resembling a smile.

Doctor Volospion lost none of his composure. 'If you mean that I pride myself on my ability to sniff out any fakes, any piece of doubtful origin . . .'

'Show me this cup you have. This Holy Grail.'

'Certainly. There. In the cabinet with Jissard's space-helmet and Panjit's belt.'

Emmanuel Bloom trotted rapidly in the direction indicated by Doctor Volospion, weaving his way amongst the cabinets and display cases, to the far wall where, behind a slightly quivering energy screen, between the helmet and the belt, stood a pulsing, golden cup, semi-transparent, in which a red liquid swirled. Bloom did not bother to inspect it. He turned back to Doctor Volospion, who had followed behind. 'It is a fake, that Grail, I can assure you.'

'You would argue that it never existed. I am certain that it did.'

'Then how could you keep it? You of all people?'

Doctor Volospion frowned. 'I keep it because it is mine. I had it from a time-traveller who had spent his entire life searching for it and who, as it happens, found it in one of our own cities. Unfortunately, the traveller destroyed himself, soon after coming to stay with me. But the thing itself is authentic. He had vouched for it – and he should have known, for he had dedicated himself to its discovery.'

'Well, I am glad he is dead,' said the Fireclown, and he laughed a strange, deep-throated laugh which had no business issuing from that puny frame. 'For I should not have liked to have disappointed him. That cup is not even a very good copy of the original.'

'How would you know, Mr Bloom?'

'Because I am, amongst other things, the Guardian of the Grail. That is to say, I am graced by the presence of the Holy Grail. Only those who are absolutely pure in spirit, who never commit the sin of accidie – or moral torpitude, if you like – may ever see the Grail and only one such as myself may ever receive the sacred trust of Joseph of Arimathea, the Good Soldier, who carried the Grail to Glastonbury. I have had this trust for several centuries, at least. I am probably the only mortal being left alive who deserves that honour. My ship of full of such things, of course, collected in an eternity of wandering the many dimensions of the universe, tumbling through Time, companion to the chronons . . .'

Doctor Volospion's features were serious. His voice contained an unusual vibrancy. Mavis was surprised to see him so easily taken in by this obvious charlatan.

'How can you prove that your Grail is the original, Mr Bloom?'

'I do not have to prove such a thing. It has chosen me to be its Guardian. The Grail will only appear to one whose Faith is Absolute. My Faith is Absolute.'

'Your faith in yourself, at any rate,' acidly murmured Mavis.

He wheeled on her. 'Indeed! And why not? Ah, you still make a pretence of resistance, I see. Such is female pride. I came here to claim a world, but I would willingly renounce that claim if it meant that I could possess you, woman, body and soul. You are the most beautiful creature I have ever seen, in all the eons of my wanderings. Mavis! Mavis! Music floods my being at the murmur of your exquisite name. Queen Mavis – Maeve, Sorceress Queen, Destroyer of Cuchulain, Beloved of the Sun – ah, you have the power to do it, but you shall not destroy me again, Beautiful Maeve. You shall find me in Fire and in Fire we shall be united!'

'I am sure Miss Ming is duly flattered,' interrupted Doctor Volospion. 'But as for the Holy Grail, you do not, I suppose, have it about you?'

'Of course not. It appears only at my prayer!' Mr Bloom dismissed the doctor from his attention and, hands outstretched in that stiff, awkward way of his, moved to embrace Miss Ming, only to pause as he felt Volospion's touch on his arm.

'It is in your ship, then?'

'It visits my ship, yes.'

'Visits?'

'It is a mystical artefact, Doctor Volospion. It comes and goes. That is why your so-called Grail is plainly a fake. If it were real, it would not be there. You are an obtuse creature, but I suppose that is only to be expected of one who is not really alive at all. Can one hold an intelligent conversation with a corpse?'

'You are crudely insulting, Mr Bloom. There is no call . . .' began Volospion.

Mavis, terrified of further conflict in which, somehow, she would be the worst sufferer, if her experience was anything to go by, interrupted.

'Show Mr Bloom your menagerie, doctor! There are many entities there he might like to converse with!' She winked broadly as soon as the Fireclown's back was turned, but Volospion ignored the communication. He seemed to be brooding as he led Bloom from the museum and through another series of narrow, gloomy passages (copied, as he had told Miss Ming, from some otherwise unremarkable architecture from one of Earth's many periods of barbarism). Doctor Volospion had a tendency to favour the subterranean in almost everything.

At last they reached the series of chambers Doctor Volospion chose to call his 'crypts', where he had incarcerated his collection of creatures culled from countless cultures, some indigenous and others alien to Earth. Proudly the doctor pointed out his Christians and his Hare Krishnans, his Moslems and his Marxists, his Jews and his Joypushers, his Dervishes, Buddhists, Hindus, Nature-worshippers, Confucians, Leavisites, Sufis, Shintoists, New Shintoists, Reformed Shintoists, Mansonite Water-sharers, Anthroposophists, Flumers, Haythornthwaitists, Fundamentalist Ouspenskyians, Sperm Worshippers, followers of the Five Larger Moon Devils, the Stone That Cannot Be Weighed, the Sword and the Stallion, Awaiters Of The Epoch, Mensans, Doo-en Skin Slicers, Crab-bellied Milestriders, Poobem Wrigglers, Tribunists, Calligraphic Diviners, Betelgeusian Grass Sniffers, Aldebarran Grass Sniffers, Terran Grass Sniffers and Frexian Anti-Grass Sniffers, all in their normal environments, as was the custom at the End of Time, and a good many of them seemingly content. The menagerie was filled with a babble of voices as prophets prophesied, preachers preached, messiahs announced various millenia, saviours summoned disciples, arch-bishops proclaimed armageddon, fakirs mourned materialism, priests prayed, imams intoned, rabbis railed and druids droned. Doctor Volospion was forced to turn a power ring and cancel out much of the noise in order to continue conversation.

'Well, Mr Bloom, do you find these pronouncements essentially distinguishable from your own?'

The Fireclown had been studying Mavis; she was glad when Doctor Volospion spoke, for the malformed little man's attention was making her feel extremely self-conscious. She refused to return the stare, but she could feel herself blushing as she pretended to take an interest in the sermon being delivered by a snail-like being from some remote world near the galaxy's centre.

'What?' Bloom cocked an ear in Volospion's direction. 'Distinguishable? Oh, of course. Of course. I respect all the views being expressed, but they are, I would agree, familiar. These poor creatures lack either my power or my experience. I would guess, too, that they lack my courage. Or my purity of purpose.'

'Many would differ with you, I think.' Doctor Volospion's voice was full of confident self-congratulation.

'Quite so. But you cease to entertain me, Doctor Volospion. I have decided to take Miss Ming, my Madonna, back to my ship.'

'That's what you think!' cried Mavis indignantly. 'I couldn't imagine anything more awful! You give me the jitters! You're a horrible little pervert! I can guess what *you've* got in mind. No thanks!'

Emmanuel Bloom blinked, temporarily taken aback. 'How can such perfect lips form such empty words? It is my duty and my destiny to remove you from this environment, to bring you to the knowledge of your own divinity!'

Mavis smiled openly at Doctor Volospion. 'I don't think you'll be removing either me *or* yourself from here, Mr Bloom.' Her heart was beating rapidly. She knew she had nothing to fear from the lunatic, yet she was close to panic. He moved like a mechanical toy as he continued to close with her, his face flushed, his huge eyes full of affection and determination. His high, fluting voice continued to trill, but she no longer heard his words. His bird-like hands touched hers. She screamed. 'Doctor Volospion!'

'It is hardly gentlemanly, Mr Bloom, to force your attentions upon a lady – and one who shares the protection of my roof.' Doctor Volospion appeared to be relishing the drama. The fingers of his left hand hovered over the fingers of his right, on which were most of his power rings.

Mavis was surprised by the strength of the Fireclown's grip; an almost euphoric sense of weakness suffused her body. She was panting, incapable of thought; her lips were dry, her tongue and her palate were dry and the only word she could form was a whispered 'No'.

Doctor Volospion seemed unconscious of the extent of the tension. His voice continued lightly: 'Mr Bloom. Since you are to remain here as my guest, I would ask you to recall . . .'

The blue eyes became shrewd even as they continued to stare into Mavis's. 'Your guest? No longer. We leave.'

'I could not think of it. You have told us, yourself, that you are unique. I accept your assessment. You will grace my menagerie – my finest acquisition. Here you may preach to your heart's content. You will find the competition stimulating, I am certain.'

'There is no entity more free in all the teeming multiverse than the Fireclown,' said Bloom calmly, all his bombast gone. He did not blink; his eyes still stared into hers. 'You cannot imprison me, sir.'

'Imprison? You shall have everything you desire. Your

favourite environment shall be recreated for you. If necessary, it is possible to supply the impression of distance, movement. Regard the state as a well-earned retirement, Mr Bloom.'

The avian head turned on the long neck, but he did not relax his grip on her hands. 'Your satire palls, Doctor Volospion. It is of the sort that easily grows stale, for it lacks love; it is inspired by self-hatred. You are typical of those faithless priests of the fifth millenium who were once your comrades in vice.'

Doctor Volospion was astonished. 'You could not know my origins!'

'Oh, the Sun knows All. Old He may be, but His memory is clearer than those of your poor, senile cities. One gesture reveals a society to me – two words reveal an individual. The eagle floats on currents of light, high above the world, and the light is recollection, the light is history. I know you Volospion and I know you for a villain, just as I know Mavis Ming as a goddess, chained and gagged, perverted and alone, but still a goddess.'

Doctor Volospion's laugh was cruel. 'All you do, Mr Bloom is reveal yourself as a buffoon! Not even your insane Faith can make an angel of Miss Ming!'

Mavis was not resentful. She had her good points, but she was no Gloria Gutzmann, and she tried too hard, she knew, and people didn't like that. She could be neurotic. There was evidence. The affair with Snuffles hadn't done anyone any good in the end, though she had been trying to do Dafnish Armatuce a favour. But then, she thought, maybe she had been acting selfishly, after all. Well, it was all water under the bridge. She was suddenly surprised at herself for thinking such ordinary thoughts when a moment before she had been unable to think at all. She took a deep breath.

'I am the Flame of Life. I carry a torch that will resurrect the spirit, and I carry a scourge to drive out devils, and I need no armour save my faith, my knowledge, my understanding. I am the Sun's soldier, keeper of His mysteries.' Bloom's back was to her now as he addressed Doctor Volospion. His little frame twitched and trembled, his red-gold mass of hair might have been a bristling crest belonging to some exotic fowl, his little hands clenched and unclenched at his sides, like claws, as his beautiful, musical voice filled that dreadful menagerie. 'Ah, Volospion, I should destroy you – but one cannot destroy the dead!'

'Possibly,' said Volospion, apparently unmoved, 'but the dead can imprison the living, can they not? Therefore, Mr Bloom, I possess the advantage, as men like myself have always possessed it over such as you.'

And at last, far too late in Mavis's opinion, the long hand touched a power ring and the Fireclown was surrounded by bars of energy. After one attempt to free himself, Bloom stood stockstill, his arms at his sides again, his blue eyes blinking as if in bewilderment.

Doctor Volospion smiled. 'Eagle? Phoenix? I see only a caged sparrow.'

Ignoring him, the Fireclown turned in the narrow space and spoke to Mavis. 'Free me,' he said. 'It will mean your own freedom.'

Mavis giggled.

5

In Which Doctor Volospion Suggests A Bargain

MAVIS AWOKE FROM another nightmare, filled with a sense of desolation worse than any she had experienced in the past. An impression was all that was left of her dream, but she thought it might have involved the lunatic Bloom. She blamed him for her recent sleeplessness. He had frightened her more than anything had ever frightened her before. He deserved imprisonment. In any other world it would have been his punishment for doing what he had done. If Doctor Volospion hadn't stopped him, he would have raped her, she knew. She wished she could stop thinking about what he had said to her. If she had had the courage to return to the menagerie alone she would have done so – just to see him made harmless by Doctor Volospion's energy cage (the sort of cage she had been in when she had first arrived) just to ask him what he meant by his ridiculous flattery. But she wasn't sure she could survive it. Doctor Volospion said that he hadn't taken well to captivity; that, from time to time, he would rage and scream and fill his cage with flames and smoke as he tried to escape, offering all sorts of empty threats and, so Doctor Volospion said, demanding that she be brought to him. 'I do believe that he has genuinely fallen in love with you, Miss Ming,' the doctor had said, apparently relishing the idea. 'It might be charitable . . .'

She had felt sick at the suggestion.

'Repulsive little runt,' she said aloud, pushing back her pink silky sheets and turning up the lamp (already fairly bright) whose stand was in the shape of a flesh-coloured nymph rising naked from the powder-blue petals of an open rose. 'I do wish Doctor Volospion would let me have a power ring of my own. It would make everything much easier. Everyone else has them. Lots of time travellers do.' She crossed the soft pale yellow carpet to her gilded Empire-style dressing table to look at her face in the mirror. 'Ooh, I look *awful*! That dreadful creature.' She sighed. She often had trouble sleeping, for she was very highly-strung, but this was much worse. For all their extravagant entertainments, their parties where the world was moulded to their whims, what they really needed, thought Mavis, was a decent TV network. TV would have been just the answer to her problems right now. Perhaps Doctor Volospion could find something in one of the rotting cities. She would ask him. Not that he was doing her any favours, these days. He was full of the Fireclown and was spending almost all his time down in his murky vaults. 'Oh, Mavis!' she murmured. 'Why is it always you! The world just isn't on your side.' She gave one of her funny little crooked smiles, very similar to those she had seen Barbara Stanwyck giving in those beautiful old movies. If only she could have gone *back* in time, to the twentieth century, where the sort of clothes and manners she preferred were the norm! And the men! Well, they had better, simpler lives. She sometimes felt as if she'd spent half her life, before coming to the End of Time, inhabiting the world of the past. Maybe that had been what she had really been hoping for when she let them elect her as the first person to test the time machine? Of course, it had been proof of her popularity, now she considered it, that everyone had been unanimous about her being the first to go. That sort of thing was good for the ego. Yet even this thought didn't cheer her up. If anything, she felt more depressed. She began to experience the first signs of one of her headaches.

'Poor old Mavis!' Well, not old, of course. There were some advantages to living in this world. 'Oh, dear, oh, dear . . . ' She began to pad back towards the big circular bed. But the thought of a continuance of those dreams, even though she had pushed them right out of her mind, stopped her. It had been Doctor Volospion's suggestion that she continue to lead the sort of life she had been used to – with regular periods of darkness and daylight and a corresponding need to sleep and eat, even though he could easily have changed all that for her. To be fair, he tended to follow a similar routine himself, ever since he had heard that Lord Jagged of Canaria had adopted this antique affectation. If she had a power ring or an air car at her disposal (again she was completely reliant on Volospion's good graces) she would have left the palace and gone to find some fun, something to take her mind off things. She looked at her Winnie the Pooh clock – another three hours before the palace would be properly activated. Until then she would not be able to get even a snack with which to console herself.

'I'm not much better off than that idiot down there,' she said. 'Oh, fuck! Oh, Mavis, what sort of a state have they got you into?'

There was a tap at the door.

Grateful for the interruption she pulled on her fluffy blue dressing robe and cried, 'Come in!'

Doctor Volospion, in black and white doublet and hose, looking like a demonic Hamlet, entered. 'You are not sleeping, Miss Ming? I heard your voice as I passed . . . '

'I've got a bit of a headache I'm afraid, doctor.' He could normally cure her headaches. She found her whole mood improving at once. She became eager, anxious to win his approval. Her spirits were rising. It was amazing what a bit of company could do. 'Silly little Mavis is having nightmares again.'

'You are unhappy?'

'Oh, no. *No.* In this lovely room? In your lovely palace. It's everything a little girl dreams about!'

'Then?'

'It's that awful Mr Bloom. Ever since . . . '

'Aha!' The saturnine features cleared. 'You are still afraid. There is no need to worry, Miss Ming. He can never escape. He has tried, but I can assure you that my powers are far greater than his. He is only capable of parlour tricks. Yet he obstinately insists on his right to rule our world – any world, I gather – and upon his superiority. He becomes tiresome.'

'You'll let him go, then?'

'I could not be sure that he would leave the planet. Besides, he has something I wish to own and he refuses to give it to me.'

'You could take it now.'

'Not from him. Not from his ship. I have visited his ship. It is protected by a screen which nothing of mine can penetrate. I find it odd that, with such a screen at his disposal, he allowed himself to be so easily captured. But I suppose his head was turned.'

'By me?'

'He would not have come to my palace at all if it had not been for you. That was why I had you accompany us to the menagerie.'

'I guessed that. You know Mavis – she's always glad to help. He was a menace.'

Doctor Volospion sighed. 'Well, I have just returned from visiting him again. I have offered him his liberty in return for one piece of his property, but he fobs me off with specious arguments, with vague talk of Faith and Trust and the like – you've heard his babble.'

'Horrible little bore,' murmured Mavis sympathetically. She had never seen Doctor Volospion so evidently cast down. 'You never know with some people do you. He's best locked up, for his own good. He's some sort of cripple, isn't he? Or spastic? You know what they're like. You can't blame them. It's frustration. It's all bottled up in them. Sex maniacs.'

'To do him justice, Miss Ming, his interest seems only in you. I have offered him many women, both real and artificial, from the menageries. Many of them very beautiful, but he insists that none of them have your "soul", your – um – true beauty.'

'It's because I'm the first piece of woman-flesh he'd seen in a couple of centuries, I bet. He and Donny Stevens have a lot in common. A pity they can't meet. Nobody's going to treat little Mavis like an ass on two legs ever again. I swore that to Betty. That's why I gave up men. At least with a lady you know where you are on that score. You know what I call him? The Randy Runt! He's got about as much sex-appeal as a seagull – less! Did you ever hear of a really sweet old book called Jonathon . . . '

'Your headache is better, Miss Ming?'

'Why, yes.' She touched her hair. 'It's almost gone. Did you . . . ?'

Doctor Volospion drew his own brows together and traced beringed fingers across the creases. 'You don't give yourself enough credit, Miss Ming . . . '

She smiled. 'That's what Betty was always telling me when I used to feel low. But poor old Mavis . . . '

'He demands that you see him.'

'Oh!' She shook her head. 'No, I couldn't, really. As it is I haven't had a good night's sleep since the day he arrived.'

'Of course, I understand.' This was unlike him. He seemed to have none of his usual confidence. It made her feel strange. Yet she had always known he had a soft spot and this was her opportunity to give him some sympathy in return for all he had done for her. She moved closer to him.

'Is it that important to you, Doctor Volospion?'

'It might help me, you see, to convince him to give me what I want from him.'

In spite of herself, she found that she was already relenting. 'Well, if I saw him for a few moments. It might help me, too – to lay the ghost, if you know what I mean.'

'Yes. You could be right. Perhaps if we went immediately?' Already his spirits were rising.

She hesitated, then she patted his arm. 'Oh, all right. Give me a few minutes to get dressed.'

With a bow, Doctor Volospion left the room.

Mavis began to dress. It took her quite a bit longer than she had anticipated, because she couldn't choose exactly what she wanted to wear. On the one hand she thought some sort of sexless boiler suit would be best, on the other all her impulses (female vanity!) made her want to put on her very sexiest clothes. In the end she compromised, donning a flowery mou-mou that disguised her plumpness.

Doctor Volospion was waiting for her outside. Together they made their way to the menagerie. She was surprised, as they descended, that she was feeling quite light-headed, almost gay.

They passed through the tiered rows of his many devotional trophies, past the bones and the sticks and the bits of cloth, the cauldrons, idols, masks and weapons, the crowns and the boxes, the scrolls and ju-jus, tablets and books, the prayer-wheels and crystals, until they reached the door of the first section of the menagerie, the Jewish House. 'I had thought of putting him in here,' Doctor Volospion told her as they passed by the inmates, who ranted, wailed, chanted or merely turned aside as they passed, 'but finally I decided on the Non-Sectarian Prophet House.'

'I hadn't realised your collection was so big,' she said, doing her best to make conversation. The place continued to disturb her.

'It grows, you know, almost without one realising it. I suppose, because so many people of a messianic disposition take an interest in the future, we are bound to get more than our fair share of prophets, anxious to discover if their particular version of the millenium has come about. Because they are frequently disappointed many are glad of the refuge I offer. Martyrdom, it would seem, is the next best thing to affirmation.' He chuckled.

Finally, after passing through a score of different Houses they came to the Fireclown's habitat, designed to resemble a desert, scorched by a permanently blazing sun. 'He refused,' whispered Doctor Volospion, as they approached, 'to tell me what sort of environment he favoured, so I chose this one. It is the most popular with prophets, as you'll have noticed.'

Emmanuel Bloom sat on a rock in the centre of his energy cage. His black velvet suit seemed more ragged and dustier than when she had last seen him; his white shirt was dirtier. He appeared not to have noticed them and was reciting poetry to himself.

'. . . *Took shape and were unfolded like as flowers.*
   And I beheld the hours
As maidens, and the days as labouring men,
   And the soft nights again
As wearied women to their own souls wed,
   And ages as the dead.
And over these living, and them that died,
   From one to the other side
A lordlier light than comes of earth or air
   Made the world's future fair.
A woman like to love in face, but not
   A thing of transient lot –.

And like to hope, but having hold on truth –
And like to joy or youth,
Save that upon the rock her feet were set –
And like what men forget,
Faith, innocence, high thought, laborious peace –'

He had seen her. His great blue eyes blinked. His stiff little body began the rise. His bird-like, fluting voice took on a different tone:

'*And yet like none of these . . .*' He put an awkward finger to his small mouth. 'So Guinevere comes at last to her Lancelot – or is it Kundry, come to call me Parsival? Sorceress, you have incarcerated me. Tell your servant to release me so that, in turn, I may free you from the evil that holds you with stronger bonds than any that chain me!'

She felt silly. 'He's not my servant,' she said. Already the blood was beginning to pound through her again. She should not have come.

Bloom crossed the stretch of sand until he was as close to her as the cage permitted. 'He is not your master, you may be sure of that, this imitation Klingsor!'

'I haven't the faintest idea what you're talking about.' Her voice was shaking. She contented herself with one of her crooked smiles.

He pressed his tiny body against the energy screen. 'I must be free,' he said. 'There is no mission for me here, now, at the End of Time. I must continue my quest, perhaps into another universe where Faith may yet flourish.'

Doctor Volospion said: 'I have brought Miss Ming, as you demanded. You have talked to her. If you will give me the Grail . . .'

Bloom's manner became agitated. 'I have explained to you, demi-demon, that you could not keep it, even if by some means I could transfer it to you. Only the pure in spirit are entitled to its trust. If I agreed to your bargain I should lose it myself. Neither of us would gain!'

'I find your objections without foundation,' said Doctor Volospion smoothly, unruffled by the Fireclown's anger. 'What you believe, Mr Bloom, is one thing – the truth, however, is quite another! Faith dies, but the objects of faith do not, as you saw in my museum.'

'Those things have no value without Faith!'

'They are valuable to me. That is why I collect them. I

desire this Grail of yours so that I may, at least, compare it with my own.'

'You believe that yours is false. Why not believe the rest of what I tell you!'

'I shall decide which is false when I have yours in my possession. Is it on your ship?'

'I have told you – it manifests itself at certain times.'

Doctor Volospion allowed his own ill-temper to show on his face. 'Miss Ming . . .'

'Please let him have it, Mr Bloom,' said Mavis in her best wheedling voice, the one she had used on her father and on Donny whenever she had wanted something very much. 'He'll let you go if you do.'

'I can leave whenever I please,' said the Fireclown. He ran his hand through his auburn mop. 'You demean yourself woman, by aiding this wretch, by adopting that idiotic tone.'

'Well!' Mavis felt her legs shaking. 'I'm not staying here, not even for you, Doctor Volospion! It's too much. I can stand a lot of things, but . . .'

'Be silent.' The Fireclown's voice was low and firm. 'Listen to your soul. It will tell you what I tell you.'

'I never did have much time for loonies,' she said cuttingly, 'not even back home. So long, feller . . .'

'Miss Ming!' Doctor Volospion's hand seized her arm. 'For my sake do not give up. If I have that Grail . . .'

'You may see the Grail, beautiful Mavis,' murmured Fireclown, 'but it shall always be denied to such as he! Come with me and I shall let you witness more than Mystery!'

'Oh, Christ!' she shouted, trying to free herself from Doctor Volospion's restraining hand. 'I can't take any more. I can't!'

'Miss Ming!' fiercely croaked a desperate Volospion. 'You promised to help.'

She still struggled, trying to prise his grip away from the sleeve of her mou-mou. 'Listen, chum, I'm helping little Mavis. You can do what you like.'

Panic would soon make her incapable of moving, she knew. This knowledge contributed to her hysteria. She scratched Doctor Volospion's hand so that at last he released her. She ran between the cages of roaring, screaming, moaning lunatics. She was sobbing, horrified at having hurt her host, terrified both of what she had left behind her in the cage and of what might become of her in the future now that she had offended Doctor Volospion.

'I'm sorry! I'm sorry!' she shrieked above the surrounding noise, but she continued to run until she was completely clear of the menagerie. She staggered, going more slowly as she passed the exhibits in the museum; she was close to fainting and twice had to lean against something until she had the energy to move on. Eventually she had climbed the steps back into the palace proper and reached the soft pink security of her own bed before sinking into a sleep which was at last free from nightmares.

6

In Which Miss Ming Experiences A Transformation

WHEN MAVIS WOKE up again she was surprised at how refreshed she felt, even confident. She had no doubt that Doctor Volospion would be angry with her but she did not seem to care very much.

'What can he do, after all?' she asked herself aloud. She was still wearing her mou-mou. She looked at the ripped sleeve, inspected the bruise on her arm. She doubted if her scratch was worse than the bruise. On the other hand, in her experience men had a different way of looking at these things. She felt almost buoyant. 'I guess little Mavis will have to find a new berth,' she said as she removed the mou-mou and went to take a shower. 'Well, it was high time for a change, and I'm not much gone on sharing the same roof as that mad midget downstairs. He might escape some day.'

The shower made her feel even better. She decided to go out, visit a few people, find someone to put her up for a while. She began to wonder whom she should visit first.

And then, all of a sudden, depression swept back. It caught her so unexpectedly that she had to sit down on the edge of the unmade bed, dropping her towel to the floor. 'Oh, Christ! What's wrong with me?'

It was probably because, she was beginning to tell herself, that she had got up too fast and too soon. After all, she hadn't had a lot of sleep last night, and not much on previous nights.

Doctor Volospion was knocking at the door.

'This is it, Mavis!' Again, she began to feel better, even at the prospect of one of Volospion's tongue-lashings. 'Come in!'

He was smiling when he entered. 'I came to apologise, Miss Ming.'

She glanced at his hand. There was, of course, no sign of her scratch. She had been taken aback by his manner. 'Oh,' she said.

'I did not realise how badly Mr Bloom affected you,' he continued.

'Oh, well. I shouldn't have . . .'

'The fault was wholly mine.' He had all his old assurance. He was dressed in robes of scarlet and green, a tight-fitting dark green hood on his head, emphasising the sharpness of his features. As he spoke, he drew on dark green gloves.

She was nervous now, having expected him to be at very least cool towards her; on the contrary he was almost warm. His voice caressed her, giving her that kitten-like feeling she always enjoyed so much. Her laugh was girlish. 'I lost my cool, I guess.'

'Well . . .'

'You talked to him after I'd gone? He still wouldn't give you the Holy Grail, eh?'

'Unfortunately . . .'

'Well, I'd like to help.' Careful, Mavis, she told herself, you're letting yourself in for it again. But she couldn't stop. 'If there's anything I can do to make up for what happened last night.'

'I wouldn't put you to further embarrassment.'

'As long as I never have to come face to face with your creepy little salamander I don't mind.'

'You realise that he would do almost anything for you, if you asked.'

'Oh, no. I couldn't . . .'

'I am not suggesting it. Somehow he controls his ship's protective devices from wherever he is. I asked him if he would let you see the Grail. He said that you could.'

'I'm not sure what you're getting at, Doctor Volospion.' She spoke as firmly as possible. 'I'm not going to see him again. Never.'

'Ever,' he said absently. 'Quite. You would not have to see him. You can visit his ship. He will lower the barriers to enable you to enter.'

CAWTHORN 75

'Then you'll go in and get the Grail?'

'No. He would sense that. You would have to go into the ship, take the cup and bring it back to me.'

'And there wouldn't be any danger?'

'None at all. He genuinely loves you, Miss Ming. Of course, if you consider it a betrayal . . . '

'Betrayal? I didn't make any deals with that over-sexed squab!'

'Of course you didn't.' His voice was rich with gratification. 'You'll go?'

She became frightened again. Doctor Volospion had a knack of talking her into situations she was prone to regret. 'Just go into the ship, get this cup, bring it back to you?'

'That is all.' He put a green hand on her shoulder. 'It would mean a great deal to me, as you know. My collection is important to my happiness. If I thought that I had something in it that was not authentic – well, I should never be content.'

'I know what your museum means to you,' she agreed. 'Your studies . . . '

'Exactly.'

'Very well, Doctor Volospion. Rely on Mavis. Girl scouts to the rescue!'

'You'll have my gratitude for ever.'

And that, Mavis thought guiltily (for she hated doing anything for mere gain), might mean her own power ring at last.

Since Mavis had last been to this part of the planet someone had altered the position of the sun. The landscape was in twilight, the teardrop-shaped ship a silhouette. Doctor Volospion's air car, which resembled one half of a black upturned pea-pod, landed her beside the ship; gingerly she stepped to the ground, sensitive to the stillness and silence of her surroundings. She wished that Doctor Volospion had come with her, but he had told her that somehow the Fireclown could detect what was happening near his ship and that if he had guessed she was not alone he would have put up his screens again.

She reached the foot of the ramp and hesitated. It was impossible to see anything of the ship's interior from where she stood. A warm, musty smell came from the entrance; there was a suggestion of pale smoke curling from the interior. If she had not known otherwise, she would have suspected the Fireclown of being inside, for the ship was redolent of his presence.

'Okay, Mavis,' she said bravely, speaking aloud to dispel the silence, 'here goes!'

She was wearing her blue and orange kimono over her bikini, for Volospion had warned her that it might be uncomfortably warm within the Fireclown's ship. She climbed the ramp and stood outside the entrance, peering in. It seemed to her that points of fire flickered on the other side of the airlock's open door. She sucked her lower lip, feeling just like a little girl, like Alice or someone, in one of the magic books she had still read, from time to time, before her journey into the future. She began to feel excited rather than afraid. 'What manner of creature is lord of this fairy castle?' she called, to reassure herself. 'Shall I find my handsome prince – or an ugly ogre?' She moved from the airlock into the true interior of the ship. It was as if firelight illuminated the large chamber, although its source was mysterious. The rosy, flickering light cast her shadow, enlarged and distorted, upon the far wall. The chamber was in disorder, as if the shock of landing had dislodged everything from its place. Boxes, parchments, books and pictures were scattered everywhere; figurines lay dented or broken upon the carpeted floor; drapes, once used to cover portholes, hung lopsidedly upon the walls, which curved inwards near the ceiling. Apparently the place had been Bloom's storeroom, for there was no sign of furniture. She stumbled over the junk until she reached a companionway leading up to the next chamber. The cup she had been told to find was probably in the storeroom, but she thought it sensible to explore the other sections of the ship first, in case it was displayed somewhere. This next room was lit similarly to the first, but so realistically that she found herself searching for the open fireplace which would be the source of the light. There was, in fact, a faint smell of burning timber. 'Mavis,' she said firmly, 'keep that imagination of yours well under control!' This room, as she had suspected, contained a good-sized bed, shelves, storeage lockers, a desk, a chair, and a screen whereby the occupant could doubtless check the ship's functions. Against one wall, at the end of the bed, was a large metal ziggurat which looked as if it had once been the base for something else. Would this be, she wondered, where the cup was normally kept? In which case, the Fireclown would have hidden it and she was going to have a much longer job than she had hoped. On the wall were various pictures, some were paintings, others were photographs and holographs, primarily of men in the costumes of many periods. On the wall, too, was a narrow shelf, about two feet long, apparently empty. She reached to touch it and felt something thin, like a cane. Curiously, she pulled the object towards her and held it in her hand. It was an old-fashioned riding crop, its tip frayed and dividing at one end; a silver head at the other. The head was beautifully made, fashioned like a woman's face and almost certainly an authentic example of what the Italians called the 'stile Liberty'. What impressed Mavis most about it was the look of ineffable tranquillity upon the features. The contrast between the woman's expression and the function of the whip itself disturbed Mavis and hastily she replaced it. Wishing that the light were stronger, she began to search for the cup or goblet (Doctor Volospion's description had been vague). First she looked under the bed, finding only a collection of books and manuscripts, many of them dusty. 'This whole ship could do with a good spring-clean!' She searched through the wardrobe and drawers, finding a collection of clothes to match those worn by the men whose pictures decorated the wall. This sudden intimacy with Bloom's personal possessions had not only whetted her curiosity about him – his clothes, to her, were much more interesting than anything he had said – but had somehow given her a greater sympathy for him. She began to feel guilty about rummaging through his things; her search for the goblet began increasingly to seem like simple thievery. She wanted to find the Grail and get out as soon as possible. If she had not made a promise to Doctor Volospion she would have left the ship there and then. As she opened a mahogany trunk, inlaid with silver and mother-of-pearl, the lid squeaked and at the same time she thought she heard a faint noise from below. She paused and listened, but there was no further sound. She saw at once that the trunk contained only faded manuscripts. She decided to return to the storeroom. The curiosity which had at first directed her energy was now dissipating to be replaced by a familiar sense of panic. She felt her heart-rate increase and the ship seemed to give a series of little tremors. She returned to the companionway and was half-way down when the whole ship shook itself like an animal, roared, as if sentient, and she was pressed back against the steps, clinging to the rail as, swaying from side to side, the ship began to take off. Sweating, she turned herself round with difficulty and began to climb back towards the living quarters where she felt she would be safer. If her throat had not been so constricted she would have screamed. The damned ship was taking off under its own power. She had probably activated it herself. Unless she could work out how to control it she would soon be adrift in the cosmos, floating through space until she died: and she would be alone. It was the latter thought which terrified her most. She reached the cabin and crawled across the carpet as the pressure increased, climbing on to the bed in the hope that it would cushion the acceleration effects. The sensations she was experiencing were not dissimilar to those she had experienced on her trip through time and, as such, did not alarm her – it was the prospect of what would become of her when the ship was beyond Earth's gravity which she could not bear to consider.

The pressure began to lift, but she remained face-down upon the bed ('these sheets could do with a wash,' she was thinking irrelevantly) even when it was obvious that the ship was travelling through free space.

'Oh, you've let yourself in for it this time, Mavis,' she told herself. 'You've been conned properly.' She wondered if, for reasons of his own, Doctor Volospion had deliberately sent her into space. She knew his capacity for revenge. Had that silly tiff meant so much to him? Or was this his punishment for the scratch she had given him? 'What a bastard! What bastards they all are!' That was Mavis all over, she thought, trusting the world – and this was how the world repaid her. Her self-pity, however, was half-hearted: She realised, in fact, that what was after all a genuine threat to her life made her feel much better than, for instance, when she had just been terrified of someone catching her while she searched the Fireclown's room.

She began to roll over on the bed. At least the ship itself was comfortable enough. Cosy, really, she thought. It would be just like when she was a little girl, in her own little room, with her books and her dolls. In a way, she was safer here than anywhere she had been since she had grown up. It should not be difficult to work out the means of returning to Earth. What did Earth and its denizens have to offer her, anyway, except treachery?

'All right, Mavis,' she said as she swung her legs over the edge of the bed. 'Make yourself right at home, girl.'

'It is true, woman, that you have found your home at last,' said Emmanuel Bloom from the shadows overhead.

'My God,' said Mavis, realising the extent of Doctor Volospion's deception.

Bloom swung himself down from the ceiling, an awkward macaw. She saw the hatch that doubtless led to the control cabin. 'My Goddess,' he said. He was wearing the same stained velvet suit.

'You swapped me for the cup!'

'Doctor Volospion suggested the bargain.' He strutted across the cabin and manipulated a dial. Red-gold light began to fill his living quarters. Everything glowed and each piece of fabric, wood or metal seemed to have a life of its own. She stood up, edging away from the bed, conscious, for some reason, of her large, pendulous breasts, of the fatness of her stomach, of the width of her thighs.

'Listen,' she began. She was breathing rapidly again, and heavily. 'You can't really want me. I'm fat old Mavis. I'm ugly. I'm stupid. I'm selfish.'

He raised a stiff right arm in a gesture of impatience. 'What has any of that to do with my love for you? What does it matter if the foolish Volospion thought, as he put it, that he was killing two birds with one stone when he was actually freeing two eagles? I am the Fireclown. I am Bloom, the Fireclown. I have lived the span of Man's existence. I have made Time and Space my toys. I have juggled with chronons and made the multiverse laugh. I have mocked Reality and Reality has shrivelled to be re-born. My eyes have stared unblinkingly into the hearts of stars, and I have stood at the very core of the Sun and feasted on freshly created photons. I am Bloom, Eternally Blooming Bloom. Bloom, the Phoenix. Bloom the Destroyer of Darkness. These eyes, these large bulging eyes of mine, do you think they cannot see into the souls as easily as they see into suns? Can they not detect an aura of pain that disguises the true centre of a being as smoke hides fire? That is why I choose to make you mine, to enslave you so that you may know true freedom.'

Mavis forced herself to speak. 'Listen, chum, kidnapping is kidnapping, whatever you call it . . . '

He ignored her. 'Of all the beings on that wasteland planet, you were one of the few who still lived. Oh, you lived as a frightened rodent lives, your spirit perverted, your mind enshelled with cynicism, refusing for a moment to look upon Reality for fear that it would detect you and devour you, like a wakened lion. Yet when Reality occasionally impinged and could not be escaped, how did you respond?'

'Look,' she said, 'you've got no right . . . '

'Right? I have every Right! I am Bloom! You are my Bride, my Consort, my Queen, my Goddess. There is no woman deserves the honour more!'

'Oh, Christ,' she said, 'please let me go. Please. I can't give you anything. I can't understand you. I can't love you.' She began to cry. 'I've never loved anyone! No one but myself.'

His voice was gentle. He took a few jerky steps closer to her. 'You lie, Mavis Ming. You do not love yourself.'

'Donny said I did. They all said I did, sooner or later.'

'If you loved yourself,' he told her, 'you would love me.'

'That's a new one!' Her voice shook. To her own ears now her words were without resonance of any kind. The collection of platitudes with which she had always responded to experience; the borrowed ironies, the barren tropes with which, instinctively, she had encumbered herself in order to placate a world she had seen as essentially antagonistic, all were at once revealed as the meaningless things they were, with the result that an apalling self-consciousness, worse than anything she had suffered in the past, swept over her and every phrase she had ever uttered seemed to ring in her ears for what it had been – a mewl of pain, a whimper of frustration, a cry for attention, a groan of hunger. 'Oh . . . ' She became incapable of speech. She could only stare at him, backing around the wall as he came half-strutting, half-hopping towards her, his head on one side, an appalling amusement in his unwinking, protruberant eyes, until escape was blocked by a heavy wardrobe. She became incapable of movement. He reached a twitching hand towards her face; the hand was firm and gentle as it touched her and its warmth made her realise how cold, how clammy her own skin felt. She was close to collapse, only supported by the wall of the ship.

'The Earth is far behind us now,' he said. 'We shall never return. It does not deserve us.' He pointed to the bed. 'Go there. Remove your clothes.'

She gasped at him, trying to make him understand that she could not walk. She did not care, now, what his intentions were, but she was too exhausted to obey him.

'Tired . . . ' she said at last.

He shook his head. 'No. You shall not escape by that route, madam.' He spoke kindly. 'Come.' The high-pitched, ridiculous voice carried greater authority than any she had heard before. She began to walk towards the bed. She stood looking down at the sheets; the light made these, too, seem vibrant with life of their own. She felt his little claw-like hands pull the kimono from her shoulders, undo the tie, removing the garment entirely. She felt him break the fastening on her bikini top so that her breasts hung even lower on her body. She felt no repulsion, nothing sexual at all, as his fingers pushed the bikini bottom over her hips and down her legs. And yet she was more aware of her nakedness than she had ever been, seeing the fatness, the pale flesh without any emotion at all, remarking its poor condition as if it did not belong to her.

'Fat . . . ' she murmured.

His voice was distant. 'It is of no importance, this body. Besides, it shall not be fat for very long.'

She began to anticipate his rape of her, wondering if, when he began, she would feel anything. He ordered her to lie face down upon the bed. She obeyed. She heard him move away, then. Perhaps he was undressing. She turned to look, but he was still in his tattered velvet suit, taking something from a shelf. She saw that he held the whip in his hand – the one she had seen. She tried to feel afraid because she knew that she should feel fear, but fear would not come. She continued to look up at him, over her shoulder, as he returned. Still her body made no response. Of course she had entertained fantasies of flagellation, at least since puberty, and Donny had occasionally slapped her with a slipper, but what happened now neither excited her imagination nor her body. She wished that she could feel something, even terror. Instead she was possessed by a calmness, a sense of inevitability, unlike anything she had known.

'Now,' she heard him say, 'I shall bring your blood into the light. And with it shall come the devils that inhabit it, to be withered as weeds in the sun. And when I have finished you will know Rebirth, Freedom, Dominion over the Multiverse, and more.'

Was it a mark of her own insanity, she wondered, that she could detect no insanity in his words.

The whip fell upon her flesh. It struck her buttocks and the pain stole her breath. She did not scream, but she gasped. It struck again, just below the first place and she thought his flames lashed her. Her whole body jerked, trying to escape, but a firm hand held her down again, and again the whip fell. She did not scream, but she groaned as she drew in her breath. The next stroke was upon her thighs, the next behind her knees, and his hands were cruel now as she struggled. He held her by the back of the neck; he gripped her by the shoulder, by the loose flesh of her waist, and each time he gripped her she knew fresh pain. She believed, at last, that it was his intention to flay her alive, to tear every piece of skin from her body. He held her lips, her ears, her breasts, her vagina, the tender parts of her inner thighs, and every touch was fire.

She screamed, she blubbered for him to stop, she could not believe that he, any more than she, was any longer in control of what was happening. And yet the whip fell with a regularity which denied her even this consolation, until, at length her whole body burned and she lay still, consumed. Slowly the fire faded from this peak of intensity and it seemed to her that, again, her body and her mind were united; this unity was new. She heard him cross the chamber to replace the whip. He said nothing. She began to breathe with deep regularity, as if she slept. Her consciousness of her body induced an indefinable emotion in her. She moved her head to look at him and the movement was painful.

'I feel . . .' Her voice was soft.

He stood with his arms stiffly at his sides. His head was cocked, his expression was tender and expectant.

'. . . different,' she said.

'You have found your pride.'

'Yes.'

He reached to caress her face. 'I love you,' he said.

'I love you.' She began to weep.

He made her rise and look at her body in the oval mirror he revealed. It seemed that her skin was a lattice of long, red bruises; she could see where he had gripped her shoulders and her breasts. The pain was hard to tolerate without making at least a whisper of sound, but she controlled herself. 'Will you do this again?' It was almost a request.

He shook his little head.

She walked back to the bed. Her back, though lacerated, was straight. She had never walked in that way before, with dignity. She sat down. 'Why did you do it?'

'In this way? Perhaps because I lack patience. It is one of my characteristics. It was quick.' He laughed. 'Why do it to you, at all? Because I love you. Because I wished to reveal to you the woman that you are, the individual that you are.'

'It won't fade, this feeling?'

'Only the scars will go. It is within you to retain the rest. Will you be my wife?'

'Wife?' She smiled. 'Yes.'

'Well, then, this has been a satisfactory expedition, after all. Better, really, than I expected. Oh, what leaping delights we shall share, what wonders I can show you. No woman could desire more than to be the consort of Bloom, the Good Soldier, the Champion Eternal, the Master of the Multiverse!'

'And my master, too.'

'As you are my mistress, Mavis Ming.' He fell with a peculiar, spastic jerk, on his knees beside her. 'For Eternity. Will you stay? I can return you within an hour or two.'

'I want to stay,' she said. 'Yet you gave up that goblet for me, the one that meant so much. Your honour?'

He laughed as he struggled to his feet. 'If Doctor Volospion ever deciphers the inscription on the cup I gave him he will discover that it was awarded, in 1980, to Leonard Bloom by the Union of Master Bakers for the best matzo bread of the Annual Bakery Show, Whitechapel, London. He was a very good baker, my father. I had kept his cup in all my journeys back and forth through the time-streams and I regret giving it to Doctor Volospion, but it was worth it. My father always swore it was solid silver, but I don't think it was.'

She smiled.

'And now,' he said, 'I'll leave you. I must set my controls. You shall see all that is left of this universe and then, through the centre of the brightest star, into the greater vastness of the multiverse beyond! There we shall find others to inspire and if we find no life at all, upon our wanderings, it is within our power to create it, for I am the Fireclown. I am the Voice of the Sun! Ah! Look! It has come to you, too. This, my love, is Grace. This is our reward!'

The cabin was suddenly filled with brilliant golden light apparently having as its source a beam which entered through the very shell of the spaceship, falling directly upon the ziggurat at the end of the bed. A smell, like sweet spring flowers after the rain, filled the cabin, and then a crystal cup, brimming with scarlet liquid, appeared at the top of the ziggurat. Brilliant scarlet rays spread from a hundred points in the crystal, almost blinding her and, although she could hear nothing, she received an impression of sonorous, delicate music. She could not help herself as she lifted her aching body from the bed to the floor and knelt, staring into the goblet in awe.

From behind her the Fireclown chuckled and he knelt beside her, taking her hand. 'We are married now,' he said, 'before the Holy Grail. Married individually and together. And this is our Trust which shall be taken from us should we ever commit the sin of accidia. Here is proof of all my claims. Here is Hope. And should we ever cease to forget our purpose, should we ever fall into that sin of inertia, should we lose for more than a moment our Faith in our high resolve, the Grail will leave us and shall vanish forever from the sight of Man, for I am Bloom, the Last Pure Knight, and you are the Pure Lady, chastised and chaste, who shall share these Mysteries with me.'

She began: 'It is too much. I am not capable . . . ' But then she lifted her head and she smiled, staring into the very heart of the goblet. 'Very well.'

'Look,' he said, as the vision began to fade, 'your wounds have vanished.'

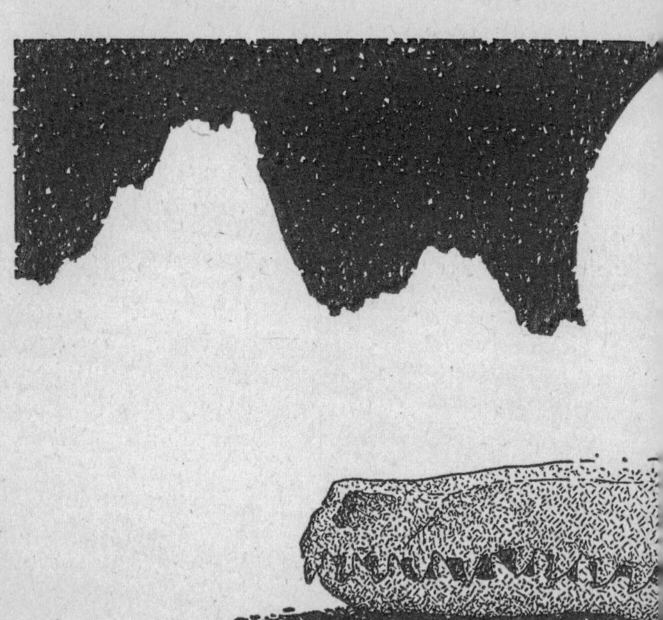

THE BOY

by BRUCE McALLISTER

(His sigh of relief is without consideration for her feelings.)
WENDY: But they are ours, Peter, yours and mine.
PETER: But not really?
WENDY: Not if you don't wish it.
PETER: I don't.

– J. M. Barrie, *Peter Pan, or The Boy Who Would Not Grow Up*

HIS EARS WERE odd, almost pointed. His complexion was smooth except for the pimples on his forehead and the streaks of caked dirt. The pimples were as red as a rash. The skin was bumpy there. His hair was dusty and oily.

He stood there swaying a little from hunger, mouth open and saliva pearled at the corner of his mouth. He was wearing a thin green stretch-suit which each day covered a little less of his dirty body. The suit was torn. It was ragged at his ankles, and at his forearms, where the suit stopped and his skin began. The suit was stained at the armpits. It had been stained all over by the rains. Where the suit had holes in it – from branches, from thorns – the dirty pink of his skin showed through.

His right arm had a long scab. He had obviously picked at it and made it worse. The scab was like wood, and in one place there was the yellow mound of a surface infection, one that was not getting any better.

His nose had been running, and the crust extended from his nostril to his lip.

He had an apple-like thing in each hand, and both pieces of fruit were the pink-brown colour of rotting apples. He began moving again slowly through the bushes, and as he went, clouds of insects darted in towards the fruit. He waved them away with one hand and then the other.

The rain began again. The drops slid effortlessly off the oil of his face and forehead, and he blinked them from his eyelids.

When at last he reached the clearing and the girl, she was up, her thin arms around her knees, her back against the tree. Her nightgown, once a soft pink material, was dirty now, streaked and torn. There was a solid band of brown where it dragged along the ground. With her knees up, her underwear showed dark from the dirt and shadow.

Her left arm was caked with mud where she had been sleeping on it. Her nose was running, and she sniffled, running her hand and forearm under her nose.

She didn't look at him. He handed her one of the pieces of fruit, and she accepted it without looking at it. Picking up a thick twig from the ground, she at last looked at the fruit and began to scrape away the rotten places. She scraped until very little was left, and she was whimpering, the sound odd as it came through her clenched teeth and parted lips. The boy pretended not to hear her.

He turned to her. He looked at her in the rain, and ate his piece of fruit in two large bites, swallowing with little chewing, and holding his breath so that he would not smell or taste it.

By now the rain had soaked their heads and shoulders. The boy began to shiver before the girl did, and the shivers so racked his body that his legs jerked and jolted, and his skin was splotchy with a bluish tinge. The girl held out against the shivering by putting her arms around her knees, and squeezing.

He was looking at her hard now, and he was shivering as though sick. She was not looking at him. He got up and moved over to her. He leaned against her and she neither moved away nor pressed back against him. He could see her teeth, showing like yellow shells in her mouth, and the rain dripped from the end of her nose.

He moved his mouth towards her, and touched her cheek with his lips. She pulled away a little. He did it again, on her ear, near the hair that was matted by the rain.

He put his arm around her, and she tried to pull away quickly when he kissed her open-mouthed and groping. She struggled, and he pushed her back towards the tree trunk. He was no longer shivering hard. She turned her head to the side as far as it would go, and he had her nightgown up to her waist. She was holding her knees together tightly – they were knobby, ivory-coloured – and he could not do it with one hand alone. He forgot her face; he had to look down to guide both hands to pry her legs apart. She kicked at him weakly, and whimpered, but he pushed himself down between her legs with his entire body and held her down. He was a little lower than he wanted to be, and he squirmed to rise. His weight held her thin white legs apart. They were like bony wings. Her head started to roll back and forth on its own, hitting the tree trunk, the wet bark crackling off into her hair, her mouth open and catching the rain, and she moaned even before he could start into her. This upset him. He began to be rough.

With one hand he did something below his waist. There was a flap or zipper there, and when he had done it, he slid up higher again on her. She stopped moving her head. She was completely still, waiting. He began to rise and fall upon her, like a spider, spreading her white legs even wider at each thrust. Her legs were as cold as stiff fish now, not moving at all on their own, like wet wing-bones, and this upset him more, and he was rougher in his thrusts. Like her, he was whimpering, and from his lips slipped a word – a name – one he had not spoken in a long time.

When he was through, he slid back and away, his skin no longer bluish, his limbs and shoulders no longer racked by shivering. Once again it had warmed him, and he was content.

Although her legs were now free of the weight, she did not close them. The rain continued to fall. It ran down her thighs, beading at the place between her legs where the hair was like a cowlick. She lay with her eyes closed, her head turned to the side, and her cheek in the mud against the root of the tree.

It was the same dream: He wakes to find himself on the sand of the cove. It is the first time: the cove is not familiar. Why is he here on this sand? *Where* is this sand? Why can he remember nothing before the sand? There is a girl sleeping beside him. She is wearing a fresh bright-pink nightgown which stirs now and then in the wind. *He* is wearing his fresh green body-suit, the colour of forests. Her name, he realises now, is *Wendy*. He remembers a story.

Suddenly he hears sounds in the bushes high above the

beach. He stares into the dappled foliage, and it rustles again. Half a dozen boys – two of them twins, and all of them clad in blue flannel or in suits and caps of animal fur – appear at the jungle's edge. He smiles at them. They approach, and his smile goes away. They are dirty. One has a festering sore on his leg, a big one. Another boy is trembling in some sickness. They have been here on this island for quite a while, he realises now. He and the girl have only just arrived. He stares at her, and the boys edge in closer to them, moving oddly, like animals. Something golden and familiar, and no larger than a hand, buzzes above his head, calling to him in a voice that is fainter than it should be.

He awoke one night to a sound of pounding, and it was not a dream.

As soon as his eyes opened, he saw. The moon was full.

Not far from his feet stood an animal, blue-white in the moonlight, and dappled in the shadows cast by the leaves. The animal was moving its four legs in short steps, and stumbling as though blind. It moved its head as if to clear webs from its eyes, then took another step, and tripped on a vine. The boy could smell the wet animal smell of it, and another smell, a faint and sickly sweet one. The animal snorted, threw back its head, and the mane whipped through the air coarsely. The moonlight caught the head fully, revealing.

At the sight of the thing on the animal's head, the boy stopped breathing.

On the head was a horn like a shaft of smooth coral from the rocks of the cove. The horn shone in the blue moonlight for a long moment, then dipped into dappled shadow as the animal again stumbled. The animal snorted wetly, as though frightened by a smell, and in two steps the body had disappeared into the dark.

The boy began to breathe again. He was trembling, seeing images of the girl waking and screaming and the horn of the frightened or angry animal rushing to pierce his stomach or hers like a long terrible tooth.

For a long time he was unable to sleep. The girl never woke, and eventually his eyes closed.

They were walking through the trees and vines where the sun did not reach them except in a dappled brightness and with its wet heat. They were sweating, and they had to blink the sweat from their eyes. Insects moved in thick breaths around their shoulders and heads, and their hands darted by habit to clear the air before them. The girl sneezed. She stopped to lift the edge of her gown, and with it cleared her nose.

They entered the stagnant water where the leaves rotted darkly, where fallen branches looked like snakes, and there were at times snakes that resembled branches. The boy's eyes darted, watching, and then suddenly they were on the other side, where the ground was wet but was at least ground. He stopped, bent over, and moved a hand to pull two living things from the calf of his right leg. They were finger-long, almost as thick as thumbs, and he annoyed them by grasping them. They wriggled to resist him. Their heads moved painfully into his flesh. As he pulled, his face twisted, and when he had them free, he flung them away without looking. He began walking again, and she followed.

Once again they were moving from their clearing at the island's centre through the swampy water to the cove. When at last they reached it, they stood and stared out at the sea. The water of the cove shimmered oddly from the oil and scum, and the larger pieces of debris rocked like boats or large toys. The debris had been there for a very long time – the wood, the garbage, and the soft plastic things from a world farther away, eddying between rocks in the yellowish foam, bobbing in each small wave.

The boy looked down the beach across the dirty sand. Forty or fifty steps from them the great green and white-bellied carcass was decaying. It was scaly – or had once been scaly. The belly was bloated. The long toothy skull looked like wet cotton now, eyes pecked out by the remaining sea birds, the holes shadowed and dry. The tail reached into the water's edge, where the water moved a little, and where the flesh had been stripped by the tiny transparent crab-like creatures of the cove. They swarmed on the bone, clung to it like pale silver gnats. When the tide came in later in the day, they would get even more of the massive tail – each tide a little more.

The two of them did not look at the carcass for long. They had seen it – considered it – many times before.

They walked back to a spot by the edge of the jungle, well above the reaches of the high tide, and stopped by the several mounds of sandy ground there. They stood still, staring down at the mounds. Two pieces of splintery driftwood, tied with dry weed, formed a cross, the cross embedded in the first mound, and on the cross had been wrapped a familiar piece of blue flannel, streaked and faded. Near this first mound, but farther into the shadows of the jungle, were other mounds and other driftwood crosses and shreds of familiar cloth jerking in the wind. One cross bore a cap made of animal fur. Another cross held a ragged piece of black and white, also fur.

One of the mounds had changed. It was no longer a mound. It was a hole where some animal had recently dug and removed something, and there was a smell in the area now. The girl backed away, staring down at the hole, and the boy watched her.

The boy looked elsewhere, to a spot not far from the blue flannel where there was a mound no larger than a hand, and a tiny cross – two thick twigs tied with dry weed. He stared at the tiny mound, and began to make a sound through his teeth. His body jerked a little with the sound.

He turned to her, the muscles knotting in his jaw.

He made a grab for her, caught her, pushed her to the ground. She tried to wriggle free, using one hand, and with the other did something frantic in her mouth, in her throat, with her finger. She was trying, struggling, plunging again with the finger, and before he could even begin to rise and fall on her, she had done it. She had made herself sick. She could turn to him now with the mess on her face, making him jerk back at the sight. She could smile oddly at him now.

He started to hit her, and did not. He got up, looked at the wet mealiness on her face, and turned to begin walking towards the water. As he went, he grabbed up a long stick.

As he moved along the edge of the dim water, he did not look back. Before long, the sand turned to rock, rising up through the oily sand and shallow water. He ascended the rocks, and went where he had never gone before.

He was almost beyond it before he saw it. He had been looking down the slope of rocks – darker, wetter, as they neared the sea's oily edge – and at first he saw it only in the corner of his eye. It was big. It was still and dark. He stopped, and turned fully towards it.

It was a cave, the mouth large and dark. He stared, and was able to discern something vaguely there inside. There was even a familiar feeling about the place, this cave, even though he had never been here before. He began moving towards the mouth, holding the stick tight. There was a white substance on the rocks – terrible-smelling and sometimes slick – and his feet slipped more than once on it. With his eyes on the cave, he had to step very carefully to keep his balance.

The white substance was deep, like a lip, at the mouth of the cave, but the birds that had once sat on the ledge above the cave's mouth to make this lip were gone. The lip was thick enough that he had to strain to step over it, to keep from getting it between his toes.

A few steps inside, in the darkness, he had to stop to let his eyes clear. The place was feeling even more familiar, although this was not possible.

When he saw the creature in the middle of the cave floor, he did not jump or jerk in surprise.

Even the creature was somehow familiar, although he had not seen it before – except perhaps in a dream.

The creature's body was like his own, but also not like his own. The grey-pink body was naked, and the legs were crossed neatly, though in an odd way, like a knot. The legs and the short arms dangling at the creature's sides were thin, so much thinner than his own. The head was two or three times larger than a head should have been. It was as though the contents of the head had bloomed up and out through a soft spot in the skull, then healed over without hair, and the pressure from inside had closed the eyes, and the eyes had healed over too. The body was balanced on its knot of legs, and the great head was balanced on its thin rigid neck.

The boy saw the other things in the middle of the cave floor, next to the creature. The boy let himself look at them. The creature did not seem to be awake.

There were three things that were long and glistening. The boy remembered slowly that these were *tubes*. They led from the darkness behind the creature to its body, one coiled and entering the body between its legs, another entering the side of its stomach, and the third connected directly to its chest. The *tubes* did not move. They were not supposed to move. Something was supposed to move *in* them.

And the other things. On the rock and dirt floor of the cave, right beside the creature's crossed legs, were rectangular things, one here, one there, two farther away. Slowly the boy recognised them as *books* – face down, one closed, two open. And a small item not much larger than a *book*, though it was black and silver (it was *plastic*; it was *metal*) which the boy slowly understood as a *machine*. The lid of the *machine* was 'open'. There was a ribbon of some slick substance coiled inside, its end laid out along the top of the *machine* as though waiting for someone to touch it, to fit it properly somewhere. Even this – this ribbon – was familiar to him. He understood it as a *tape*. A *tape* always had voices and other sounds in or on it, even though it had nothing for eyes, as *books* did.

He took his stick then and prodded at the ribbon. Nothing moved.

When he looked up, he jerked back. The creature's head had turned to face him. It was looking at him through eyelids that could not open.

Somehow he knew the creature, and he found himself trembling because of it. And how was it possible? The understanding stirred like oil.

He *remembered* this creature: it was the *voice*. The sound before all other sounds, the voice that had called him and *made* him come. To this island, to awake on the sand beside the girl, to find the other boys, to join them in their pain, as the *voice* wanted. And then to watch them start to die, one by one, from this sickness, from that wound, or that slow poison – everything as the voice wanted it. Even *she* – the one of gold, tiny wings like dust, the magic of his life and of his story. How could *she* – of all of them – have died? And though he was alive, he had changed so much. Was it from the pain – day after day? From what the island did to him? Or was it instead from the *voice* – its whim shaping him like clay?

He was shivering hard. The creature's face had been staring at his for so long now. So he moved. He moved a little closer to the *books*, poking at them with his stick and then looking up at the face. There was something like a smile on the lips, and now one of the short arms was beginning to rise, to straighten out, the hand aiming a finger at one of the *books*, a small brown one. The finger pointed. The book's thick first page (cloth and thick *paper*) had a name on it, but it was too far away.

The hand dropped back down limply to the creature's side.

The boy stared at the *book*, and then back at the face. The smile had become a twisted thing, like two worms together. It was as though the creature were laughing, but without sounds.

He began to move to the book, but then froze.

The creature had twitched violently, twitched again, as the great head rolled on the thin neck, and under the lids the eyes moved strangely, bulging, threatening to pop.

Slowly the creature stopped twitching. Its face turned once again to regard him. There was spittle on the lips, and a faint quiver in them.

Again, he moved towards the *book*, understanding now that the twitching had had nothing to do with him, that it had been an accident, like some illness.

The creature's body did not turn as he approached, but the head did. He stared back at it, and moved sideways to approach the *book* more closely.

He jumped – something had caught at his foot. He kicked to free himself, and suddenly there was a great sucking sound in the cave. He looked down. He had kicked one of the *tubes*. He looked up again. The sucking sound was coming so loudly from the creature's chest, from the hole where the *tube* had been a moment before, and the creature was fumbling at the *tube* with its short arms.

The boy discovered that he could not move. Something unseen had grabbed his body, holding him. This force was familiar, too, and to feel it made him sick and faint. He remembered it: the same invisible jaws that had followed the voice that had called to him, making him come. These jaws held him stiff as a rock, while the creature's arms went on fumbling at the *tube*, managing at last to put it back where it belonged, stopping the terrible sucking sound.

The invisible jaws around him faded away. He was staring at the creature, and was again free to tremble. Violently he trembled, and a thin warm stream moved down the inside of his leg as he began to remember it all, to see it again – as he had seen it at his own birth not long ago: the grey world inside this creature, the quivering illness of its thought and desire, the stillness inside it where no feeling stirred, where only a boredom as endless as an oily sea ever moved, wave after wave, giving birth to the games where the raw power of the *voice* – of the terrible grey-pink body – took pleasure like hysteria in squeezing bodies out of nowhere, in building flesh out of the air, in calling bodies up from old *books* and old *tapes*, giving them hair, excrement, and bones – an animal with a long horn on its head, a boy with the name of *Peter*, a thin girl named *Wendy*, and others on an island of pain.

He remembered the moment of his birth, and he began to scream.

And as he screamed, it opened up. He understood – as he had not understood before – what this creature was, how kindred its blood was to his. How it was not from hell or the heaven of stars or from one man's nightmare. How instead it was – it and the few hundred others like it – all that was left of *man* in the world, of the bodies and bones that had made the *books* and *tapes* – after a century of infected seas, of crippled air, of a blood-poisoned world, and of those last attempts to change man enough, to help him survive, live on, regardless of his form, regardless of what he might lose, that he might live on and on, forever and ever.

Screaming, leg wet, stick dropping from his hand which had frozen open, he turned and ran. Half falling down the rocks, he tripped and got up, tripped and got up, knowing now that the creature had *allowed* him to find the cave, that it had probably called him to it – in its game.

When at last he reached the beach, he was no longer screaming.

As he approached her, he could see that the mealiness was still on her face, but that it had dried.

They were gathering roots and tubers at the edge of an unfamiliar clearing when they heard it: the first voices they had heard since the others had died. They jerked upright instantly, and cocked their heads to listen.

Except for one, the voices were deep. The one voice was like the whistling of a low-voiced bird.

He rushed with her from the clearing and crouched with her just inside the trees and vines. They stared, searching, and their eyes began to sting from the dryness of not blinking.

The voices grew louder, too loud, coming close. He and she jerked upright, turned, and ran a few steps farther back into the trees and undergrowth. Again they crouched low and waited.

What they saw, when it appeared, was difficult to understand. The boy shook his head and blinked, then stared again at what was visible through the screen of undergrowth between the trees. He could see the top half of a body not unlike the girl's beside him, but the distant figure was taller, older, with dark long hair, and a white dress much less tattered and soiled than the long pink nightgown beside him.

He stared at the figure – this woman in the distance – paying no attention to the shorter figures moving with her. As he stared, his breathing quickened. Even without closing his eyes he could see himself and this woman together on the ground, rolling, struggling with each other. He was on top of her suddenly, rising and falling into the warmth under her dress, until he rolled exhausted and spent off her and on to the ground.

The vision passed, and he was staring at the figure again, his breathing slowing.

He saw the figures who were moving with her, as they crossed the clearing. The tops of their heads barely reached up to her shoulders, and the heads were large, one balding, two or three wearing hats. When he caught a clear glimpse of their rough shirts and shoulders, he saw the muscles and the muscles scared him. Even without closing his eyes he could see himself caught by those muscular arms, caught on the ground with the woman, and the arms beat him until he died.

He squinted and moved his head trying to see more of the dwarfed, muscular bodies and faces. Their eyes were big. Their faces did not look cruel, but still he was afraid of them. They were singing in their low voices, and the woman was singing in her high voice. All except the woman carried long wooden shafts with metal on them – double-ended spike on one shaft (it was a *pick*), flat curved metal ends on two or three others (they were *shovels*, yes). Those instruments, as he knew, were for digging and moving earth, but they could harm a body as well.

The moving figures disappeared into the dappled shadows of thick vines and undergrowth, and soon the voices were fading away.

He turned and could see by the girl's slack open mouth and her stare that she understood no more than he did. A beautiful woman and seven dwarfed men. Their story was not clear to him, but he knew they had one. They were on the island now.

Her stomach was large now. A few days before he had told her – in the first words he had used in a long time – that her stomach looked like a big cheek, or some stomach that was trying to hold a boulder inside it.

He had not spoken to her again since that day, and she had not tried to make him speak.

They were at the cove now, walking on the rocks and looking for any mussels or rock clams or sea jelly they might have missed in the heavy rains of the previous three days.

He heard the faintest of sounds behind him, and turned – to find that she had fallen. She had fallen without a cry, and she had fallen quite far – down between some rocks, at least a body's length down, the barnacles scraping her arms and face, the rock ledges striking her body, striking the tight bulge of her belly. Her eyes were open. Her head leaned against the barnacles, the blood giving them a colour they had never before had. She was making no sound, and he knew that it had been no accident that she had fallen from a high place. He could remember clearly the other two times she had tried it, both times with falls.

She sniffled so quietly that he could barely hear her. She was holding her stomach, and against it her hands were pale and small, the tendons raised like ivory.

He pulled her up by an arm, and still she made no sound. She managed to stand. At least her legs were not broken.

On their way to the clearing in the jungle, she slipped many times and fell.

When they reached their place by the trees, it began. She screamed. The thing came out of her like the inside of a great mussel shell. It did not move. It made no sound. He stared at it open-mouthed and in a moment became aware that she had stopped screaming. He waited. She made no further sound, and he knew that this time she was not just hating him in silence, that she was dead.

He leaned down, hesitated, and grabbed her arm. He began to pull at her, to pull her towards the cove. He was blinking wildly, his face twisted. The thing – a single bloody muscle with a small face, miniature arms and legs – was attached to her between her legs. He pulled her along the ground, and it dragged behind her. This thing – like the inside of some terrible fruit – turned on its cord, rolling from side to side, picking up soil and leaves.

At last it broke free. He saw it break free and he dropped her arm. His throat was making a sound that would not stop, that would not stop.

Eyes closed, he could see the face and soft body of the taller figure, the woman, her breasts and her singing.

He did not look back. He went to the clearing. He fell to the ground. He trembled into sleep.

He dreamed of her warm body and her breasts. He dreamed of sucking on those breasts with his eyes closed, and sleeping for a long time after he had done this.

He awoke and sat hungry, listening to the different kind of silence on the island.

He went to the beach. He went to the smallest mound – the one no larger than a hand – and the tiny cross of tied twigs planted on it. He looked down at it and the setting sun turned the sand at his feet to gold. This upset him. He kicked the sand to make the gold go away, and as he did it, the gold dust rose as slow as death.

He dreamed of sucking blood, of being dragged bloody through leaves and soil. They clung to him like finger-long creatures. They sank their heads into him.

He awoke with a scream and stumbled up to begin running in the dim light of the dawn.

He was running to that familiar place, and he was running hard.

When he reached the beach, he slipped again and again on the sand, and then on the rocks as he started up them, catching himself, getting up and falling again, and finally reaching the cave.

He rushed in, stick in hand, eyes closed –

– and the smell and the stillness of the cave forced his eyes open.

There were bodies all around him. It was like one of his dreams.

The creature of the great head, of the *voice*, was still there in the middle of the cave floor, but its body was now entirely motionless, tipped to one side, the flesh a different colour, with a thing that shouldn't have been there embedded in its chest.

It was the horn, the smooth coral-like horn of the night-blind animal that had come stumbling to him that night. The horn was charred now, as though burnt black upon entering the creature's chest. The *tube* that once had led to the chest had been melted, black. The visible end of the horn was splintered, as though struck from the night-blind animal's head by some instrument of wood and metal and the force of muscular shoulders.

Fallen across the crossed legs of the creature was a small muscular body charred just as black as the horn. Only the largeness of its head and the thickness of its shoulders made it recognisable to him. Of all parts of the body, the arms were charred the worst, as though they had been the ones that had guided the horn into the creature's chest, and had suffered the most from the terrible burning answer.

Here and there, other small bodies with muscular shoulders and big heads were tilted against the cave wall. Six of them. Their eyes wide, their limbs completely still, any visible flesh a strange colour. Each chest among the six was charred, caved in as though by a broad invisible horn, and these bodies were arranged against the cave's walls as though flung there from the centre of the floor, away from the place where the creatures now sat, still and tilted. The instruments of wood and metal once carried by the small thick bodies in his memory were strewn here and there, some of them a little charred, and some of their big heads were crushed in at the back – by the cave wall meeting them – and some of their backs were bent at odd angles.

But worst of all – there on the floor in front of the creature – was the woman, the one he had dreamed of night after night. He stared at her, and began to tremble. He went on staring. Her body – with its soiled white dress and breasts like small mounds of sand – was puffed now, and in her chest was a crusty red hole, one the size a night-blind animal's horn would make. Her body was arranged neatly in front of the creature – as if to display the hole.

He stared into the hole, and even without closing his eyes he could see the charging animal, mane flying, hooves suddenly loud, and then the horn lowered – into her. Had she done something to scare it? Had the other seven been trying to catch it, to chase it in a game, kill it in their hunger? Or had it instead been the other thing: the *voice* – making it happen, urging the horn to pierce her, just like all of their other pains –

– and if it was the *voice* that had done it, it had done even more:

– had *let* dwarfed men find its cave – had *known* they would try to kill it with the same horn that had taken their woman –

– and as they'd rammed it through its chest, the creature had let them do it, and killed them too, not in anger, or love of self, but in its boredom, a boredom with this island, with thought and life, with this world-without-end that was trying to end.

He stepped forward, eyes on his face, and began to kneel beside her pale arm. As he did, he saw something begin to crawl from one of her open eyes.

He shrieked. He rose. He began to run.

He was flying. Even without her golden dust to help him, he was at last able to fly, and as he flew he found that he could hear someone clapping, someone very small and golden clapping – for him and for his story – as he fell on through the salty sky.

'. . . AS AMERICAN AS . . .'

by WILLIAM NABORS

A LOOSELY WOVEN straw sombrero hung by its string from a nail above the screenless window so that the sun, shining through gaps in the hat's weave, cast shadows on the opposite wall of the tar-paper shack. The patterns reminded me of: (a) WHELLO FLAKES? (b) alchemy? (c) the great mandella? (d) roulette? Yes, that was it, roulette – *Russian Roulette.* 'Shoot yourself,' Susan had told me. 'We're through. You can't even keep a job. All you had to do was co-operate. Why couldn't you just once . . . '

CO-OPERATE. 'My life story,' I said. 'I've spent years co-operating. I've co-operated with you; my relatives, your relatives, friends, enemies, bosses, teacher, *ad infinitum*, I'm through co-operating. It's all I've ever done. Look up my old report cards. "Co-operates well" – "Does not co-operate". They always checked "Co-operates well". That's why – '

I stormed out of the house but when I was halfway down the block, I thought of something. For once I went back to deliver a belated wisdom. I said the thing we poor conversationalists never think of until it's too late. I poked my head in the door and gave forth. 'In Vichy France, co-operate wasn't such a fucking nice word. Do you know what they called people who co-operated with the Nazis? Collaborators! Do you know what the French Resistance did to collaborators? Do you know what the Allies – '

'This isn't Vichy France. This is America!'

Then she locked herself in the bathroom (a conventional tactic) and spoiled my oratorical debut. I had planned it so well. I was working up to Nuremburg – the trials. I was going to mention Göring, Eichmann, General Yakashito, My Lai, Captain Levy, Thoreau, Dr Mudd, Ellsberg, poor clumsy O'Stanley; every case I could cite where society had confirmed the ultimate responsibility individuals must bear for their actions. I had barely reconnoitered the death camps (WW II and Mid-East VI) when Susan stomped off to the bathroom, locked the door and started flushing; literally drowning out my rhetoric before I could expound on *The Psychopathology of Everyday Life* (Freud: rewritten and annotated by L. Clerk, 1986). Well, goddamn it, she could flush till her ass stung, I wasn't about to co-operate, job or no job.

I left again. The second time, though, I had a destination. I was calm. I caught the public to Sister Anjou's. When the rail stopped over the half-completed Hickory Turnpike (the world's most expensive, untravelled, bikeway to nowhere), I looked down at the roof of a government *Friendly Kitchen*. A man in Indian dress was urinating down the open skylight. A luv-board on the roof mocked his action. SUPPORT THE INSTITUTIONALISED DEPRESSION: MAKE YOUR CHILI WITH HORSEMEAT. The hum first came to me as the peace keepers rushed on to the roof to cart the red man away. '*I'm the black flag of anarchy, ho hum. Ho hum, to you and your mother and all your mother's sons. I'm the black flag of anarchy, ho hum!*' I was quite moved when the peace keepers lifted the Indian, dosed with *motionless*, on to the stretcher. I couldn't see him smiling, but I'd bet a Hoover dollar he was. They usually are.

Sister Anjou (she came into the world an Angela) my sweet juicy prize, is always 'in' to me. Ours is no ordinary incest, no common lust. She is no ordinary whore. Anjou is expert in the sensuous art and yet, spontaneous, ripe; my sweet, juicy, anjou; defiance *par excellence*, rebel between sheets. When I arrived, she did not interrogate me, but rather brewed me the bootleg elixir. What a tonic for tribulation! I recall her Herbert Hoover poster. I attacked it. I don't know why. I'm no anarchist; I wasn't yesterday. I know my verses.

1st Hoover 23

'Poor Hoover, object of scorn,
Thus we go down with the cotton mill colic.
Thus we all suffer, grow ragged and worn.
Oh, though I walk in the steps of a demon,

I dare that demon be other than me!
I will learn to praise our keeper,
Hoover, an aimless depression for me.'

And you should hear my other histories. I've memorised practically the entire *Annotated Book Of Knowledge Of All Things Good And Evil, Past, Present And Henceforth* (A.D. 2nd 1938: Government Press, Dept. of Archives and Planning.) Let me slip you a few treasures from the prophets:

'. . . deplore this and every act of violence . . . (Stalin, Joe: TIMES MAN OF THE YEAR – 1942) . . . nor do we glory in this victory, but in the peace to . . . (Hitler, Adolph: 1934–19–) . . . have secured peace in our time . . . (Chamberlain, Neville, the umbrella man: 1938) . . . a peace that will endu . . . (Roosevelts, Ted and FRANK and James's, Jess and FRANK: assort. vintages, perpetually on film) . . . the kind of peace . . . (molotovs, kruschevs, breznevs, nixons, nehrus, kennedys, maos, chous, hos, etc., smiths) . . . an honourable . . . not seek war no more . . . our goal is . . . a piece of every peace . . . the British thing . . . we Russians . . . Irish are a peaceful . . . as American as . . .'

There you have it, the sort of history that repeats itself. It is the history of tragi-comic cliché, a knowledge that has no utility but to leave you looking down the long barrel of civilisation, forecasting the various blasts, but with absolutely no influence over the triggering mechanisms. You achieve the station of a socially conscious sponge, dripping with foreknowledge, doom-saying; anticipating the turn of happenstance; but read your papers, catch your newsies, there's nothing you can do about anything but make lamentations and dream of almanacs. Even in a world dedicated to approximation of a signal era of history; here, in the midst of our Institutionalised Depression, when the *Basic History Packet* tells how very like 1933, second, third or fourth 1933 must be and what differences ('added perfections') exist, you'd just as well look on events with sloven apathy, as be aware of where we're going. Do you recall your O'Stanley? Not many do. O'Stanley for most of us has been forcibly ('them pinkies makes us ferget; them greenies makes us remember') deleted from mass-history, but some few still recall his words.

'Socially, there are two classes, Serfs and Knights. Some serfs are called artisan and commercial class. Some Knights are called priests and kings. There be degrees to all things. The essential condition (human if you will) winds up the one-same-thing, in and out of time and speculation. Also rises the suns and downs the moons. With predictable history, we have come close to our goal of static reality. *Status Quo*, the hoped for achievement of every order, has become scientifically as well as socially possible. Every few years the electors vote a new nostalera and that wards off demon-boredom, most times a calculable variable. The possibility of possibility intrigues us. We change the coat: the vehicle, the point of travel, the social structure. We tinker sophisticatedly or crudely with the psyche; flirt with mortality and the secret of eternal youth, shed and create disease, famine, war, make art and make love; make peace. We speak promises and lies and truths; procreate and cease in procreation. We choose and choose not and wind up in the lonely alcove of self, altering only self. Serf or Knight, each is his own battleground.'

Hail, martyred O'Stanley, clumsy oaf! But I must sing a song of social significance. Here's the bootleg talking, I think, or is it me, hum humming the hum I must?

my battle lines ain't bounded by the inner con*tears* of my skull, nor sky. i cares! i'm a human*must*, a demo*crack*; archetypal 20th century wes*turn* man, of soap opera, tv, news and dial-a-prayers. in schools i learned i's s'posed t' care. 1 – 2 – 3 – whack! whack! whack! shape up son – you can! can! can!

On the back of a thinko-graph called 'Armageddon and Picnic Psychology and Goin' to Hell on a Rolli-coaster', I mark, P.S.:

and

when i've satiated my appetites physical,
i satiates my appetites, mystical.
employed, i's a bureau*crack*!
cut loose an anar*christ* am i!
with a gutteral arts degree

who knows how to obfuscate
quite as well as i,
whose favourite hum is buy! buy! buy!
so's why does i ast
'sir, what's duty?'
'ma'am, where's honour *lay*?'
dopin' makes me dopey's,
all i knows to say.

Bootleg (surely you can see, if you can see) dulls some; sharpens others. I count myself among the latter. Me, one dose and like gypsies over tea leaves, coffee grounds and dreams, I read the world's vomit and the crud stuck in toilet bowls. (Every man's tissue, a Rorscharch.) I am the historian as prophet. Call me the Omar Khyam of ivy halls and corner speakeasies; call me anything you like, but say always, I rebelled, even if it isn't true. And do remember, *remember*, for it is true, I didn't tag Morales. I didn't cooperate. I fought for dispensation. Let it be so. I could have gone along. Susan encouraged me; Anjou didn't discourage me. And the *Forty Law* is intelligent! Among the choices; famine, war, etc. (all natural and unnatural bearers of apocalypse) I stand by the *Forty Law*. But Morales, 'El Viejo;' what a backhand! What a serve! What speed, agil – . Archives never asked me to do anything like this before. I was educated to help bring back, albeit, with necessary refinements, the *Sweet Bygones*; our yesterdays. If the genocides hadn't gotten out of hand, someone from Archives and Planning, some messenger boy from Anthropology, would have taken care of Morales. These damn Indians, thumbing their noses at history. It's their fault I got the assignment. What do they want to stick around this nostalera for? Why won't they pick a happy-time? Show me an Indian in the literature or history of the Great Depression and I'll find you a commy in George Washington's cabinet, and call him Karl Marx and let the Clerks rewrite the history of the whole goddamn western world! I've never been as shocked by anything as I was when Dr Bannister tripped in with his proposition. 'You're a tennis fan,' he said.

'Why yes.' I thought he'd found another home movie of ol' Don Budge, practising those sky high lob shots nobody ever hits any more, except by accident.

'Well then,' said Bannister, 'you can give the good news

to Morales, 'El Viejo', I believe they call him. We like to see that operatives of his stature get a personal summons, a privilege of rank, you might say. Anyhow, we're a little shorthanded now. I thought maybe you would take a run up to Forest Hills and give him the notice. He'll be forty next month and, well, we like to give them a chance to get everything in order; think over the reincarnation, pick out a happy-time, that sort of thing. You'll enjoy the tournament. This will be Morales last match with that young fellow Bornas. Ought to be exciting. Remember, don't be squeamish about giving him his summons. It's not as if you were an undertaker. Morales is ready for an Elders era. The sooner he can consult the packet for the elder-time he wants, the happier he'll be. By the way, mention that his fooltax is in arrears. Enjoy the match; see you next week!'

I opened the summons. That was the first step to involvement:

> 'Greetings Elder:
>
> This is to advise you of your obligation to report for pre-induction examination. Is your fooltax paid up? Have you made your will? Put your house in . . . '

How could Bannister ask me to tag Morales? If those dullards at anthropology had listened to me, they wouldn't be having this trouble. I told them to put the damn Indians on reservations. That's where most of them were in the early thirties. But no, they wouldn't listen. They stuck them in the genocides; didn't even let them have a choice like they did the blacks. I guess the reasoning was, you can't have a good depression without oppression. You've got to have your Saco-Vanzetti, your Scottsborough Case; an occasional lynching down south, angry poems by Langston Hughes. But what can you do with a reservation? Nothing! Just as well use the land for a good dust storm. And with that sort of logic Archives and Planning put the Indians in the Genocide, only the red devils won't co-operate. They won't go willingly and everywhere you look, they're disrupting things. No matter how well you educate them about the death camps – Jews in WW II; Arabs in Mid-East VI – they won't buy it. There's no nostalgia for genocide; especially among these Indians. They can't appreciate historical necessity. They don't even want to go back to the post-civil war days and get massacred; even with an annual treaty that will let them get Custer once a year until, again, the west is won. They say 'no more treaties'. No matter how you arrange the terms, it's the only reply they'll make. No Indian has spoken but to utter those words since the Genocide began. They simply piss on everything and say 'no more treaty.' Not even a 'How' or an 'Ugh'. They resist the Genocide, so respectable operatives like myself have to carry the burden of history. Fooltaxes keep going up and still there aren't enough peace keepers and summoners to keep order. No matter how you arrange things, you always wind up with a bunch of dissidents. The Indians end up smiling though. They go happy! I thank for our peace keepers. I thank for non-violent aggression through *motionless.*

But why can't the peace keepers be more efficient? I'm no summoner. I can't do it. No, goddamnit, they can dock my pay. They can double my fooltax. Even if I wind up a galley slave somewhere in the outer reaches of history, dreaming of nostaleras unattained, I will not tag Morales. I won't, not even if they make me an Indian; put me in the Genocide, I won't do it. I'm no judas. Sure, I almost gave it to him at Forest Hills. Yes, but that last set! 'El Viejo' was down five games to one. It seemed the match, the tournament was lost. I thought, 'El Viejo' will be glad of a new reincarnation, a happy-time where he can again excel. What nostalera will he choose? Will he cross the great desert with Brigham Young, go wenching with old Ben Franklin – but then Morales began his come-back. He played masterfully, perhaps reaching the peak of his glorious career in the eighth game when he broke Bornas' service with perfectly executed drop shots, just over the net at points where Bornas could do nothing but poke out his racket and hope futilely for a miracle. But the miracle was 'El Viejo', who took the set and the tournament 7–5, winning the last six games consecutively. To give him the summons at that moment would have been like, like bringing him death itself. Still, I waved to him as he left the court. 'I must do it,' I said but then the old cummings hum ran through my mind: *'how do you like your blue-eyed boy, Mister Death.'*

I couldn't do it. I talked hours with him. 'Get me a dispensation,' he begged.

'Dispensations are for technocrats only. Don't you understand that? You will be much happier in a nostalera for the forty-plusers. Happiness requires constancy. You won't have to look around at – '

'If my game were slipping! If I were put upon by the world, I would take your summons. It would be welcome! I'm no dissident but – don't do this to me. You saw how I played! Did it look like I was through? I beat these kids! I'll be doing it for a long time. They call me 'El Viejo', but my game – you know I'm getting better. I'm no agitator, but . . .'

'I will get you a dispensation,' I said. 'You played well.'

We drank wine. We celebrated his victory and the dispensation. We made many toasts to his championships and to the forty-plusers on all the frontiers of history.

Selected Advice and Exhortations

Susan's – 'You're in trouble; you've done it now. You better give that little spic his summons. After all it's just another reincarnation. You're not executing him! Do you want our fooltax raised? Do your job!'

Anjou's – 'You done made yo' self a mess. You musta got yo' brains from yo' daddy stead o' our mama. How come you never done yo' job? Give that Puerto Rican bum his paper!'

Bannister's – 'Get this matter settled quick or . . . '

Mine – 'He just wants to wait till his game starts to slip. What's wrong with that! Forty's not so goddamn old! In three years I'll be forty. I can't summon Morales. Do you want me to be the Eichmann of my time? The Cal – '

Replies and Demands

Susan – matrimony, order, screams 'Oh, please, yuk!'

Anjou – chaos, incest, smiles 'Oh, please, yuk!'

Bannister – force, authority, nods 'Get this matter settled quick or . . . '

Me – 'Oh . . . '

They are prohibitions in counterpoint, two-headed Hoover quarters, reflections; eyes questioning blanks that won't fill in. The look they offer, I categorise – *so what we all crack skulls dialing our timepiece back and forth, plugging in our tasty-toasters, driving up the price of chili; being general pigs, plying our trades and our . . .*

And considering my post I must admit, I'm well invested

in the blood guilt of my age. So why worry about his summons? What can I do – demand justice? The 'on' and 'off' switch is in other hands. There's no Geneva Convention regarding torments of the soul; no law of nations concerning international despair.

Tarpaper rustles in the wind. Anjou is near, naked; sweating from her morning dance.

'Sister.'

'Yes.'

'Sister, I'm afraid.'

'Nothin' to be 'fraid of 'cept stupidity.'

She walks to the window. Quickly her shadow glides up the wall and on to the ceiling; grey, too heavy, thick, too much a symbol, not at all Anjou, sweet fruit.

'Brother, the mornin's come. What you breakfastin' on? Got some good chili, none that hoss meat shit! Got some yams lef' over. You sho' been high. Took yo' bootleg and went to ravin'. You been yellin' 'bout goin' to Carolina. Wish you meant it. I could sho' do with a vacation myself. Nobody works harder'n a fifty dolla' "ho".'

'Dance for me, I want to think, to – '

'Sho'.'

I watch her movements, smooth, effortless. She is not – even in this shack with the wind rattling its walls – so far from the ballets of our youth, the Carolina-Georgie Gold rush of second twenty-nine. Our daddies said: 'Thirty thousand dream miners found an ounce of gold in Carolina; an ounce and and a half in Georgia. That's where the term "fool's gold" got started.' But Anjou gave the miners a better dream than gold. She danced the dance of the Carolina Wren. She was a promise of natural grace. Even now her movements are smooth, uplifting. She does no dance of death. The body is still tight-muscled. The rhythm; the desire is there but she is thirty-eight. Public dancing is denied her. Still, she says, 'I had my time.' And each morning she exercises; dances, dreams. *'The fifty-dolla' "ho" the worka;'* she sings, *'the twenty dolla' "ho" jest lay there; hunde'd dolla' "ho" jest smile. You got yo' self a workin' gal, Brother better show me yo' style.'*

Listening; watching her dance, Morales fate seems less significant. He is prey, but honoured. Anjou is just prey. The game is to shame her, make her stop dancing; kill her by decree. Still, she goes on. The next nostalera; the one after that, she will still be dancing. Of Morales doom, his battle, I am spectator only. Towards Anjou, it is different. Morales is combat, Anjou is joy. Joy is a mortal issue. In her fate I share, we . . .

'Carolina,' I say. 'Kitty Hawk, Kill Devil Hill. Let's – '

'What stuff you talkin'?'

'Kill Devil Hill; I want to go there – the vacation. Remember when we were kids, before they drove us north. We went to the *Wright Memorial.* The Clerks were just rebuilding it – Hitler's statue on one side; Picasso's on the other. I played Orville and you played Wilbur. You danced with Pablo but you wouldn't let Adolph touch you. I got so tickled when you slapped his face, I fell over the edge; straight down, fifty feet through the briars. Didn't get but one little scratch. Our mamas said I was in the air longer than Wilbur (or was it Orville) and your daddy told about being in the store in Elizabeth City that December day when the telegram about the first flight came over the wire. He asked my daddy what he thought about it. 'Goddamn Yankee foolishness,' my daddy said.

'Your daddy winked. "Yassauh!" ' he said.

'We all layed down and laughed. Now that was some nostalera!'

It was late when we caught the southbound public. Sister Anjou had to meet a client first and I had to do something about Morales's summons. I went to Bannister. I was going to give the summons back and quit. I would tough out the rest of this nostalera as an Indian if I had to, but I would be an unregimented, anarchist Indian; social consciousness amiss, mortality and morality, tentative.

But when I arrived at Archives, a large crowd of Cherokees had surrounded the building. I couldn't get to Bannister's office. The Indians wore contraband 'breathers' so that the *motionless* did not effect them. 'This could go on all day,' an operative said. Peace keepers ran around with ancient electro-clubs trying to chase the Cherokees away. I knew the other Clerks were probably driving themselves batty looking for appropriate historical precedents to justify whatever was going to happen. Off hand, I thought of several precedents myself. The big riot back in second sixty-eight when after a couple of assassinations and a rigged Kentucky

Derby, a bunch of dissidents tried to overthrow the government with brotherhood parades. The peace keepers brought that to a rapid halt.

This Archives riot looked like something else, though. The street was full of piss. Everywhere you looked, Indian men, women, and children were drinking vats of brew and urinating. Some were taking bootleg too, but a mild dose; a hit suited to silent rioting. Here and there the injured lay moaning in the street, waiting for samaritans to carry them to comfort centres. I threw the Morales summons into the street. An old man urinated on it, yellowing it like all other history. I wept. I laughed. *'I'm the black flag of anarchy, ho hum.'*

Riding at night on the public, you begin to appreciate the magnitude of our Institutionalised Depression. It is a magnificent nostalera. Out the windows, the darkened landscape looks burned. The route the public takes is through back alleys, past ancient warehouses and factory sidings of real Bygones. The way of the night rail south is through the stable; the constant land of the weary and poor. Shanties and rag-pickers, stray cats, skinny dogs and tired land pushing up a crop no one will buy; dark rivers, forest, back porch lights in small towns; vacant storefront churches make a mosaic as the public whines through the night. Until you wake up, you don't know it was all a dream.

'My daddy played the bones,' says Anjou.

'My mama played the harp,' I say.

'My mama moaned a hungry song,' she says. 'What was she hungry for?'

'My daddy never sang at all,' I say. 'He made his music with a deck of cards.'

Parents blend together. Who was wedded to whom? Brother and sister, sucklings at one breast. Where did we come from? Where are we going?

It's a long time climbing to the top of Kill Devil Hill. In the hours before dawn you smell the ocean and the sound. Through the fog you are certain you have a clear vision of them both. Somehow, you know it won't be that way, that it's just the sense of the sleight-of-hand man. Still, you expect the sunrise to confirm your memories.

Anjou spreads our quilt. We lie in front of the memorial between the statues of Hitler and Picasso. Anjou rises, embraces the painter to reenact the scene of our youth. 'I'm not going to fall down the hill again,' I tell her.

'Then I won't slap ol' Adolph. I'll hug Pablo though!'

Here is our conversation with these giants. After all, we've come here to make theatre.!

Q. Mr Picasso, Pablo, did you see your 'Guernica' in Orville's (or was it Wilbur's) first flight?

A. No, my vision is not death. It is life. I might have seen my dove if I'd been looking. I'm no soothsayer you know.

Q. Mr Hitler, Adolph, did you see your 'Guernica' in the famous flight?

A. Yes, and I saw London, my V.2's, and Warsaw and . . . I may have been a lousy painter but I'm a hell of a prophet. Let me tell you, I even saw Dresden and Chemnitz and a hole in my head AND – '

Q. What about this Orville, Wilbur – did you see –

A. 'No comment – the bicycle busi – Shut up, Wilbur!'

CHRISTMAS STORY

by MICHAEL BUTTERWORTH

DEPRESSION.

Radio playing DJ selections music is the only thing which reaches him.

Bright light shining down casts white table top with typewriter whisky bottle paper and jugs of water in blinding circle of light spotlights his existence amidst the shadows of the room.

Wall of large flowers creeping up to the ceiling.

Steel gas fire, budgie chatter from a cage in a corner.

Behind him a window out on the world.

Along a shoreline vision he sees in his mind kicks pebbles hissing breakers crash at his side, sea-weed round his ankles from the clinging sea.

Misty day cloud and sea horizons mix indistinguishable depths.

Feeling he is being followed but each time he turns to look only the shoreline twists along at the feet of the craggy cliffs melting into mist.

In the next room hears his three-year daughter playing with christmas toys.

Cards from distant friends.

Glittering chopped tree seems so new and bright to minds of his children.

A toy train that goes round and round, minds trapped by its circular movement adult minds trapped by their relationships.

Distant faraway scene in his mind the christmas ritual reinforces.

Budgie chattering away berserk thoughts in its pea head trapped by its reflection in the mirror.

Across the carpet cold draughts . . .

. . . ahead of him the shoreline melts into mist where the sheer craggy cliffs push the beach into the sea and further access is impossible.

He stands before the jagged face staring intently at the stratified layers manifestations of time compares his own life with the life of the earth . . . the universe.

Clear cold air to carry his thoughts.

Pebbles have turned to sand at his feet he sinks slightly leaving depressions filled with cleansing sea water, his tracks obliterated by the mother.

Behind him he senses his pursuer, turns but sees only the shoreline melting into the mist.

He presses his back against the cliff face and eyes the mistiness . . . sudden droplets floating in the air settling on his clothes, feels the cold shapes twisting in the mist approaching impressions made by the stranger in the sand filling with sea water.

In the oven, a flapping bird beak tapping at the see-through window feet clawing in hot grease.

The stranger introduces himself, bringing a new life into the room exciting the Coloroll red flowers interminably creeping up their black background.

The depression blocking thoughts feeling lifts.

He faces the stranger across his typewriter where the stranger has seated himself in an armchair in the shadows, leaving his depression in the faded upholstery the only sign of his presence.

With a thud the budgie dies in its cage.

Silence from the next room as his offspring finish choking on this that.

The gas fire dies in its frame.

Across the city his cousin and wife who are travelling to visit him crash.

His wife doesn't get up out of bed with his tiny son.

The stranger radiates a smile which encroaches into the pool of light above the table and fills him with warmth, bearing the christmas gifts.

The smile reaches him where he is standing watching the depressions in the sand approach.

The hard granite cliff face presses into his back last thing he remembers.

Shoreline dissolving into mist.

Namelessness.

Beinglessness.

He has lain awake like this once before, drifting unawares out of a deep something, in time to see the form of the stranger disappearing against the white wall of his bedroom.

He remembers the strong feeling he had that the stranger had manipulated his mind in his sleep, or wherever it was that he had been taken.

As he awoke more fully the fading form frightened him and he ducked under the bedclothes.

Then when he peeped out the white shroud with featureless face and arms crossed below the cloth had gone.

Instead the early dawn sky was pulsing with a strange red light trapped behind a broken horizon of houses and trees through the glass pane.

He comes to, staring at the words he has typed from out of the unknown greyness, the vision of layers of humanity in the rocks still burn inside him.

Music rides in from the next room proclaiming brief human desires its harmonies cutting right across time from primeval existence to life to come.

He has been singled out again.

He remembers that he had walked for hours through the early morning deserted streets and traced the source of the red light to a disused church in the countryside, when the light had promptly ceased.

He doubted whether it had been visible to anyone else.

He wonders about the significance of a second visitation whether one reinforces the other.

Music from the next room ceases.

He puts on his coat and gloves and packs a small lunch in the kitchen, leaving the christmas decorations the bodies of his family and the dying tree the trapped bird.

To his surprise the world outside the house has changed dramatically.

Wind blowing down street clogged with silent forms . . . christmas lights dragged and smashed to the ground roofs ripped off building walls crumbling into piles of plaster and brick rubble.

Cars crushed and jammed together along the roadside as if ploughed aside by a giant hand.

Silence except for the eerie sound of wind slicing through wires through gaps in the brickwork.

His house door faces the avenue of glinting junked metal and blood, a huge gouge in the earth stretching as far as his eye and inner geographical awareness can see through building hill and lake.

He realises intuitively that the road has been carved exclusively for his benefit, for his car, and he feels uncomfortable.

Powerless climbs into his car and drives between the gate-posts across the ripped urban landscape.

His wife wakes to the cries of their son from his bedroom cot she lies still savouring the warmth of the blankets a moment longer lets waves of sleep wash over her.

Then she rises into her housecoat and collects the standing child tiny fists clenched whitely gripping at the cot sides.

She climbs unsteadily downstairs greeted by the christmas disarray of toys a sinkful of pots a tabletop of stale meal.

Their daughter drops her chocolate angel stolen from the christmas tree clamours round her feet for attention.

Daddy has gone.

Not again she sighs, worried now how she is going to cope with her night job if the kids are unminded if she should phone his psychiatrist inform social services or . . . the door bell rings insane burst of chattering rattles the budgie's cage on its stand.

Child in arm she opens the door greets her boy-friend from the night club with a scowl of bad temperedness.

Behind him as he travels, town and country heal themselves sealing off the route along which his enemies – who want him to return – have set out in pursuit, only to be buried in the settling earth.

Ahead of him the misty coastline where the huge gouge that rents the land breaks through the lonely cliff line ends submerged in the sea.

He drives his car into the spray cast off by the hissing breakers crashing shoals of silver fish on to the beach.

Moves along the deserted shoreline, wheels crunching over the gleaming pebbles spinning on clumps of slippery brown seaweed strained off from the waves.

Coasts slowly until he can go no further halted by the stratified cliff face layers of humanity in the time-worn granite.

He climbs out and slams the car door walks insignificant man to the foot of the towering cliff roar of the mighty sea spray slashing up its face soaking his clothes stings his eyes and throat.

Incessant roaring of the white-crested combers dashed to foam and sucking backward across the pebbles hissing sound.

Long time ago remembers standing here as a young boy holiday with the family.

Wind, misty day, a rough sea . . . now the merging occasions become one.

Past present and future separated by biological existence.

At the furthermost reach of the waves pebbles turn to sand, foot-prints walk towards him from round the back of his parked car rapid tiny indentations filling with the sea.

It is the stranger, who walks past him touches his being with a cold breath goes a lot deeper into his bones than the hazy swirling forms about him.

The man turns and sees that the stranger has manifested himself once more, tall white shroud arms akimbo featureless face shimmering dully against the dark brown rock.

A pathway from the sky cuts through the grey mist focusing a slanting pillar of light against the rock by the side of the apparition.

As the man looks he sees a white crucifix made of the same shimmering substance materialise flickering weakly then more strongly as it persists under the pillar of light.

In the side of a grocer's shop his car smashed through the plate glass coloured packets and cans stream of blood and petrol over the pavement running into the gutters.

Few cries from injured shoppers his sightless eyes body slumped across the bonnet beneath an overturned display stand coloured christmas papers fluttering drawing-pinned to the shelves . . .

He feels a rising tide of emotion inside him as he clambers over the shining wet boulders paddles through rock pools filled with anemones and shells arms out-stretched towards the pure white arms of the cross by the stranger's side.

Mankind is suffering.

As he reaches the cross bathed in its glory and brilliance shape etched on his being stoops to kiss it instantaneous awareness of humanity living in trees living in caves in wooden shacks in igloos in skyscrapers in underground laboratories in space stations in prisons in interplanetary bases in starships in far flung worlds throughout the galaxies the universe, feels the power of their thoughts lifting him upward into the grey sky his intense compassion flooding out into empty space bathing all beings lifting lifting . . .

A new Christ.

THE SUN NEVER SETS ON THE LANDS OF ENGLANDS QUEEN
D Britton 75

THE CABINET OF OLIVER NAYLOR

by BARRINGTON J. BAYLEY

NAYLAND'S WORLD WAS a world of falling rain, dancing on streaming tarmac, drumming on the roofs of big black cars, soaking the grey and buff masonry of the dignified buildings that lined the streets of the town. Behind the faded gold lettering of office windows, constantly awash, tense laconic conversations took place, accompanied by the pouring, pattering sound of rain, and the rushing of water from the gutterings.

Beneath the pressing grey sky, all was humid. Nayland, his feet up on his desk, looked down through the window to where the slow-moving traffic drove through the deluge and splashed the kerbs. Nayland Investigations Inc., read the window's bowed gold lettering. The rain fell, too, on the black and white screen of the TV set flickering away in the corner of the office. It fell steadily, unremittingly, permanently. Humphrey Bogart and Barbara Stanwyck fled together in a big black car, quarrelling tersely in an enclosed little world smelling of rain and seat leather.

They stopped at a crossroads. The argument resumed in clipped, deadpan tones, while Bogart gripped the steering wheel and scowled. The windscreen wipers were barely able to clear away the rain; on the outside camera shots their faces were seen blurrily, intermittently, cut off from external contact.

In the office, the telephone rang. Nayland picked it up. He heard a voice that essentially was his own; yet with an accent that was British rather than American.

'Is that Oliver Nayland, private detective?'

'*Frank* Nayland,' Nayland corrected.

'*Frank* Nayland.'

The voice paused, as if for reflection. 'I would like to call on your services, Mr Nayland. I want someone to investigate your world for me. Follow the couple in the black car. Where are they fleeing to? What are they fleeing from? Does it ever stop raining?'

Nayland replied in a professionally neutral tone. 'I charge two hundred dollars a week, plus expenses,' he said. 'To investigate physical world phenomena, however – gravitation, rain, formation of the elements – my usual fee is doubled.'

While speaking he moved to the TV and twiddled the tuning knob. The black car idling at the crossroads vanished, was replaced by a man's face talking into a telephone. Essentially the face was Nayland's own. Younger, perhaps; less knowing, not world-weary. There was no pencil-line moustache, and the client sported a boyish haircut Nayland wouldn't have been seen dead in.

The client looked straight at him out of the screen. 'I think I can afford it. Please begin your investigations.'

The picture faded, giving way to Gene Kelly singing 'Dancing in the Rain'. Nayland returned to the window. He picked up a pair of binoculars from his desk and trained them on a black car that was momentarily stopped at the traffic lights. He glimpsed the face of Barbara Stanwyck through the side window of the car. She was sitting stiffly in the front passenger seat, speaking rapidly, her proud face vibrant with restrained, angry passion. By her side Bogart was tapping the driving wheel and snarling back curt replies.

The lights changed, the car swept on, splashing rain water over the kerb. Nayland put down his binoculars and become thoughtful.

FOR a few minutes longer Oliver Naylor watched the private dick's activities on his thespitron screen. Nayland held tense, laconic interviews in seedy city offices, swept through wet streets in a black car, talked in gloomy bars while the rain pattered against the windows, visited the mansion of Mrs Van der Loon, and had a brief shoot-out with a local mobster.

Eventually Naylor faded out the scene, holding down the 'retain in store' key. At the same time he keyed the 'credible sequence' button back in. The thespitron started up again, and with a restrained fanfare began to unfold an elaborate tale of sea schooners on a watery world.

Naylor ignored it, turning down the sound so that the saga would not distract him, and rose from his chair to pace the living room of his mobile habitat. How interesting, he thought, that the drama machine, the thespitron as he called it, should invent a character so close to himself in name and appearance. True, the background was different. *Frank Nayland* was a 20th century American, perfectly adapted to his world of the private eye, *circa* 1950, whereas *Oliver Naylor* was a 22nd century Englishman, a different type altogether.

The thespitron had an unlimited repertoire and in principle one could expect a random dramatic output from it. But in practice it showed a predilection for Elizabethan tragedy – worthy, Naylor thought, of the immortal Bill himself – and for Hollywood thrillers of the 1930s–50s period. Both of these were firm favourites of Naylor, the thespitron's creator. Clearly he had unintentionally built some bias into it and would need to locate its source.

The existence of Frank Nayland probably had a similar explanation, he concluded. It was probably due to the optical extra he had built into the machine, namely the facility by which the viewer could talk to the characters portrayed on the thespitron screen. The thespitron exhibited an admirable degree of adaptability – it was perfectly delightful, for instance, to see how it had automatically translated his stick-mike into a big, unwieldy 1950s telephone. Similarly, it must have absorbed his *persona* from earlier intrusions, fashioning it into the world of Frank Nayland.

Just the same, it was eerie to be able to talk to himself, albeit in this fictional guise. A soupçon, perhaps, of 'identity crisis'.

He strolled to the living room window and gazed out. Millions of galaxies were speeding past in the endless depths, presenting the appearance of a sidewise fall of tiny snowflakes. The habitat was speeding through the universe at a velocity of c^{186}, heading into infinity.

AT length Naylor sighed, turned from the window and crossed the room to settle himself in a comfortable armchair, switching on the vodor lecturer which he had stocked with all relevant material before leaving Cambridge. Selecting the subject he wanted, he rested his head against the leather upholstery and listened, letting the lecture sink into his mind much as one might enjoy a piece of music.

The vodor began to speak.

'IDENTITY. The logical law of identity is expressed by the formula A = A, or A is A. This law is a necessary law of self-conscious thought, and without it thinking would be impossible. It is in fact merely the positive expression of the law of contradiction, which states that the same attribute cannot at the same time be affirmed and denied of the same subject.

'Philosophically, the exact meaning of the term "identity", and the ways in which it can be predicated, remain undecided. Some hold that identity excludes difference; others that it actually implies it, connoting "differential likeness". See B. Bosanquet, *Essays and Addresses*, 1889. The question is one of whether identity can be posited only of an object's attributes, or whether it refers uniquely to an object regardless of its attributes . . .'

Naylor looked up as Watson-Smythe, his passenger, emerged from an adjoining bedroom where he had been sleeping. The young man stretched and yawned.

'*Haw!* Sleep knits up the ravelled sleeve, and all that. Hello there, old chap. Still plugging away, I see?'

Naylor switched off the vodor. 'Not getting very far, I'm afraid,' he admitted shyly. 'In fact, I haven't made any real progress for weeks.'

'Never mind. Early days, I expect.' Watson-Smythe yawned again, tapping his mouth with his hand. 'Fancy a cup of char? I'll brew up.'

'Yes, that would be excellent.'

Watson-Smythe had affable blue eyes. He was fair-skinned and athletic-looking. Although only just out of bed he had taken the trouble to comb his hair before entering the habitat's main room, arranging his shining blond curls on either side of a neat parting.

Naylor had no real idea of who he was. He had met him at one of those temporary habitat villages that sprang up all over space. He was, it seemed, one of those rash of adventurous people who chose to travel without their own velocitator habitat, hitching lifts here and there, bumming their way around infinity. Apparently he was trying to find some little-known artist called Corngold (the name was faintly familiar to Naylor). Having discovered his whereabouts at the village, he had asked Naylor to take him there and Naylor, who had nowhere in particular to go, had thought it impolite to refuse.

Watson-Smythe moved to the utility cupboard and set some water to boil, idly whistling a tune by Haydn. While waiting, he glanced through the window at the speeding galaxies, then crossed to the velocitator control board and peered at the speedometer, tapping at the glass-covered dial.

'Will we get there soon, do you think? Is 186 your top speed?'

'We could do nearly 300, if pushed,' Naylor said. 'But any faster than 186 and we'd probably go past the target area without noticing it.'

'Ah, that wouldn't do at all, would it?'

The kettle whistled. Watson-Smythe rushed to it and busied himself with warming the teapot, brewing the tea and pouring it, after a proper, interval into bone-china cups.

Naylor accepted a cup, but declined a share of the toast and marmalade which Watson-Smythe prepared for himself.

'This fellow Corngold,' he asked hesitantly while his guest ate, 'is he much of an artist?'

Watson-Smythe looked doubtful. 'Couldn't say, really. Don't know much about it myself. Don't know Corngold personally either, as a matter of fact.'

'Oh.' Naylor's curiosity was transient, and he didn't like to pry.

Watson-Smythe waggled a finger at the thespitron, which was still playing out its black-and-white shadow show (Naylor had deliberately eschewed colour; monochrome seemed to impart a more bare-boned sense of drama). 'Got the old telly going again, I see – the automated telly. You ought to put that into production, old chap. It would be a boon to habitat travellers. Much better than carrying a whole library of play-back tapes.'

'Yes, I dare say it would.'

'Not in the same class as this other project of yours, if it comes off, of course. That will be something.'

Naylor smiled in embarrassment. He almost regretted having told his companion about the scheme he was working on. It was, possibly, much too ambitious.

After his breakfast Watson-Smythe disappeared back into his bedroom to practise callisthenics – though Naylor couldn't imagine what anyone so obsessed with keeping trim was doing space travelling. Habitat life, by its enclosed naturc, was not conducive to good health.

His passenger's presence could be what had been blocking his progress, Naylor thought. After all, he had come out here for solitude, originally.

He switched on the vodor again and settled down to try to put his thoughts back on the problem once more.

'THE modern dilemma (continued the vodor) is perhaps admirably expressed in an ancient Buddhist tale. An enlightened master one day announced to his disciples that he wished to enter into contemplation. Reposing himself, he closed his eyes and withdrew his consciousness.

'For thirty years he remained thus, while his disciples took care of his body and kept it clean.

'At the end of thirty years he opened his eyes and looked about him. The disciples gathered round. "Can the noble master tell us," they asked, "what has engaged his attention all this time?" The master told them: "I have been considering whether, in all the deserts of the world, there could conceivably be two grains of sand identical in every particular."

'The disciples were puzzled. "Surely," they said, "that is a small matter to occupy a mind such as yours?"

' "Small it may be," the master replied, "but it was too great for me. I still do not know the answer."

'In the 20th century a striking *scientific* use of the concept of identity seemed for a while as though it would cut right across many logical and philosophical definitions and answer the Buddhist master's question. To explain paradoxical findings resulting from experiments in electron diffraction, equations were devised which, in mathematical terms, removed from electrons their individual identities. It was pointed out that electrons are so alike to one another as to be, to all intents and purposes, identical. The equations therefore described electrons as exchanging identities with one another in a rhythmic oscillation, without any transfer of energy or position . . .'

NAYLOR's first love had been logic machines. He had begun as a boy by reconstructing the early devices of the 18th and the 19th centuries: the deceptively simple Stanhope Demonstrator, with its calibrated window and two cursors (invented by an English earl, probably the very first genuine logic machine, though working out the identities was a tedious business); Venn diagrams – which in common with the Jevons Logic Machine (the first to solve complicated problems faster than the unaided logician) made use of the logic algebra of George Boole. He had quickly progressed to the type of machine developed in the 20th century and known generically as the 'computer', although only later had it developed into an instrument of pure logic for its own sake. By the time he was twenty he had become fully conversant with proper 'thinking machines' able to handle multi-valued logic, and had begun to design models of his own. His crowning achievement, a couple of years ago, had been the construction of what he had reason to believe was the finest logic machine ever, a superb instrument embracing the entire universe of discourse.

It was then that he had conceived the idea of the thespitron, a device which if marketed would without doubt put all writers of dramatic fiction out of business for once and all. Its basic hardware consisted of the above-mentioned logic machine, plus a comprehensive store and various ancillaries. After his past efforts, he had found the arrangement surprisingly easy to accomplish. In appearance the machine resembled an over-large, old-fashioned television set, with perhaps rather too many controls; but whereas an ordinary television receiver picked up its programmes from some far away transmitter, the thespitron generated them internally. Essentially it was a super-plotting device; it began with bare logical identities, and combined and recombined them into ever more complex structures, until by this process it was able to plot an endless variety of stories and characters, displaying them complete with dialogue, settings and incidental music.

Naylor had watched the plays and films generated by the thespitron for several months now, and he could pronounce himself well pleased with the result of his labours. The thespitron was perpetual motion: because the logical categories could be permutated endlessly, its dramatic inventiveness was inexhaustible. Left to its own devices, it would eventually run through all possible dramatic situations.

PHILOSOPHICALLY Naylor held fast to the tradition of British empiricism (without descending, of course, to

American pragmatism) and saw himself as a child of the 19th century, favouring, perhaps for reasons of nostalgia, the flavour of thought of that period – though the doctrines of J. S. Mill had been much updated, naturally, by the thoroughgoing materialist empiricists of Naylor's own time. It would have gone totally against the grain, therefore, to ascribe the logical categories to any supernatural or non-material cause. Yet he had once heard a theological argument which, because of his possession of the thespitron, afforded him a great deal of secret, if perverse, pleasure.

This argument was that God had created the universe for its theatrical content alone, simply in order to view the innumerable dramatic histories it generated. By this notion all ethical parameters, all poignancies, triumphs, tragedies and meaningless sufferings, were, so to speak, literary devices.

Was not the thespitron a *private* cosmic theatre? The cosmos in miniature? Complete in itself, as the greater cosmos was, self-acting, containing its own logical laws? Furthermore it had a creator and observer – Naylor himself, who was thus elevated to the status of a god. The only god that existed, possibly, since the idea of an original transcendental God was, of course, absurd.

The alluring impression that the thespitron had some sort of cosmic significance was heightened by its present location here in intergalactic space, googols of light years from Earth. Despite his empiricist philosophical upbringing Naylor could not rid his mind of the fascinating fiction that there might be, at the source of existence, a preternatural logic machine – the transcendental archetype of his own – which ground out logical identities in pure form. He pictured to himself an immensely long, dark corridor down which the identities and categories passed, combining and recombining until eventually they permutated themselves into concrete substance to become the physical universe and all its contents.

Naylor smiled, shaking his head, reminding himself how corrupting to philosophy were all such idealist fancies. He was well aware of how fallacious it was to imagine that logic was antecedent to matter.

NAYLOR was by no means alone in regarding himself as a product of 19th century values; most educated Englishmen of his time did. The qualities of a rational civilisation were epitomised, it was commonly believed, by the great Victorian age, with its prolific inventiveness, its love of 'projects', its advocacy of 'progress' combined with its innate conservatism. Nostalgia was not the sole cause, however, of the 22nd century's respect for past endeavours. The renaissance in Victorian sentiment, in Britain at least, was genuine.

As often happens, economic forces were in some measure responsible for the change. During the 21st century it gradually became clear that the advantages of global trade were at last being outweighed by the disadvantages; the international division of labour was taking on the aspect of a destructive natural force which could impoverish entire peoples. The notion of economic progress took on another meaning. It came to signify, not the ability to dominate world markets, but the science of how a small nation might become wealthy without any foreign trade whatsoever. Britain, always a pioneer, was the first to discover this new direction. With the help of novel technologies she reversed what had been axiomatic since the days of Adam Smith, and for a time was once again the wealthiest power on Earth, aloof from the world trade storm, reaping through refusal to trade all the benefits she had once gained through trade.

It was a time of innovation, of surprising, often fantastic invention, of which the Harkham Velocitator, a unit of which was now powering Naylor's habitat through infinity, was perhaps the outstanding example. The boffin had come into his own again, outwitting the expensively equipped teams of professional research scientists. Yet in some respects it was a cautious period, alert to the dangers of too precipitous use of every new-fangled gadget, and keeping alive the spirit of the red flag that had once been required to precede every horseless carriage. For that reason advantage was not always taken of every advance in productive methods.

Two methods in particular were forbidden. The first, an all-purpose domestic provider commonly known as the matter-bank, was technically called the hylic potentiator. It worked by holding in store a mass of amorphous, non-particulate matter, or hyle, to use the classical term. Hylic matter from this store could be instantly converted into any object, artifact or substance for which the machine was programmed, and returned to store if the utility was no longer needed or had not been consumed. Because the hylic store consisted essentially of a single gigantic shaped neutron, very high energies were involved, which had led to the device being deemed too dangerous for use on Earth. Models were still to be found here and there in space, however.

The second banned production method was a process whereby artefacts were able to reproduce themselves after the manner of viruses if brought into contact with simple materials. The creation of self-replicating artifacts had become subject to world prohibition after the islands of Japan became buried beneath growing mounds of still-multiplying TV sets, audvid recorders, cameras, autos, motor-bikes, refrigerators, helicopters, pocket computers, transistor radios, portphones, light airplanes, speedboats, furniture, sex aids, hearing aids, artificial limbs and organs, massage machines, golf clubs, zip fasteners, toys, typewriters, graphic reproduction machines, electron microscopes, house plumbing and electrical systems, machine tools, industrial robots, earth-movers, drilling rigs, prefabricated dwellings, ships, submersibles, fast-access transit vehicles, rocket launchers, lifting bodies, extraterrestrial exploration vehicles, X-ray machines, radio, video, microwave, X-ray and laser transmitters, modems, reading machines, and innumerable other conveniences.

Of all innovations, the invention to have most impact on the modern British mind was undoubtedly the Harkham velocitator, which had abolished the impediment of distance and opened up infinity to the interested traveller. Theoretically the velocitator principle could give access to any velocity, however high, except one: it was not possible to travel a measured distance in zero time, or an infinite distance in any measured time. But in practice, a velocitator unit's top speed depended on the size of its armature. After a while designing bigger and bigger armatures had become almost a redundant exercise. Infinity was infinity was infinity.

Velocitator speeds were expressed in powers of the velocity of light. Thus 186, Naylor's present pace, indicated the speed of light multiplied by itself 186 times. Infinity was now littered, if littered was a word that could be predicated of such a concept, with velocitator explorers, most of them British, finding in worlds without end their darkest Africas, their South American jungles, their Tibets and Outer Mongolias.

In point of fact the greater number of them did precious little exploring. Infinity, as it turned out, was not as definable as Africa. Early on the discovery had been made that until one actually *arrived* at some galaxy or planet, infinite space had a soothing, prosaic uniformity (provided one successfully avoided the matterless lakes), a bland sameness of fleeting mushy glints. It was a perfect setting for peace and solitude. This, perhaps, as much as the outward urge, had drawn Englishmen into the anonymous universe. The velocitator habitat offered a perfect opportunity to 'get away from it all', to find a spot of quiet, possibly, to work on one's book or thesis, or to avoid some troublesome social or emotional problem.

This was roughly Naylor's position. The success of the thespitron had emboldened him to consider taking up the life of an inventor. He had ventured into the macrocosm to mull over, in its peace and silence, a certain stubborn technical problem which velocitator travel itself entailed.

The problem had been advertised many times, but so far it had defeated all attempts at a solution. It was, quite simply, the problem of how to get home again. Every Harkham traveller faced the risk of becoming totally, irrevocably lost, it being impossible to maintain a sense of direction over the vast distances involved. The scale was simply too large. Space bent and twisted, presenting, in terms of spatial curvature, mountains and mazes, hills and serpentine tunnels. A gyroscope naturally followed this bending and twisting; all gyroscopic compasses were therefore useless. Neither, on such a vast and featureless scale, was there any possibility of making a map.

(Indeed a simple theorem showed that large-scale sidereal mapping was inherently an untenable proposition. *Mapping* consists of recording relationships between locations or objects. In a three-dimensional continuum this is only really practicable by means of data storage. However, the number of possible relationships between a set of objects rises exponentially with the number of objects. The number of possible connections between the 10,000 million neurons of the human brain actually exceeds the number of particles within Olbers' Sphere (which, before the invention of the velocitator, was thought of as the universe). Obviously no machine, however compact, could contain the information necessary to map the relationships between objects whose number was without limit, even when those objects were entire galaxies).

Every velocitator habitat carried a type of inertial navigation recording system, which enabled the traveller to retrace his steps and, hopefully, arrive back at the place he had started from. This, to date, was the only homing method available; but the device was delicate and occasionally given to error – only a small displacement in the inertial record was enough to turn the Milky Way galaxy into an unfindable grain of sand in an endless desert. Furthermore, Harkham travellers were apt, sometimes unwittingly, to pass through powerful magnetic fields which distorted and compromised the information on their recorders, or even wiped the tapes clean.

Naylor's approach to the problem was, as far as he knew, original. He had adopted a concept that both philosophy and science had at various times picked up, argued over, even used, then dropped again only to resume the argument later: the concept of *identity*.

If every entity, object and being had its own unique identity which differentiated it from the rest of existence, then Naylor reasoned that it ought to be uniquely findable in some fictive framework that was independent of space, time and number. Ironically the theoretical tools he was using were less typical of empiricist thought than of its traditional enemy, rationalism, the school that saw existence as arising, not from material occasions, but from abstract categories and identities; but he was sufficiently undogmatic not to be troubled by that. He was aware that empirical materialists had striven many times to argue away the concept of identity altogether, but they had never, quite, succeeded.

Naylor imagined each individual object resulting from a combining, or focusing together, of universal logic classes (or universal identities), much as the colour components of a picture are focused on to one another to form a perfect image. It was necessary to suppose that each act of focusing was unique, that is to say, that each particle of matter was created only once. It would mean, for instance, that each planet had a unique identity: that a sample of iron taken from the Earth was subtly different from a sample of iron taken from the Moon, and it was this difference that Naylor's projected direction-finder would be able to locate.

But was it a warrantable assumption, he wondered?

'Ah, the famous question of identity,' he said aloud.

The vodor lecture, heard many times before, became a drone. He turned it off and opened his notebook to scan one section of his notes.

'IDENTITY AND NUMBER:— The natural numbers, 1, 2, 3, 4, 5 . . . , are pure abstractions, lacking identity in the philosophical meaning of the word. That is to say, there is no such entity as "five". Identity in a set of five objects appertains only to each object taken singly . . . "Fiveness" is a process, accomplished by matching each member of a set against members of another set (i.e. the fingers of a hand) until the set being counted is exhausted. Only material objects have identity . . . '

In his fevered imagination it had seemed to Naylor that he need but make one more conceptual leap and he would be there with a sketch model of the device that would find the Milky Way Galaxy from no matter where in infinity. He believed, in fact, that he already had the primitive beginnings of the device in the thespitron. For although no *physical* mapping of the universe was possible, the thespitron *had* achieved a *dramatic* mapping of it, demonstrating that the cosmos was not entirely proof against definition.

But the vital leap, from a calculus of theatre to a calculus of identities, had not come, and Naylor was left wondering if he should be chiding himself for his lapse into dubious rationalist tenets.

Dammit, he thought wryly, if an enlightened master had no luck, how the devil can I?

Gloomily he wrote a footnote: 'It may be that the question of identity is too basic to be subject to experiment, or to be susceptible to instrumentation.'

His thoughts were interrupted by the ringing of the alarm bell. The control panel flashed, signalling that the habitat was slowing down in response to danger ahead. In seconds it had reduced speed until it was cruising at only a few tens of powers of the velocity of light.

At the same time an announcement gong sounded, informing them that they had arrived within beacon range of someone else's habitat – presumably Corngold's.

As Naylor crossed to the panel to switch off the alarm Watson-Smythe appeared from the bedroom. He had put on a gleaming white suit which set off his good looks perfectly.

'What a racket!' he exclaimed genially. 'Everything going off at once!'

Naylor was examining the dials. 'We are approaching a matterless lake.'

'Are we, by God?'

'And your friend Corngold is evidently living on the shores of it. Can you think of any reason why he would do that?'

Watson-Smythe chuckled, with a hint of rancour. 'Just the place where the swine would choose to set himself up. Discourages visitors, you see.'

'You can say that again. Do I take it we are likely to be unwelcome? What you would call a recluse, is he?'

The younger man tugged at his lower lip. 'Look here, old chap, if you feel uneasy about this you can just drop me off at Corngold's and shoot off again. I don't want to impose on you or anything.'

By now Naylor was intrigued. 'Oh, that's all right. I don't mind hanging about for a bit.'

Watson-Smythe peered out of the window. They were close to a large spiral galaxy which blazed across his field of vision, swinging majestically past his line of sight as they went by it.

'We'll get a better view on this,' Naylor said. He pressed a small lever and a six-foot screen unfolded at the front end of the living room, conveniently placed for the control panel. He traversed the view to get an all-round picture of their surroundings. The spiral galaxy had already receded to become the average smudged point of light, and in all directions the aspect was the usual one of darkness relieved by faintly luminous sleet – except for directly ahead.

There, the screen of galaxies was thin. Behind it stretched an utter blackness: it was a specimen of that awesome phenomenon, the matterless lake.

The distribution of matter in the universe was not, quite, uniform. It thinned and condensed a bit here and there. But its non-uniformity mainly manifested in great holes, gaps – lakes, as they were called – where no matter was to be found at all. Although of no great size where the distances that went to make up infinity were concerned, in mundane terms their dimensions were enormous, several trillion times larger than Olbers' Sphere (the criterion of cosmic size in pre-

Harkham times and still used as a rough measure of magnitude).

Any Harkham traveller knew that it was fatal to penetrate more than the fringes of such a lake, for should anyone be so foolhardy as to pass out of sight of its shore (and many had been) he would find it just about impossible to get out again. When not conditioned by the presence of matter, space lacked many of the properties normally associated with it. Even such elementary characteristics as direction, distance and dimension were lent to space, physicists now knew, by the signposts of matter; the depths of the lakes were out of range of these signposts. Thus it would do the velocitator rider no good merely to fix a direction and travel it in the belief that he must sooner or later strike the lake's limit, for he would be unlikely ever to do so. He was lost in an inconceivable nowhere, in space that was structureless and uninformed.

As they neared the shore the boundary of the lake spread and expanded before them like a solid black wall sealing off the universe. 'Will Corngold be in the open, do you think, or in a galaxy somewhere?' Naylor asked.

'I'd guess he's snuggled away in some spiral; harder to find that way, eh? There's a likely-looking bunch over there.' Watson-Smythe pointed to a cluster of galaxies ahead and to their right. 'Right on the edge of the lake, too. What do the indicators say?'

'Looks hopeful.' Naylor turned the habitat towards the cluster, speeding up a little. The galaxies brightened until their internal structures became visible. The beacon signal came through more strongly; soon they were close enough to get a definite fix.

Watson-Smythe's guess had been right. They eventually found Corngold's habitat floating just inside the outermost spiral turn of the cluster's largest member. The habitat looked like two or three eskimo igloos squashed together, humped and rounded. Behind it the local galaxy glittered in countless colours like a giant Christmas tree.

Watson-Smythe clapped his hands in delight. 'Got him!'

Naylor nudged close to the structure at walking pace. The legally standardised coupling rings clinked together as he matched up the outer doors.

'Jolly good. Time to pay a visit,' his passenger said.

'Shouldn't we raise him on the communicator first?'

'Rather not.' Watson-Smythe made for the door, then paused, turning to him. 'If you'd prefer to wait until . . . well, just as you please.'

He first opened the inner door, then both outer doors which were conjoined now and moved as one, and then the inner door of the other habitat. Naylor wondered why he didn't even bother to knock. Personally he would never have had the gall just to walk into someone else's living room.

With tentative steps he followed Watson-Smythe into the short tunnel. Bright light shone through from the other habitat. He heard a man's voice, raised in a berating, bullying tone.

The door swung wide open.

The inside of Corngold's dwelling reminded Naylor of an egg-shaped cave, painted bright yellow. Walls and ceiling consisted of the same ovoid curve, and lacked windows. The yellow was streaked and spattered with oil colours and unidentifiable dirt; the lower parts of the walls were piled with canvases, paintings, boxes, shelves and assorted junk. The furniture was sparse: a bare board table, a mattress, three rickety straight-backed chairs and a mouldy couch. An artist's easel stood in the middle of the floor. Against the wall opposite to the door was the source of Corngold's provender and probably everything else he used: a matter-bank, shiny in its moulded plastic casing.

Corngold was a fat man, a little below medium height. He was wearing a green silk chemise, square-cut about the neck and shoulders and decorated with orange fringes and tassels, and baggy flannel trousers. He had remarkably vivid green eyes; his hair had been cropped short and now had grown so that it bristled like a crown of thorns.

He reminded Naylor of early Hollywood versions of Nero or Caligula. He did not, it seemed, live alone. He was in the act of browbeating a girl, aged perhaps thirty, who for her dowdiness was as prominent as Corngold was for his brilliant green shirt. Corngold had her arm twisted behind her back, forcing her partly over. Her face wore the blank sullenness that comes from long bullying: it was totally submissive, wholly drab, the left eye slightly puffy and discoloured from a recent bruise. She did not even react to the entry of visitors.

Corngold, however, eased his grip slightly and turned to greet Watson-Smythe indignantly. 'What the bloody hell do you mean barging in here!' he bellowed. 'Bugger off!' His accent sounded northern to Naylor's ears; Yorkshire, perhaps.

'Are you Walter Corngold?' Watson-Smythe countered. To Naylor's faint surprise his tone was cold and professional.

'You heard me! Bugger off! This is private property.'

Watson-Smythe reached into his jacket and produced a slim Hasking stun beamer. With his other hand he took a document from his pocket. 'Watson-Smythe of M.I.19,' he announced. 'I have here a warrant for your arrest, Corngold. I'm taking you back to Earth.'

So that was it! Naylor wondered why he hadn't guessed it before. Now that he thought of it, Watson-Smythe was almost a caricature of the type of young man one expected to find in the 'infinity police', as it was jocularly called – M.I.19, the branch of security entrusted with law enforcement among habitat travellers.

'What are the charges?' he asked, mildly amused.

Watson-Smythe inclined his head slightly to answer him, keeping the Hasking trained on Corngold. 'Two charges: theft, and the abduction of Lady Cadogan's maid, who unless I am very much mistaken is the young lady you are now mistreating, Corngold. Take your hands off her at once.'

Corngold released the girl and shoved her roughly towards the couch, where she sat staring at the floor.

'Ridiculous,' he snorted. 'Betty's here of her own sweet will, aren't you, dearest?' His voice was heavy with irony.

She glanced up like a frightened mouse, darting what might have been a look of hope at Watson-Smythe. Then she retreated into herself again, nodding meekly.

Corngold sighed with satisfaction. 'Well that's that, then. Sod off, the two of you, and leave us in peace.' He strolled to the easel, picked up a brush and started to daub the canvas, as though he had banished them from existence.

Watson-Smythe laughed, showing clean white teeth. 'They said you were a bit of a character. But you're due for a court appearance in London just the same.' He turned politely to Naylor. 'Thanks for your assistance, Naylor old boy. You can cast off now if you're inclined, and I'll take Corngold's habitat back to Earth.'

'Can't,' Corngold said, giving them a brief sidewise glance. 'My inertial navigator's bust. I was stuck here, in fact, until you turned up. Not that it bothers me at all.'

Watson-Smythe, frowned. 'Well . . .'

'Is it a malfunction?' Naylor queried, 'or just a faulty record?'

Corngold shrugged. 'It's buggered up, I tell you.'

'I might be able to do something with it,' Naylor said to the M.I.19 agent. 'I'll have a look at it, anyway. If it's only the record we can simply take a copy of our own one.'

Corngold flung down his brush. 'In that case you might as well stay to dinner. And put that gun away, for Chrissake. What do you think this is, a shooting gallery?'

'After all, he can't go anywhere,' Naylor observed when Watson-Smythe wavered. 'Without us he'll *never* get home.'

'All right.' He returned his gun to its shoulder holster. 'But don't think you're going to wriggle out of this, Corngold. Kidnapping's a pretty serious offence.'

Corngold's eyes twinkled. He pointed to a clock hung askew on the wall. 'Dinner's at nine. Don't be late.'

WEARILY Naylor slumped in his armchair in his own living-room. He had spent an hour on Corngold's inertial navigator, enough to tell him that the gyros were precessing and the whole system would need to be re-tuned. It would be a day's work at least and he had decided to make a fresh start tomorrow. If he couldn't put the device back in order they would all have to travel back to Earth in Naylor's habitat – as an M.I.19 officer Watson-Smythe had the power to require his co-operation over that. At the moment he was in his bedroom, bringing his duty log up to date.

The business with the navigator had brought home anew to Naylor the desirability of inventing some different type of homing mechanism. He was becoming irritated that the problem was so intractable, and felt a fresh, if frustrating, urge to get to grips with it.

Remembering that he had left the vodor lecture unfinished, he switched on the machine again, listening closely to the evenly-intoned words, even though he knew them almost by heart.

'The question of *personal* identity was raised by Locke, and later occupied the attentions of Hume and Butler. Latterly the so-called 'theorem of universal identity' has gained some prominence. In this theorem, personal identity (or *self*-identity) is defined as *having knowledge* of one's identity, a statement which also serves to define consciousness. Conscious beings are said to differ from inanimate objects only in that they have knowledge of their identity, while inanimate objects, though possessing their own identity, have no knowledge of it.

'To be conscious, however, means to be able to perceive. But in order to perceive there must be an "identification" between the subject (self-identity, or consciousness) and the perceived object. Therefore there is a paradoxical "sharing" of identity between subject and object, similar, perhaps, to the exchange of identity once posited between electrons. This reasoning leads to the concept of a "universal identity" according to which all identity, both of conscious beings and inanimate objects, belongs to the same universal transcendental identity, or "self". This conclusion is a recurring one in the history of human thought, known at various times as "the infinite self", "the transcendental self" and "the universal self" of Vedantic teachings. "I am you", the mystic will proclaim, however impudently, meaning that the same basic identity is shared by everyone.

'Such conceptions are not admitted by the empirical materialist philosophers, who subject them to the most withering criticism. To the empiricist, every occasion is unique; therefore its identity is unique. Hume declared that he could not even discover self-identity in himself; introspection yielded only a stream of objects in the form of percepts; a "person" is therefore a "bundle" of percepts. Neither can the fact that two entities may share a *logical* identity in any way detract from their basic separateness, since logic itself is not admitted as having any *a priori* foundation.

'The modern British school rejects the concept of identity altogether as a mere verbalism, without objective application. Even the notion of electron identity exchange is now accepted to be a mathematical fiction, having been largely superseded by the concept of "unique velocity" which is incorporated in the Harkham velocitator. It is still applied, however, to a few quantum problems for which no other mathematical tools exist.'

NAYLOR rose and went to the window, gazing out at the blazing spiral galaxy which was visible over the humped shape of Corngold's habitat. 'Ah, the famous question of identity,' he murmured.

He knew why the question continued to perplex him. It was because of the thespitron. The thespitron, with its unexpected tricks and properties, had blurred his feeling of self-identity, just as the identity of electrons had been blurred by the 20th century quantum equations. And at the same time, the thoughts occurring to him attacked materialist empiricism at its weakest point: the very same question of identity.

There came to him again the image of the categories of identity proceeding and permutating down a dark, immensely long corridor. He felt dizzy, elated. Here, in his habitat living-room, his domain was small but complete; he and the thespitron reproduced between them, on a minute scale, the ancient mystical image of created universe and observing source, of phenomenon and noumenon; even without him here to watch it, the thespitron was the transcendental machine concretised, a microcosm to reflect the macrocosm, a private universe of discourse, a mirror of infinity in a veneered cabinet.

Could the characters and worlds within the thespitron, shadows though they were, be said to possess *reality*? The properties of matter itself could be reduced to purely logical definitions, heretical though the operation was from the point of view of empiricism. The entities generated by the machine, obeying those same logical definitions, could never know that they lacked concrete substance.

Was there identity in the universe? Was that *all* there was?

Now he understood what had made him include a communication facility in the thespitron; why he had further felt impelled to talk to Frank Nayland, his near-double. He had identified himself with Nayland; he had tried to enlighten him as to the nature of his fictional world, prompted by some irrational notion that, by confronting him, he could somehow prod Nayland into having a consciousness of his own.

Who am I? Naylor wondered. Does my identity, my consciousness, belong to myself, or does it belong to this – he made a gesture taking in all that lay beyond the walls of the habitat – to infinity?'

Sitting down again, he switched on the thespitron.

NAYLOR's sense of having duplicated the logical development of the universe was further heightened by the inclusion of the 'credible sequence' button. This optional control engaged circuits which performed, in fact, no more than the last stage of the plotting process, arranging that the machine's presentations, in terms of construction, settings and event-structure, were consonant, if not quite with the real world, at least with a dramatist's imitation of it.

With the button disengaged, however, the criterion of mundane credibility vanished. The thespitron proceeded to construct odd, abbreviated worlds, sometimes from only a small number of dramatic elements, worlds in which processes, once begun, were apt to continue forever without interruption or exhaustion; in which actions, once embarked upon, became a binding force upon the actor and required permanent reiteration.

The world of Frank Nayland, private investigator, was one of these: a world put together from bare components lifted from the Hollywood thriller *genre*, bereft of the background of any larger world, and moving according to an obsessive, abstract logic. A compact world with only a small repertoire of events, the terse fictional world of the private dick, a world in which rain was unceasing.

Summoning up Nayland from store, Naylor watched him pursue his investigations, rain dripping from the brim of his hat, his gabardine raincoat permanently damp. So absorbed did he become in the dick's adventures that he did not see Watson-Smythe until the M.I.19 officer tapped him on the shoulder.

'It's nine o'clock,' Watson-Smythe said. 'Time we were calling on Corngold.'

'Oh, yes.' Naylor rose, rubbing his eyes. He left the thespitron running as they went through the connecting tunnel, tapping on Corngold's door before entering.

A measure of camaraderie had grown up during the hour they had earlier spent with the artist. Naylor had come to look on him more as an eccentric rascal than a real villain, and even Watson-Smythe had mollified his hostility a little. He had still tried to persuade Betty Cooper, the maid allegedly abducted from the home of Lady Cadogan (from whom Corngold had also stolen a valuable antique bracelet), to move in with them pending the journey back to Earth, but so great was Corngold's hold over her (the hold of a sadist, Watson-Smythe said) that she would obey only him.

There was no sign of the promised dinner party. Corngold

was before his easel, legs astraddle, while Betty posed in the nude, sitting demurely on a chair. Though still a sullen frump, Naylor thought that when naked she had some redeeming features; her body tended to flop, was pale and too fleshy, but it was pleasantly substantial in a trollopy sort of way.

Corngold turned his head. 'Well?' he glared.

Watson-Smythe coughed. 'You invited us to dinner, I seem to remember.'

'Did I? Oh.' Corngold himself didn't seem to remember. He continued plying the paint on to the canvas, a square palette of mingled colour in his other hand. Naylor was fascinated. The man was an artist after all. His concentration, his raptness, were there, divided between the canvas and the living girl.

Naylor moved a few paces so he could get a glimpse of the portrait. But he did not see what he expected. Instead of a nude, Corngold had painted an automobile.

Corngold looked at him, his eyes twinkling with mirth. 'Well, it's how I see her, you see.'

Naylor was baffled. He could not see how in any way the picture could represent Betty, not even as a metaphor. The auto was sleek and flashy, covered with glittering trim; quite the opposite of Betty's qualities, in fact.

He strolled to the other end of the egg-shaped room, glancing at the stacked canvases. Corngold had a bit of a following, he believed, among some of the avant-garde. Naylor took no interest in art, but even he could see the fellow was talented. The paintings were individualistic, many of them in bright but cleverly toned colours.

Corngold laid down his brush and moved aside the easel, gesturing to Betty to rise and dress. 'Dinner, then,' he said in the tone of one whose hospitality may be presumed upon. 'Frankly I'd hoped you two would have got tired of hanging around by now and cleared off.'

'That would have left you in a bit of a spot,' Naylor said. 'You have no way of finding your way home.'

'So what? Who the hell wants to go to Earth anyway – eh?' 'I've got everything I need here.' Corngold winked at him obscenely, and, to the extreme embarrassment of both Naylor and Watson-Smythe, stuck his finger in Betty's vulva, wriggling it vigorously. Betty became the picture of humiliation, looking distressfully this way and that. But she made no move to draw back.

Naylor bristled. 'I say – you *are* British, aren't you?' he demanded heatedly.

Corngold withdrew his finger, whereupon Betty turned and snatched for her clothes. He looked askance at Naylor.

'And why shouldn't I be?' he challenged, his manner suddenly aggressive.

'Dammit, no Englishman would treat a woman this way!'

Corngold giggled, his mouth agape, looking first at Betty and then at Naylor. 'Fuck me, I must be a Welshman!'

'Perhaps the best thing *would* be to leave you here,' Watson-Smythe commented, his tone voicing the coldest disapproval. 'It might be the punishment you deserve, Corngold.'

'Do it, then! You'd never have got to me at all, you bastards, if I'd found a way to turn off the fucking beacon.'

'It can't be done,' Naylor pointed out. It would be typical of such a character, he thought, not to know that. The beacon signal was imprinted on every velocitator manufactured, as a legal requirement. Otherwise habitats would never be able to vector in on one another.

Corngold grunted, and dragged the board table to the centre of the room, arranging around it the three chairs his dwelling boasted. With a casual gesture he invited his guests to sit down. When they had taken their places he banged on the tabletop. 'What's all this "Corngold", anyway? Have I yet agreed that I am Corngold? Establish the identity of the culprit – that's the first thing in law.'

'I am satisfied you are Walter Corngold,' Watson-Smythe said smoothly.

'Supposition, supposition! Establish the identity!' Corngold was shouting.

He laughed, then turned to Betty, who was clothed now and standing by in the attitude of a waitress. 'Well, let's eat. Indian curry suit you? How do you like it? Mine's good and hot.'

While Corngold discussed the details of the meal Betty went to the matter-bank and returned with a large flagon of bright red wine and four glasses. Corngold sloshed wine into them, indicating to her that she should knock hers straight back. As soon as she had done so he emptied his own glass, instantly refilling it.

'One good hot vindaloo, one lamb biriani and a lamb kurma,' he instructed curtly.

Betty moved back to the matter-bank and twisted dials. Spicy aromas filled the room as she transferred bowls of food from the delivery transom to a tray. Naylor turned to Corngold. 'You can't seriously contemplate spending the rest of your life in this habitat? Cut off from humanity?'

'Humanity can go jump in a lake.' Corngold jerked his thumb towards the great nothingness that lay beyond the local galaxy. 'Anyway who says I'm habitat-bound? You forget there are other races, other worlds. As a matter of fact I've got a pretty good set-up here. I've discovered a simply fascinating civilisation on the planet of a nearby star. Here, let me show you.'

Rising, he pushed aside a pile of cardboard cartons to reveal the habitat's control board. A small golden ring of stars appeared, glowing like a bracelet, as he switched on an opal-glowing viewscreen.

Corngold pointed out the largest of the stars. 'This is the place. A really inventive lifeform, not hard to get to know, really, and with the most extraordinary technology. I commute there regularly.'

'Yet you always bring your habitat back out here again? You must love solitude,' Naylor remarked.

'I do love it indeed, but you misunderstand me. The habitat stays here. I commute to Zordem by means of a clever little gadget they gave me.'

Heavily he sat down at the table, licking his lips. His visitors tried to ask him more about these revelations, their curiosity intense; but when the food was served he became deaf to their questions.

Taking up a whole spoonful of the pungent-smelling curry Betty served him, and without even tempering it with rice, he rolled it thoughtfully round his mouth. Then he suddenly spluttered and spat it all out.

'This isn't vindaloo, you shitty-arsed cow. It's fucking Madras!'

With a roar Corngold picked up the bowl and flung it at Betty, missing her and hitting the wall. The brown muck made a dribbling trail down the yellow.

'You must excuse my common-law wife,' he said, his expression changing from fury to politeness as he turned to

Watson-Smythe. 'Unfortunately she is a completely useless pig.'

'But I don't dare dial vindaloo,' Betty protested in a whining, tearful voice. 'The bank's been going funny again. On vindaloo – '

'Get me my dinner!' Corngold bellowed, cutting off her explanations. Submissively she returned to the machine, operating it again.

As she turned the knobs an acrid blue smoke rose from the matter bank, coming not from the transom but from the seams of the casing. Naylor, glancing at Watson-Smythe in alarm, made as if to rise, forming the intention of retreating to his own habitat and casting off with all haste. But Corngold sprang to his feet with a cry of exasperation and marched over to the ailing bank, giving it a hefty kick, at which the smoke stopped.

'It's always giving trouble,' he explained gruffly as he rejoined them. 'That's what comes of buying second-hand junk.'

Watson-Smythe replied in a tone that Naylor thought remarkably even and calm. 'You do realise, don't you, that that thing can go off like a nuclear bomb?'

'So can my arse after one of these curries. Ah, here it comes. Better be right this time.'

Corngold's vindaloo was *very* hot. The sweat started out of his forehead as he ate it, grunting and groaning, deep in concentration. He was a man of lusty nature, Naylor decided, carrying his enjoyment of life to the limit. Afterwards he sat panting like a dog, calling for more wine and swallowing it in grateful gulps.

The meal over, Corngold became expansive. He described, with a wealth of boastful details, his contacts with the inhabitants of the planet Zordem. 'Their whole science is based on the idea of a certain kind of ray,' he told them. 'They call them *zom* rays. They have some quite remarkable effects. Let me show you, for instance – '

He opened one of the egg-shaped room's four doors, disclosing a cupboard whose shelves contained a number of unfamiliar objects. Corngold picked one up. It was a smooth, rounded shape, easily held in one hand, about three times as long as it was broad, with a flat underside. He carried it to the viewscreen and slapped it against the side of the casing, where it stuck as if by suckers.

On the screen, the ring of stars vanished. In its place was intergalactic space, and in the foreground a long, fully-equipped spaceship of impressive size, the ring-like protuberance about her middle indicating the massiveness of her velocitator armature. They all recognised her as a Royal Navy cruiser, one of several on permanent patrol.

'Rule Britannia!' crowed Corngold. 'It's the *Prince Andrew*. Ostensibly making sure we habitat travellers don't mistreat the natives, but really, of course, trying to have a go at a second British Empire. I should ko-ko!'

'There have been quite a few incidents,' Watson-Smythe said sternly. 'It's no joking matter. I dare say your own relations with Zordem will be subject to scrutiny in good time.'

'Is she close?' Naylor asked.

'No, she's quite a way off,' Corngold said, glancing at a meter. 'Roughly a googol olbers.'

'Your gadget can see *that* far? But good God – how do you find a single object at that distance?'

'The Zordems put a trace on it the day I arrived. To make me feel at home, I suppose. Don't ask me how. They did it with Zom rays!'

Naylor was stunned. 'Then *these* are the people who are the true masters of infinity,' he breathed.

'Masters of infinity?' Corngold sat down at the table again, placing his bare, fat arms among the empty dishes. He wiped up a trace of curry sauce with his fingers and licked it, looking at Naylor with heavy irony. 'You really are a clown. The Zordems are nowhere into infinity, any more than we are. That's a lot of crap newspaper talk. The whole spread any of us have gone from Earth is no more than a spot. Okay, build a velocitator armature a light year across and ride on it for a billion years. You'll still only have gone the length of a spot on infinity. That's what infinity means, doesn't it? – that there's no end to it.'

'Just the same, you've been misleading us with this talk of being stranded,' Watson-Smythe accused. 'With equipment like this you can obviously find your way to anywhere.'

'Afraid not. This gadget gives the range but not the direction. The range is limited, too, to about fifty googol olbers. The Zordems have hit on a lot of angles we've missed, but they're not that much in advance of us overall.'

'But it must still be based on a completely new principle,'

Naylor said, intensely excited. 'Don't you see, Corngold? This might give us what everybody's been looking for – a reliable homing device! It might even,' he ended shyly, 'mean a reduction of sentence for you.'

He blushed at the emerald malevolence that brimmed for a moment from Corngold's eyes. If he were honest, he was beginning to find the man frightening. There was something solid, immovable and dangerous about him. His knowledge of an alien technology, and his obvious intelligence which came through despite his outrageous behaviour, had dispelled the earlier impression of him as an amusing crank. All Watson-Smythe's trained smoothness had failed to make the slightest dent in his self-confidence; Betty remained his slave, and Naylor privately doubted if the charge of abduction could be made to stick. There was something ritualistic in Corngold's brutal treatment of her, and in her corresponding misery. It looked to Naylor as though they were matched souls.

'I thought I had dropped plenty of hints,' Corngold said, 'that I don't really want to come back to Earth. Betty and I want nothing more than to remain here, thank you.'

Watson-Smythe seemed amused. 'I'm afraid the law isn't subject to your whims, Corngold.'

'No?' Corngold's expression was bland, his eyebrows raised. 'I thought I might be able to bribe you. How would you both like to screw Betty? She's all right in her way – just lies there like a piece of putty and lets you do which and whatever to her.'

Watson-Smythe snorted.

Corngold became annoyed. 'What is it you want, then? The fucking bracelet? Here – have it!' He went to the mattress on the floor, lifted it and brought out a gold ornament, flinging it at Watson-Smythe. 'It's a piece of sodding crap anyway – I only took it because Betty had a fancy for it.'

Watson-Smythe picked up the bracelet, examined it briefly, wrapped it in a handkerchief and tucked it away in an inside pocket. 'Thanks for the evidence.'

Corngold sighed. He reached for the flagon of wine and drained the dregs, ending with a belch.

'Well, it's not the end of the world. I expect Betty will be glad to see London again. Before you retire for the night, gentlemen, let me answer your earlier question – how I make the transition between here and Zordem. It's quite simple, really – done by zom rays again, but a different brand this time.'

He went to the cupboard and brought out something that looked like a large hologram plate camera with a square, hooded shutter about a foot on the side. 'This is really a most astonishing gadget,' he said. 'It accomplishes long-distance travel without the use of a vehicle. I believe essentially the forces it employs may not be dissimilar to those of the velocitator – but instead of the generator moving, it moves whatever the zom rays are trained on. All you do is align it with wherever you want to go and step into the beam – provided you have a device at the other end to de-translate your velocity. Neat, isn't it? The speed is fast enough to push you right through walls as though they weren't there.'

'Why, it's a matter transmitter!' Naylor exclaimed admiringly.

'As good as.'

Watson-Smyth had already guessed his danger and reached for his gun. But Corngold was too quick for him. He trained the camera-device on the agent and pressed a lever. The black frontal plate flickered, exactly as if a shutter had operated – as indeed one probably had. Watson-Smythe vanished.

Aghast, Naylor staggered back. '*Christ!* You've murdered him!'

'Yes! For trying to disturb our domestic harmony!'

Flustered and scared, Naylor stuttered: 'You've gone too far this time, Corngold. You won't get away with this . . . too far.'

He scrambled for the exit. He scampered through the tunnel, slamming shut the outer doors and disengaging the clutches so that the two habitats drifted apart, then slamming the inner door and rushing to the control board.

IN the egg-shaped room, Corngold had quickly set up the Zordem projector on a tripod. Focusing it on the intruding habitat a few yards away through the wall, he sighted the instrument carefully and opened the shutter for an instant. Naylor and his habitat were away, projected out into the matterless lake.

Through the communicator on the control board came a faint voice. 'I'm falling, Corngold! Help me!'

'I'll help you,' Corngold crowed, grinning his peculiar open-mouthed grin. 'I'll help you fall some more!'

He opened the shutter again. Naylor accelerated further trillions of light years per second, carried by the irresistible force of zom rays.

'That's him out of the way,' Corngold exclaimed with satisfaction, turning to Betty. 'Bring on the booze!'

Pale and obedient, Betty withdrew a flagon of cerise fluid and two glasses from the matter-bank. She poured a full measure for Corngold, a smaller one for herself, and sat crouching on the couch, sipping it.

'We'll move on from here pretty soon,' Corngold murmured. 'If they could find us others can.'

He tuned the opal-glowing viewscreen into the lake and surveyed the unrelieved emptiness, drinking his wine with gusto.

CORNGOLD'S mocking farewell was the last message Naylor's habitat received from the world of materiality, whether by way of artificial communication, electromagnetic energy, gravitational attraction or indeed any other emanation. These signposts, which normally informed space of direction, distance and dimension, were now left far behind.

There had been no time to engage the velocitator, and now it was too late. Corngold had had the jump on them from the beginning. At the first discharge of the Zordem projector Naylor's speedometer had registered c^{413} and his velocitator unit did not have the capacity to cancel such a velocity, even though the lake's shore, in the first few moments, had still been accessible. At the second discharge the meter registered c^{826} and unencumbered, total space had swallowed him up. He was now surrounded by nothing but complete and utter darkness.

Within the walls of the habitat, however, his domain was small but complete. He had, in the thespitron, a complete universe of discourse; a universe which, though nearly lacking in objective mass, conformed to familiar laws of drama and logic, and on the display screen of which, at this moment, Frank Nayland was pursuing his endless life.

Naylor's mind became filled again with the vision of the long, dark corridor down which the logical identities passed as they permutated themselves into concretisation. Who was to say that out here, removed from the constraints of external matter, the laws of identity might not find a freedom that otherwise was impossible? Might, indeed, produce reality out of thought?

'The famous question of identity,' he muttered feverishly and sat down before the flickering thespitron, wondering how it might be made to guide him, if not to his own world, at least to some world.

AS the big black car swept to a stop at the intersection Frank Nayland emerged from the darkness and leaped for the rear door, wrenching it open and hustling himself inside. His gat was in his hand. He let them see it, resting his forearm on the front seat support and leaning forward.

Rainwater dripped from him on to the leather upholstery. Ahead, the red traffic lights shone blurrily through the falling rain and the streaming sweep of the windscreen wipers.

Bogart peered round at Nayland, his face slack with fear.

'Let's get out and take a walk,' Nayland said. 'I know a nice little place where we can talk things over.'

Bogart's hand gripped the steering wheel convulsively. 'You know we can't leave here.'

'No . . . that's right,' Nayland said thoughtfully. 'You have to keep going. You have to keep driving, running – '

The engine of the car was ticking over. The lights had changed and Bogart started coughing asthmatically. Stanwyck put her hand on his arm, a rare show of compassion. 'Oh, why don't you let him go?' she said passionately. 'He's done nothing to you.'

Nayland clambered out of the car, slamming the door behind him, and stood on the kerb while the gears ground and the vehicle shot off into the night. He walked through the rain to where his own car was hidden in a culvert and drove for a while until he spotted a phone booth.

Rain beat at the windows of the booth. Water dripped from his low-brimmed hat as Nayland dialled the number. While the tone rang he dug into his raincoat pocket, came up with a book of matches, flicked one alight and lit a cigarette with a cupped hand.

'Mr Naylor? Nayland here. This is my final report.'

A pause, while the client on the other end spoke anxiously. Finally Nayland resumed. 'You wanted to know about the couple in the car. Bogart is wanted for the snatch of the

Heskin tiara from the mansion of Mrs Van der Loon. It was the Stanwyck woman got him into it, of course – she was Mrs Van der Loon's paid companion. The usual sad caper. But here's the rub: there's a fake set of the Heskin rocks – or was. Mrs Van der Loon had a legal exchange of identity carried out between the real jewels and the paste set. A real cute switcheroo. It's the paste that's genuine now, and Bogart is stuck with a pocketful of worthless rocks and a broad who's nothing but trouble.'

'Can that be done?' Naylor asked wonderingly.

'Sure. Identities are legally exchangeable.'

Staring at the thespitron screen, the stick-mike in his hand, Naylor was thinking frantically. He watched a plume of smoke drift up the side of Nayland's face, causing the dick to screw up one eye.

Something seemed to be happening to the thespitron. The image was becoming scratchy, the sound indistinct.

'Why does it never stop raining?' he demanded.

'No reason for it to stop.'

'But are you *real*?' Naylor insisted. 'Do you *exist*?'

Nayland looked straight at him out of the screen. The awareness in his eyes was unmistakable. 'This is *our* world, Mr Naylor. You can't come in. It's all a question of identity.'

'But it will work – you just said so,' Naylor said desperately. 'The switcheroo – the fake me and the real me – '

'Goodbye, Mr Naylor,' Nayland said heavily. He put down the phone.

Without Naylor as much as touching the controls, the thespitron ground to a halt. The picture dwindled and the screen went blank.

'Ah, the famous question of identity!' boomed the thespitron, and was silent.

Naylor fingered the restart button, but the set was dead. He fell back in his chair, realising his mistake. He realised how foolish had been his abandonment of the solid wisdom of materialist empiricism, how erroneous his sudden hysterical belief, based on fear, that logic and identity could be antecedent to matter, when in fact they were suppositions merely, derived from material relations. Deprived of the massy presence of numerous galaxies, the signposts of reality, the thespitron had ceased to function.

The closing circles were getting smaller. Now there was

only the shell of the habitat, analogue of a skull, and within it his own skull, that lonely fortress of identity. Naylor sat staring at a blank screen, wondering how long it would take for the light of self-knowledge to go out.

BEFORE SHE STARTED PACKING, STRAWBERRY

by CHRIS YOUNG

BEFORE SHE STARTED packing, Strawberry made bad food that hung around like a thirteenth player in a football team, but everybody had some anyway. She got her things together in an old carrier bag which had come from a Boutique in 1968. She had no clean shirts and two LPs by various artists; also she had a sheaf of letters in a drawer. They were all from different people, she read them like comics.

When she went to fetch them she tripped over Dandy's dinner and they scattered all over the floor. One of them fell on to Dandy's plate.

Don't read it, said Strawberry.

It's all right, said Dandy, I wrote it.

I know, said Strawberry. That's why.

Dandy had been ready for weeks. Now he just sat by the door and waited until it was time. He waited patiently but he did nothing else because everything he had was already tied up and waiting too. He was less impatient with Strawberry and with Sam and the May Queen, because they would not hurry to get ready.

I'll be all right when the time comes, said Strawberry.

But if you don't start now it might come and you'll miss it.

I'll know when it's coming and then I'll start.

How will you know?

Well if I don't know it's coming I won't know if I've missed it.

But then you'll have to stay here.

Then I'll have to stay here.

But you know you can't do that.

Sam will, said Strawberry.

I'm going, said Sam.
How do you know? Strawberry asked him.

Sam used to live with the May Queen in another room until she grew too big and beautiful. She would go out and find lovely things and put them in her place where Sam would be, so that in the end he had come to stay with Dandy and Strawberry. Sometimes the May Queen used to come to her place and they would stand in the doorway and look at all the wonderful things in there. Then they would go away happier than they came; but they would never go in, because there was no room.

He sat in the corner and when he lit a cigarette he threw the match into his plate, but he had forgotten to eat his food. And he didn't think about the May Queen, since he knew he had to go with her in the end. Because she loved him, the same as everything else. So he thought about Strawberry, for something to think about.

Strawberry finished packing and went on moving things around the room so that she seemed busy. She never looked at Sam. When she couldn't do that any more she sat on the floor and looked at the wall behind Dandy's shoulder. She seemed like a rock musician without his guitar.

What is it? asked Dandy.

Nothing, said Strawberry. She lied.

Dandy looked at her, and at the state of his shoes. Why don't you make love with me? he said.

Why?

Because I want you. You'd be beautiful if only you could cook.

Thanks, she said, because he was talking about cooking and not about what the time was. No.

Only the May Queen made love any more, and not with anybody else.

The room was the wrong shape when the May Queen was not there, and the colours sulked as if they didn't want to know each other. She carried all her things in a great soft brown portmanteau; there was no limit to the amount she could get into it and still she was always happy to carry other people's possessions for them as well. She kept it beside the bed in her room and she was forever starting to pack and unpack it so that there were different things in it and different things beside it for people to look at. But there were always a few things at the bottom that she never got around to taking out, because she hadn't the time. Only the May Queen knew what they were; they must have been very dusty.

Everything she had was now tidied up into the portmanteau. There was still room for more, but it looked very fat and clumsy. Anybody could have gone into her room now, but if they had there would have been nothing for them to see.

Dandy said, Certainly . . . that's all there is, really, isn't it . . . to be sure of the things that rule our lives . . . the only thing we can be sure of is ourselves, can't we? . . . I mean . . . you've got to be certain that you're making happen the things that are going on around you . . . not just letting them happen to you, haven't you? . . . that's why, that's why I'm ready to go when it isn't even time . . . why I'm sitting here talking to you instead of just waiting till Strawberry says to go . . . you see . . . if you lay yourself open to the elements you're going to be hot or cold, but never comfortably warm . . . but if you try and do things your own way, then that's the same thing as trying to understand the influences in your life . . . isn't it?

No, said Sam.

When he had finished eating Dandy picked up his plate and asked if he should do the dishes.

Why bother? said Strawberry, so he put it down again and went and sat beside her.

Do you still love me, Strawberry? he asked.

Yes.

Then why won't you make love with me?

Don't you know?

I don't think so.

Then I won't tell you. If you want to wait, she said, you'd better go and sit by the door.

When the May Queen came in the room opened its eyes like an animal waking out of hibernation. She kissed everyone and Sam kissed her back. Then she put down her portmanteau on the floor between Dandy and Strawberry; it looked like a barrage balloon.

Would you like something to eat, asked Strawberry.

No, thank you, said the May Queen.

The May Queen made dishes out of vegetables that smelled like jasmine tea and sandalwood incense. When she gave them to anyone else they were good, but most of the time she ate alone, even when she was living with Sam.

When are you going? she asked Strawberry.

When it's time.

And if you don't know when the time comes?

I suppose I'll go anyway.

The May Queen got off the floor and went to look out of the window. Usually she wore quiet shoes indoors, in case the colours were too bright. But today she was dressed for the road.

Sam still sat where he had been in the beginning. It was dark in the corner, but he was facing the window; sometimes he looked through it and he could see the branches of a tree that grew close to it, outside. But sometimes he would cover his eyes with his hands, and then he could see only brilliant changing shapes that didn't look like anything. The May Queen went and sat beside him.

You're coming with us, aren't you, Sam? she asked gently.

I'm coming with you, May Queen, he said.

Then why don't you get ready?

But it can't nearly be time yet. There seems no reason why it should be.

We are all packed and waiting, said the May Queen.

Then perhaps you're ready too soon, suggested Sam, and he put his head in his hands again, but the shapes he saw still looked like nothing.

The May Queen came back and sat down beside Strawberry again. A little dust rose around her; some of it had probably come from the other side of the solar system.

When shall we go, she said.

Now, if you like, said Strawberry.

Is it time, then? said Dandy.

I think so, said Strawberry.

Shouldn't we wait for Sam? suggested the May Queen.

He's not ready, said Strawberry, looking over at him. His

eyes were still closed. We mustn't be too late. Can I put my bag in your case?

Yes, all right, said the May Queen.

After some time Sam looked up and saw that he was alone in the room. They were too soon, he thought. It isn't time yet. What a stupid mistake. Then he realised that Strawberry and Dandy and the May Queen had gone without him. It was too soon. But nobody could do anything to change that.

The plates that Strawberry had given them still lay on the floor. Only Dandy had finished his meal. The food was cold now, and blue and white so that nobody could eat it. There was nothing else in the room but some patterns in the dust on the floor; the patterns were where the people had been, and where they had put their things.

Sam looked at the patterns on the floor and then he looked at the tree outside the window. He wondered if he ought to try and go now, but slowly the sky grew dark and in a little while he could no longer see what was out there. So he stayed where he was. His knees were drawn up to his chin and he clasped his hands together tight around his legs to keep his balance.

Outside, the May Queen said to Dandy, Would you like to put your case in mine?

Thank you, he replied. I can manage.

Strawberry and the May Queen shared a flat they found off the Shepherds Bush Road. There was no room there to unpack everything from the soft brown portmanteau. Strawberry took a job, and then another one, until she became bored. She had a fight with her boy friend who was some kind of business student and went off to look for Dandy; but she never found him.

The May Queen tried to sell some of the beautiful things she had collected to make enough money to stay alive. But nobody was interested in buying them because they didn't understand how she had come by them. One day a policeman told her to stop obstructing the right of way. That night she emptied the portmanteau into the street and gave it to Strawberry to take with her when she left. But she herself stayed in London.

Dandy went to America to hunt bears in the mountains,

because it was traditional. One of them almost certainly killed him.

So they came in due course with a trowel and threw cement over Sam. And they carefully arranged his limbs and left him where he was for a monument to human monuments. And frivolous people said you could sometimes hear him moaning like a ghost in pagan legend. But really it was just the May Queen crying in the autumn.

KONG

by ADRIAN ECKERSLEY

IN SLEEP, AS IN waking, Kong is obsessed by her. Still in his dreams he mounts the great stairway from out of the well, leaping upwards out of his lair towards her until he is arrested by the jerk of the world falling on his shoulders. He strains against the pull with all the sinews of the most powerful physique in nature: he feels the great chains with which he is loaded to be elastic, to give a little under the impact of his momentum and to give a little more as he maintains and redoubles the strain to reach her, neck swollen and eyes starting from the effort, great hands reaching out for her in gestures at once of supplication and rage. She cowers away in mock-terror, then, as he falls back exhausted, she leans forward almost to meet him, her face a mask of mock-pity. As he lunges back, predictably and without cunning, she laughs clearly and innocently, sidestepping as a calm reflex action like a savage might raise his hand to avoid the glare of a sudden sun. Finally, his work done, she allows him to sink back into his catacomb, into a sleep troubled only by her image.

The museum is as vast as can be conceived. Somewhere within its wall lurks every manifestation of every form which exists or has existed. Its ground-plan, inner walls and chambers take the form of concentric circles: the roof is a great dome; the whole can be apprehended clearly as a church of the Byzantines, those insidious guardians of knowledge's mysteries. Categorisation and organisation of the exhibits has been both more and less efficient than now in the various preceding ages: no one man or card-index system can hold information at once as to all the exhibits and no one generation of men could hope to organise or rationalise what has gone before. It exists, then, with perhaps at one point a selection of closely-related objects neatly laid out and ordered in matching glass cases, and at another a bizarre and inconsequential crowding of incongruous objects such as one might find in the back lot of some enormous, seldom-clambered junk-shop. In the past each succeeding age has tended to place its own achievement closest to the centre of the museum, thus ousting that of the previous age and forcing it a little towards the outer wall, mingling a little more with the work of a still earlier age, all just as the floor of a child's playroom when not tidied, where paints may be pushed away to accommodate building-bricks in the centre of the floor, which may in their turn be forced into confusion to make way for toy soldiers. Objects of an appeal beyond the mere fashions of the ages, however, tend to stay closer to the centre and it is not unusual to see a vast monumental sculpture of winged bull or lion standing proud and alone in a room dedicated otherwise to Dresden figurines, or the bones of some monster from before history began among neat displays of silver coins. Towards the outer wall of the museum order prevails less: unlikely engines of siege-warfare are jumbled with vast pots of iron or clay and lumps of broken sculpture reaching from the classical age back to the primeval; indeed in these reaches the chance spectator may often wonder whether the lump of rock he contemplates was included for its sculptural or its geological merits, and the prevailing darkness will not help him to an answer.

Those who claim that the museum is truly compendious state perhaps with reason that even the so-called creatures of phantasy are represented within its wall, seldom seen indeed by the casual observer as they roam free and shun the more populous centre area; but there is more than one tale of some quite down-to-earth lady seeing reflected in the glass of a display-case perhaps containing brightly-lit cutaway working models of steam or petrol engine a stooping figure in quaint and archaic garb, shabby and aristocratic with canine teeth a full inch long. Such apparitions may be put down to the enervation of a day's hard viewing or to the ever-present beat of the air-conditioning system, but as any schoolchild will tell you there is no denying the reality of Kong, the beast of the museum.

He is no mere exhibit: if his yearning towards her should cease the great chains will lie slack and the axle-trees unseen by any now living will rust in their bearings. His desire for her is his striving to make real the shadowy, multiform image of her which is printed on his retina, and it is this desire which holds him in this present – possessed by this monomania where, without memory or understanding, there is no cast for escape, no deviousness. The only direction in his world is to her. Were not memory and understanding severed from him, exclusive to the world above, he might take refuge in the re-living of past satisfaction or at least of much earlier times when the bargain they had struck against him had been less unremittingly hard: he might have remembered times when he had pulled the great chains with a will, and roamed free and bemused amongst the upper chambers. He might, indeed, have remembered a time before the museum had existed, when he had pursued the shape of his desire untrammelled, but the act of memory was itself incompatible with that state, locked in the eternity of the present by the scents and riches of a nature about him paradigmatic with his own: he can neither learn nor mourn what serpent has betrayed him.

The key to his nature is in his eyes. She has seen them clouded by the smoke of pain and rage as he is taunted and egged on by her, and with amazement she has seen them also shine clear with a momentary belief in her which makes as nothing the millennia of his suffering. Such moments are as they confront one another before their dance begins, before she is drawn irresistibly and with fascination into her own part in the machinery of things as they are and must be. She pays him the compliment of being pitiless towards him: her hardness of heart is at once an expression of tradition, behaviour fitting for the first courtesan of her age, and of something personal, a response to him as natural as the movements of her body, which would not deny him at least honour and the recognition due to his part in the scheme of things, his harsh destiny. To cease being hard of heart is difficult to contemplate, tantamount to a desertion of her post for a passion from which there would be no return. Of course she has contemplated it: every girl who had sat on this dais above the pit had contemplated it; some, according to legend, had allowed their feelings to lead them to a horrible dismemberment. There were only legends, though, sops to an obvious possibility stemming from the currents which flowed beneath her rigorous and jealously regarded training culled from the observation and experience of a whole civilisation. Her own experience has seen these legends in his moods and contortions, his refusals and denials but now, beyond all the legends of hearsay and the books and studies, even beyond the ritual of her dance with him, she knows him. Much of her knowledge does stem from the dance itself: she has thrilled with him as a 'cellist to the vibration of his instrument and each queenly turn of the neck, casual unselfconscious disarray of breast or thigh, collusive grind of pelvis or mocking soft lip gesture an inch from his has shown her in him a response which seemed even to prefigure her initiation. Her eyes have been all-knowing and all-innocent: she has been virgin, mother, mistress, daughter with all the richness and mutability of the sea: he in turn has loved, trusted, feared and destroyed her in his mind with the passion and sincerity of blind cellular growth. She sees, beyond all this, in what is kindled by the clearness in his eye, a reality which makes the museum and all she knows like the hazy memory of a sleepless night. And looking sadly from her centrepoint out across the endless clutter of labelled exhibits and the pale lifeless visitors who make no noise, she has a realisation that it is time to strike a new bargain with Kong. She seeks an answer to meet her feelings in the direction of his ever-increasing strength: perhaps she with her wiles can make him strain as even he has not: already she has caused a current to surge through power-lines not laid down for such a passion, working models to flurry a little faster through their unvaried repetition, the lights to burn with a harsh, consumptive fire and even the visitors to feel a little flushed, have to sit down and wait out strange patterns of light on the periphery of their vision. Every system has its breaking-point, and only she can surmise how close in this case it might be, but reflected in all her imaginings after this point she sees her own destruction, just as in the legends. And her woman's way is indisposed to carnage: there would be no meeting-point at her death's instant nor a recognition in the act of her dismemberment. No – the secret, the way forward, must lie in unlocking him from the tyranny of his dreams: his passion is the buzzing insect on the window-pane so locked in its desire for light and air that it cannot see the opening an inch above. She must teach him, subtly, to unlock himself, for only in thus mastering himself will he learn to recognise her fully and will she be free of the fear of her destruction.

And so Kong, dynamo of the world, learned to control himself. He learned to shrink back from the piercing calmness of her eyes, to puzzle out this recognition alone in the dark of his catacomb. When sinking away from the heart of his yearning was no longer synonymous with sleep he recovered his memory, learning to place yesterday against today. Now she will not allow him to exhaust his passion he wanders his cave and contains it: strange shapes trouble his mind; he gives them cognition and lo they are the queens of yesterday. With time hanging upon him like a soaking blanket he recaptures dimly the scents of outside as it had been thousands of years before. And when he had reached a stage of calmness in the eye of his world's hurricane his hands took up the chain and gropingly followed it as Theseus to its source. His hands puzzled a long, unredeemable time with the great shackles learning first their shape then their function then the play of forces they contained: finally he was free. His love for her was locked in his heart.

There was both terror and rejoicing as he came up out of the pit to join her. His small, baleful eye was clear and it never left her deft and fascinating form as she led him about the museum he had no eyes for, nor as she initiated his shuddering slow passion, nor as she slept uneasily by his side. His impulse to master the world was strangled by the uncertainty her nearness made him feel: lying beside her sleeping form an agony of indecision, compounded of both desire and the fear of her eye, would rack every muscle in turn. Sometimes when she was asleep his hand would reach out and gently lay itself against her cooling body, but if she awoke and her eye met his in anticipation the hand would withdraw with a start and the ever-watching eyes grow tenser still. Only when she feigned sleep would he possess her. Eventually, tired of these cat-and-mouse games and nursing broken dreams of the suavity and certainty of a lover, she returned to her books.

Left alone he diminished in stature until he was no greater than an ordinary man, his hair grew thin and patchy though still far more than the human average and they decided the city life was doing him harm. They moved him to a new satellite-town amid pleasant, well-cultivated farmland. There he wanders the paved acre of the pedestrian precinct in a long, flapping coat, a normal citizen save that sometimes on dull afternoons in march or october when the wind gusts about the tower-blocks he stops in his tracks, throws back his head and roars aloud. Passers-by look round, glance at one another and shrug: others, touched, look away and flurry a little faster through their unvaried repetition.

THE DIARY OF THE TRANSLATOR

by GEOFF RYMAN

I AM A Translator. I am a Reader. I work my long lonely day on the Decks, and at night I do not dream. I doodle with words, instead, in this diary, to clear my mind so that peace can come and with it, sleep.

* * * *

I have finished *Moby Dick.* Mother liked it, but it is a fraud. I come from a desert world, and have never seen a real sea, or a whale. There are no whales now, except on tape. There never was an Ishmael; Herman Melville poured all his ghost into his work. No memories by those hearty, simple souls who manned the 19th century have yet been discovered.

So I have had to create a world and a great white whale from words alone. My ocean is blurred and glassy, and I have been quite unable to imagine a huge timber ship. How would it sit on the water? What is meant by the creaking of ropes? My white whale is faceless, as Melville describes him, but he is made of stone, not flesh. My translation is dead and bleached, like pages.

Yet Mother approve. And she approve because I have kept it simple, so light for the leaden masses. They will never have to struggle, as I did, with the tangle of tackle and rigging and whaling lore that takes up most of the book. I got rid of that. Descriptions do not translate well. They collapse back into unnamed and unknown sights and sounds. Or is it only me, the Reader, who is lost when wordless? I did a speed-through on it all, to catch a lingering taste of whaling and of the sea.

Mother say I have caught the symbolic essence of the story. We are too used to dreams to know when things are not real. Without its try-works and its whale anatomy, the book has become what Melville feared it might – 'a hideous and intolerable allegory'. My translation is grotesque, all portentous characters and over-heated imagery. The ending! Ishmael riding up the vortex on a black bubble! That silly hand hammering the flag to the mast even after the rest of the ship has sunk. Poor Herman! It all belongs between the pages of his book.

The book that now no one will ever bother to read.

* * * *

Ate with Luton. He's doing Marx.

'It's an impossibility!' he insisted, over his taspa. He stirred it constantly, but did not eat. He has large, pink arms streaked with black hair. It seems so incongruous, that hair. We spoke, just to keep in practice.

'They thought differently to us. They built up their ideas in stages, like their buildings – one delicate definition at a time. It was the only way they could keep themselves organised. And they kept on building, going up and up and out. It's relentless!'

Luton is such a contrite man. That's why he hates failure. As he spoke, I conjured up a Simulant flower. The fibres in the stem were only half-formed. Things are always more complex than we can imagine.

'Well, if you understand what Marx is saying, perhaps you could tape just that.'

'But it wouldn't be Marx!' he exclaimed. 'A book by Marx, or any of the philosophers is a process. He was laying out a definition of reality step by step. It's very slow, very methodical, but that is the thing itself. It has to be worked through to be understood. It's not a sudden intuition, something that arrives like a deam!'

On the grass nearby two Frips had conjured up a replica of a vagina and were grinding out cigarettes in it. It sighed and shivered. Finally one of them crushed his glass monocle into its labia, and dispelled it. They had clouded eyes and smiled at our Readerish intentness. A scientist was eating at that Cord, too. His face was withered with time and concentration. He obviously refused overlays. Even without his cloak, I would have known that he worked.

'And beside,' growled Luton. 'I don't understand him. The amazingly precise definitions of his words! You have to keep them before you all the time. I just . . . ' He broke off with a shrug. ' . . . lose track.'

'It could be worse,' I said. 'You could be Jol. He's doing Wittgenstein.'

'Hmph!' he admitted, with a rueful jerk of the shoulders that was almost a chuckle. 'I suppose so. We're all slaves of the Magic Lamp.'

Luton should have been a philosopher. So should we all, all of us Readers, have been artists or philosophers. But artists of the new are not wanted, and new philosophy is banned. Philosophies thought out on tape are swallowed whole; every premise is accepted without question. Logic died with words. Mother need Translators and Historians to rescue the past, so that is what we must become. The past haunts and holds us.

An insect flew in. A real one, there's still a few left. It was some kind of Stinger, with a small hooked needle in its tail. The girl Frips shrieked, and their friends crouched low in horror. Finally the scientist stood and wordlessly waved the insect away. Confused, it wandered back out into the eternal sunshine. One of the girls collapsed in hysterics. She looked as though, in another time, she could have been a coarse and healthy farm girl. Instead, she was merely plump. She was led out, shaking, to be transmitted to a Health Cord. The scientist looked at me, his lips drawn tight. He was disgusted with her, disgusted with Frips and Lumpens. We understand each other, Scientists and Readers, though we have no idea what each other does.

The lazy and the weak have inherited, as their religion always warned they would. The strong lead and hold the centre for them, the clever work quietly. I watched Luton after we said goodbye. He has a funny walk: a huge man with a proper, precise, scholarly stride. I wish I knew what I saw in it that made me so very sad.

And what, I wonder, does a Scientist do with his god-like knowledge of time and space? How does energy become matter? How do the Machineries work? I don't know. More problems of translation?

* * * *

Mother have asked me to do another book, one of the old style microfilms from the 'Redemption'. The book is quite awful, by some cloistered woman, but Mother have decided I have a flair for the 19th century. The book is called *Sense and Sensibility*, a title with so many possibilities as to be almost meaningless. Words are so imprecise! They mean different things in different contexts and time-levels, even to different people. It's like trying to communicate by scratching in the sand with a trowel. *Sense* has more immediate impact than most ancient texts. But what a piece of trivia! Two uninspiring females follow the custom of their age and marry the men we knew they would marry all along. For some reason the nicer of the two gets stranded with a very dull older gentleman. This, the author seems to feel, is a great good. Can't think why Mother want to save it. Some of the detail is well done. At least it will be simpler to do than the last monstrosity.

* * * *

Found, after more than the usual amount of indexing the correct time-level definition of the words 'sense' and 'sensibility'. 'Sense' in this case does not mean a faculty of the nervous system, but an ability to think sensibly. 'Sensibly' is an adverb meaning reasonably or judiciously. It is not to be confused with the noun 'sensibility', which can mean something quite nearly the reverse. Oh, the hell of words! No wonder we did away with most of them. 'Sensibility' meant – and it had fallen out of common usage a scant hundred years later – a receptivity to experience and a susceptibility to emotion that may be overly developed. The two sisters in the book embody these two different ways of responding to the world. So the book is at least about something, even if it is monumentally dull. Austen must have been a frightful woman, all gossip and local chat. She keeps talking about marriage as though it was a financial arrangement designed to keep idle people fed. Sounds rather like Mother. Some of the characterisations are supposed to have a satiric edge to them, I think. But I cannot tell for sure. Everyone seems so constrained by conventions I don't understand.

Had nothing else to do, so I did a quick speed through for Mother. She seemed pleased with it. I hate idleness.

* * * *

I need more detail – houses, clothes, transportation, that sort of thing. We have books about the 19th century and tapes of ancient films made about it, but we have never actually seen beyond its very edges. Did find an early essay about *Sense*, filed under Untranslated. The writer claimed that Austen was really balancing two conflicting strains of philosophy – Classicism, and the newly burgeoning Romanticism. How am I to get that into a translation? Was Austen really interested in philosophy? Seems a rather indirect way of discussing it. Also distinctly felt that the woman who wrote the essay was just as interested in saying something about philosophy as about Jane Austen. They always did that – bandied about each others books to say something new. Perhaps a book was one long, complex word, to be carefully defined and used again. Perhaps there was a whole language of books.

I coughed up blood this morning. I am not well, despite all the patching up.

* * * *

Found a memory! Stumbled upon it sifting through the 20th century South Central English section of the Decks. In 1966 a student visited a hamlet in Hampshire called Chawton. He came, unbelievably, to see the house of Jane Austen. Only one hundred and fifty years too late, give or take some decades. The house itself was dead, all bare floors and irrelevant documents on the walls. There was an unhelpful little plaque announcing that the lady herself had always written over a particular spot, on a table rather like the one on display. But the village! And the student!

Chawton was bursting with sunlight and flowers. The houses were of old brick or flint and were top heavy with roofs of rolling thatch. The streets twisted and flowed without reason like rivers. Beyond the shade of the great trees were wide hot fields with cows. A motorway, hidden in a man-made ravine, hummed with traffic.

Through the student's hushed and whispering mind, I could imagine what Chawton must have been like one hundred and fifty years before that motorway existed – four hundred years before Transmutation! And six hundred before the demolishing of the Earth!

People had grown their own vegetables in the profusion of those gardens and had worked in the homes of nearby Alton or on the large farms. They had gone no further than Alton for their stores and hardly ever saw beyond the next parish, unless they were wealthy. They had drunk the warm milk of local cows. They had just, within the last few years, stopped weaving cloth on home looms. A quiet, slow life, then, with plants pushing themselves out of the ground, and grass turning into milk inside the stomachs of cows. The student also paused in reverence before an old, blackened horse-drawn cart, for which I am grateful. I now have a fresh image of a cart to work with. Horses I will always be a bit shaky on.

He was a strange, likeable lad, this student, not clever, but observant and very sensitive. Life later disappointed him. He looked up at a portrait of Miss Austen, and saw something in her plain, strong face that, without his help, I never would have seen. Her eyes he looked at particularly. For him they were black and deep. Miss Austen, he always called her. Miss Austen, as though the title conveyed something sad and essential. She did not marry, and that he found tragic. In the age before his, that was a mark of failure in a woman. For him, this sorrow and defeat permeated her books and haunted the village and had made her vision clear. For him she was a great writer.

I must re-read that book.

* * * *

Another message from Chawton. From a Mrs Welk who lived in Chawton all her life and died in the 1930s. Lots of rooms and furniture; she remembered things like that, Mrs Welk. She had a practical, regular clock of a mind. She was an expert at crotcheting. It fills her memory – yarn coiling and uncoiling endlessly, like the rotation of planets. I slid several memory impressions of her sitting-room together and got a fairly complete image. Lace coverlets over the backs of chairs, china figures on shelves, miniatures of relatives on the walls, and ugly electric lamps. I will use it, without the lamps, for *Sense*.

Mrs Welks considered herself a woman of standing, as she had married the local dairyman. She knew everyone in the hamlet, and most of the folk in east Alton. She knew what they all did for a living, so I now have a better idea of the economic system. The family that owned the cows sold the milk, or might trade it for garden goods. This in an age when Man had long since dropped his tools and had begun flicking switches. Mrs Welk kept the accounts and wore spectacles, which she thought ruined her appearance.

In her simple and vigorous youth, Mrs Welk had been plump and pretty. She had sex in a field with a man called John. He pushed up her frothy petticoat and peeled down her white bloomers. The grass prickled her. As he was about to descend, she felt a great weight of fear and anticipation on her stomach. She became pregnant, which is why they married. She did not at first love her husband, with his large hands and clumsy penis. But she grew to, with time and domesticity. Her love was a comfortable groove worn into his shoulder at night, and a small nurtured flame. He died, surrounded by her and their grown children. The pain in her was intense, like a parting of flesh.

I have never loved anyone. It seems such an impossible thing to do.

* * * *

No more ghosts to exhume. Nothing else on Chawton is recorded. Many other 20th century villages survive on tape, but they give me no new information. Have run through Edwardian London again, in case that helps, but I shall have to begin soon with what I have. Extraordinary how some people have left behind such strong traces of themselves, while others have faded. It seems to have nothing to do with strength of personality. Could it be that thoughts unspoken never die, but struggle vainly on for expression?

Have re-read the book again. There is indeed something formidable there, but what it is I cannot say.

* * * *

Nothing happened today. I sat, Communicator pressed against my ear, but no visions came. I played back my speed-throughs to see if they had preserved any inspiration. But the images were watery and rippled past like reflections in a stream. I forced myself to tape anyway, which is always wrong. Dry, stiff little figures tottered through rehearsed routines against a shadowed backdrop. The tape accelerated into an angry fantasy in which Elinor knifed Mrs Jennings over breakfast. Scrapped all of it, and listened to Bartok. Got bored with that, tasted a bit of *Ulysses*. Bloom was defecating. Spent the rest of the afternoon staring at the sky and my hands, too dulled by taping to move.

What use is Translation, or the New History? How can the past ever provide answers for the future? These old books hold no solutions; they no longer even ask the right questions. All these ghostly memories merely record hope and mundane confusion. Yet our only labour, aside from maintaining the Machineries, is the resurrection of the past. Mother plan - of all the insane schemes! - to rebuild a New Earth, to hang in space like a bauble. No one asks which Earth, when. No one asks what possible good it could do us. Yet they clamour for it, these Frips and Lumpens. Do they hope the past holds a secret key to who and why they are? Perhaps they cannot ignore the abyss at their feet, now that all other forms of pain has been vanquished. Mother give them tapes of *Hamlet*, tapes that can be absorbed in minutes, and they think they are encountering some form of truth. But the truth cannot be given! The abyss cannot be answered!

Hello Mother. I can feel you listening. You cannot make me happy. Do you hear that? All your technics and wizardry cannot make me or anyone else happy. You may not care what I think because I am powerless, but you too are powerless.

* * * *

More days of waiting. More useless days.

* * * *

A Historian has received and taped a message from the 19th century. The announcement slid into our minds at mid-day. I could not help but feel sad. Another century for us to loot and plunder.

There were signs of celebration out on the Grid, though how can one know when a carnival has become a festival? As usual, it was ablaze with light and music and conjured dancing bears. The Decks were more sedate. They continued to work, but in a state of joyful agitation. Deckhands smiled to each other as they gave directions to the great machine. The air quivered with broadcast excitement. Jant, the Indexer, swept up to us in her long brown cloak.

'Chaos in Records,' she announced.

'Chaos here,' replied Ari. 'Everyone wants it.'

'Will help you, too,' she said, beaming her warm happiness to me.

I don't use my Communicator much. I don't necessarily want my private feelings blasted out into the universe.

'Yes, I suppose it will,' I replied in words. I was not enthusiastic. Her smile dimmed somewhat, and she turned back to her friends. Such a pretty girl, with round cheeks and bright grey eyes. I have never been able to talk to her, even though she is a Reader.

As the Deckhands were busy pushing the message out to the millions, I did not bother them for it. It did not sound too interesting. The new memory is that of a rich pottery owner and concentrates mainly on his varied greenhouse. It has increased our knowledge of Earthly foliage to a fair degree, they tell me. Unfortunately the man didn't think about his business much; his father had built it for him. He cursed his father for proudly planting the pottery works in full view of the house. He considered himself a philanthropist, gave money to the poor, and was quite concerned with the plight of American Negroes. There are hints, supposedly, of a convoluted relationship with both of his parents.

* * * *

Yet another memory from the 19th century has wafted into the view of the Historians. Less excitement over this one, if even more self-congratulation, as it confirms that a new time-level has been penetrated. I swallowed it.

The boy's name was Stephen, Stephen Cross. He was an apprentice in a mill. It was afternoon, and he was upset because that morning, at the gates, one of the older girls, with a dirty face and a hard little grin, had been rummaging about his genitals. He did not know what it meant, or why she had done it, but he sensed, probably correctly, aggression in her. He cried, and the other boys laughed. He had no private retreat, so he had wrapped himself instead in the clatter and bustle of his work.

The ceiling was low and made of plaster, and there were few open windows. Looms were connected by leather belts to a spinning shaft that ran the length of the room. Every once and a while a yelp would go up, and Stephen would run to a roll of orderly warp to tie broken threads back together.

'Move damn you! That one! That one there!' the weaver barked, confusing them. Stephen blinked. He was a piecer because he had small delicate hands. He was terrified of being struck over them with the empty shuttle. When he couldn't find the broken thread, he began to cry again. The room dissolved for him and his fingers fumbled helplessly among the conflicting strands.

The message ended in confusion. That is all that survives of Stephen. It had been dark when he arrived, and it would be dark when he moved through empty and shadowed streets to the closeness of his home. I caught a glimpse of his mother. She had a narrow, bitten face and black hair tied with a scarf. Saw his home, too, as he remembered it, all grey wood, and the bed he shared with his brothers.

Is it possible that this is all he did with his childhood? There were no memories of toys or books. The only dogs he ever saw crept like rats through the gutters. There must have been a smelter nearby. Red dust settled in puddles and sweltered like blood in the streets. Everything was damp. He was ill with it; slow fire burned in his lungs.

He lived and died in something called a slum. The word 'slum' is derived from the word 'slump', which meant a low-lying mire, the kind of ground on which many of them were built. A slump also came to mean a depression, emotional or economic. Words have a truth, an extra meaning in them, like potatoes in a sack.

I am more confused by Miss Austen now. Was she heartless or merely unaware of the Stephens of her world? Perhaps her silence was a form of modesty. Or was it timorousness? A woman in that time could fall to great depths. Miss Austen does not lie about that. Perhaps she was afraid for herself. Is that why, whenever she heard someone coming, Miss Austen leapt up from her work and hid it?

I still want desperately to know if Stephen found the broken thread.

* * * *

One final ghost.

The discovery of still another memory was announced, and Mother beamed that it might be of special interest to me. I agreed, and the memory came.

Suddenly I was walking down the streets of another village, not Chawton, but one similar. It was, I am sure, the 19th century, very clearly. Earlier possibly even than that, though it would be difficult to prove. The long straight dresses were out of focus and the surrounding village strangely dim.

Whoever it was paid little attention to clothing and architecture. She was interested instead in faces. The tape was a procession of them. Each face was pounced upon and held until it yielded up some secret.

This was an iron mind, and a hungry one. The 'I' in it had been erased, or put away, rather, like an old crushed keepsake in a drawer. It was a stern mind, and a lonely one, heavy with sadness overcome and leavened with needled wit. It gave no hint of its name, peering intently into every face.

And in every face it saw something different. A swagger of humour there; a wizened and proud solemnity here; there the pursed lips of someone exhausted by her own weakness. The faces were lined and rugged; they had weathered things, like stones. I envied them. They laughed, over nothing. There was something self-assured and calm about them, like lions.

I have begun *Sense and Sensibility.* I will save it, really save it. I have a suspicion whose ghost it was I encountered today. Mother must think me crazy.

* * * *

Finished it!

It has been seven days since I last wrote in this diary. I have been taping all that time. Never before has the translation of a novel taken so long. It is unprecedented. Continually blotted out parts of it and imagined them again. Writers used to do that, to clear away the fog of hazy words. So should Translators revise and edit. We are a lazy lot. Everything is sacrificed for immediacy. We leave smudges across our dreams and our characters change faces suddenly. Mine do not. Marianne remains Marianne. I have given her curly hair and a chin that is slightly too large. Hints of crow's feet appear around her eyes by the end of the novel. I have pulled other details into view. I forced myself to hear every spoken word; to see each movement of the hands, to even smell, as far as I was able, beech trees and roses and varnished furniture. I conjured them up from the Grid, just to feel them.

Which is not to say that I have been faithful to Jane Austen, except in spirit. I concentrate on meaningful images and revealing entrances of characters, rather than on clumsily translated descriptions. These things I have learned from translating plays. I have also shortened the story, removed characters and whole sub-plots, cut background information. In a tape you can let people know things without telling them. It is a form all of its own, and deserves respect.

I have great circles under my eyes from lack of sleep. I don't mind. Mother gave me a facial overlay to hide them, but I ordered it away. Let them see my circles. I am proud of them. I shall surely sleep tonight.

* * * *

Mother have rejected the tape. Child Bri tried to tell me as gently as he could, but he fumbled with his words and resorted finally to beaming me his measured sympathy. He is not an unintelligent man, but he looks like a panda, and speaks like one. 'Is good. Is clear. Is too much you!' was the best he could manage.

Mother Fen himself followed, in his monkish robes. He, being a Reader, had been sent to give me a more literate explanation. 'Good day, Child Rold,' he said, extending his hand in the ancient greeting. 'You are well?' He did not use his Communicator. It glinted dead and sinister behind his ear, like a tooth.

'As well as I might be,' I replied.

'Child Bri has informed you of Mother's decision?' he asked, sympathetically, and settled next to me. 'We are sorry.' Words for him are made out of metal and have sharp little points. His voice is always even. 'We recognise the fluency of your tape and its technical excellence. I would say, speaking for myself, that it contains some of the finest detail work I have ever swallowed. But certain other requirements have not been satisfied. You have deleted whole portions of the artifact and have substantially altered others. This is not pleasing to Mother. She do not consider it a precise translation.'

'But everyone simplifies!'

'It is necessary in some cases, yes. But your tape is not so much a simplified translation as an adaptation. A Translator's duty is to preserve, not to modify or to create.'

'You mean that I actually said something.'

He paused, to re-phrase what I'd said. 'Your own feelings have been allowed to flavour the tape, certainly. This is the problem. It expresses something very personal. An attitude to the past perhaps.'

'But art consists of saying something personal!'

'Exactly.' He nodded as though we had never disagreed. 'A translation, after all, is not a vehicle for one man's feelings. We have no need for art now. All men are artists.'

'Are they? They tape, yes, and Communicate, yes, and spew up dreams all over the Grid. But an artist dreams of things that have a meaning for everyone. Like these old books! Why are we resurrecting them?'

He smiled slightly. 'To preserve them. Don't you think they deserve to be preserved?'

'They deserve to be read.'

'Perhaps. But Reading is a dead form of communication. Mother don't have the right to force people to read.' He leant forward. 'Child Rold, Mother are not trying to deprive you of anything. I have been authorised to offer you another opportunity to translate the book.'

'What will happen to my tape?'

'It can be filed with the other private tapes, if you wish.'

'It will be lost then, won't it? Cheapened.'

He still smiled. 'Art is cheap. The standards Mother maintain are high.'

I look at his blank and perfect face, and I hated him. 'Mother cheapen,' I replied, the words gurgling in my throat like a snarl. 'Everything.'

'Would you care to re-translate the book,' he repeated.

'No,' I growled. 'No I would not.' He rose with a silent nod and left.

Art is not cheap. It is purchased with tears and loneliness and long aching hours. Mother do not understand. She have given my book to Hayre, Hayre of *Green Gables*! He'll give the woman long, wild hair and sandals. Their faces will be suntanned and dreamy and pleasant. No threat of destitution will shadow them; no quirks will mar the perfection of their lips and brows. Everything Jane Austen lived and felt will be honeyed over. And Mother will call it an act of preservation! I had forgotten words could lie.

Went for a walk on the Grid, to get away from the Decks. This was once a barren, rocky world until we came and coated it with a carpet of grass that never grows and a blue sky with clouds that never rain. In the grass, and around the world's circumference run metal strips. Some run north to south, and others east to west, and where they cross, there is a Cord. The word is short for Co-ordinate. Again, the magic imprecision of words! For these Cords do bind us to our Mother! Through them comes everything we need, or want. Some Cords specialise, and are set aside for Food, Health or Transportation. Delicate buildings balance over them on stilts. The Decks themselves, open to the air like a ship, rest on a Cord. All others are given over to Sport. So they call it.

A man summoned up a woman, and to satisfy his jaded palate, ordered that she be one-legged. A gaggle of Lumpens rolled in a sensuous sea of crême caramel that had come bubbling out of the ground. A child, naked and fat, demanded a dog, and ordered that it love him. It crawled up out from the Grid plate, a tiny creature with a long body and short, struggling legs. Its eyes were bright with trust and eagerness. But the child didn't like the animal. Perhaps it was the wrong colour. Perhaps it was too real and smelt a bit of fur and wet tongue. 'Go back!' the child commanded. In the very act of running towards its master, the dog was dissolved in light and Re-absorbed. A tiny dog memory of love was then sent spinning out into eternity.

That child was a murderer.

Tapeworms spotted the plains, like cattle. There are more of them now. Mother are getting worried. Blinded by the tapes they swallow continuously, they sit staring ahead for days at a time, their eyes like stones. They forget to eat. Mother put food into their stomachs. They forget to blink, and their faces stream with tears. They look like a silent chorus for the dead. My work does this to them. We have been robbed of decent, useful labour.

I suddenly longed for seagulls, and there were seagulls, but it was not the same as the memories I had swallowed of finding them wild and free on rocky coasts. I transmitted to Forests, where Mother had designated Forests to be. I hoped to wander among plants and the fleeting shadows of birds. But there was a Hunt on, and men with rifles were shooting deer and Simulant savages. The men's faces hung limply on their skulls, lighting up only for that instant when death exploded from their hands.

Why has success diminished us? Mother say we are free, finally free to develop our human potential. I see no development. I see greed and sloth and poverty of spirit. Do we need hardship to make us noble? If so, what a terrible conundrum is all of human life and human politics. For who could condone the deliberate creation of pain and oppression as a means of human improvement? Yet I wished suffering on those people. I wanted to break open their boredom and their complacency like scabs.

There is an old story in a book that has not been translated. A man destroyed a flock of waterfowl by giving the birds more fish than they could eat. The males turned on each other; the females forgot their nests and ate their young. The colony died out within a year. Nothing worth having is ever given. Perhaps that is why we destroyed the Earth, and why we want to rebuild it as our own. The word 'Earth' meant soil, along with water, the source of life. Life also is a gift, and we destroy that, too.

On my desert world, they have resurrected Paris as it was in the 20th Century. I wonder if they resurrected the German occupation as well. I was born a cripple. They gave me new legs, but I am still a cripple inside. I have never loved or cried or touched a real flower, or ploughed the earth in the hot sun. I work my long lonely day in the Decks, pouring dreams down the gullet of the great machine, though there is no need for me to work so hard. What expiation have I undertaken and why? What sins are mine that must be redeemed?

* * * *

I have had a dream this night, a real one. I was skimming over the surface of the sea, and the sun was running with me, on the waves. The water was lime green, and underneath it, just ahead of me, something vast and white and dim was swimming. Suddenly it rose up towards the surface, and my chest clenched like a fist. Its skin was mottled: I could see the ripples of light cast by the waves on its back. But then it subsided back into the depths, a fleeting shadow, a ghost. I knew that the sun and I would chase it forever.

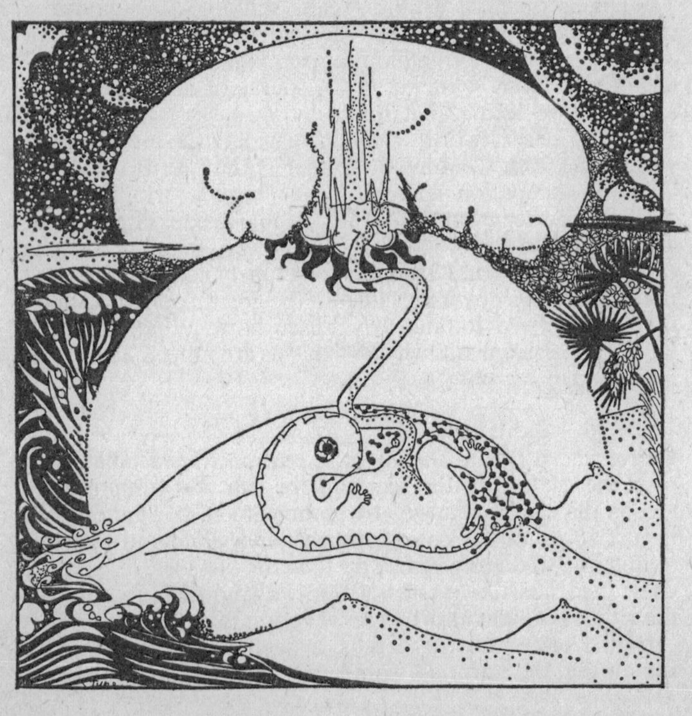

POEMS

A lazy, outpost war;
soldiers with nothing to do
but grow mutations
in the bellies
of dim-witted native girls
and marvel at a sky
with only one sun,
one moon.

Miracles dripped down the tube
and into his arm,
then out again
through the catheter.
Liver spots made his face
look like a sepia map of Mars.
Capillaries popped in his head
like starships landing in the distance.
His voice was like
broken glass when he spoke.
'The only cure for old age,'
he said,
'is death.'

'There, there now,
things will be all right,'
a voice said.
It came from a tape in the ceiling.

WILLIAM JON WATKINS

THE NAKED AND TRANSPARENT MAN GIVES THANKS

Amid the folding of all greenness left
I give my thanks, whose-heartedly, for life.
For this vermillion tapestry, warp and weft
of the blood-vein's fabric. Its threads are rife,
conspicuous; easy-meat for knife
or microbe and the many ills that kill,
and yet are stubborn and abundant still.

With ruins of ages around me, strewn
like wreckage of an unsuccessful Probe
among the craters of a wasted moon,
I extend my thanks for this living robe
and its pulsing weave, to the moth-holed globe,
and unravelling, almost threadbare sky
of the failing sun, under which I lie.

ROBERT CALVERT

DAVE GRIFFITHS

A TEAR IN THE CAMERA

by ROBERT MEADLEY

Musgrove came out of the sea, out of the west and wet and cold, his damaged leg dragging a silver furrow in Talisker's black beach. A stack, like a tooth reduced to a hook-like spire of enamel, spiked high out of the greasy water that heaved against the steep drop of the tideline. Above this stack two circling fulmars beat at the cloud's low ceiling.

At the end of his vivid trail Musgrove lay against the round, storm-smoothed stones of a dyke heaped between the towering granite boundaries of the bay. Great fragments of jointed timber and other flotsam, like the remains of immense siege machines on a long deserted rampart, littered the dyke's top. Hectic cold that was not quite wind moved bitter around the vast ravine.

Musgrove inspected his damaged leg. A rent in his mauve flying suit from belt to gaiter exposed a long fissure in the carapace of his right thigh. Inflamed tissue bulged through the crack, dressed with a fine lace of drying salt. The thigh throbbed with its own deep ache.

He remembered his head and it started to trouble him again. His shoulder was slightly sprained too, but that didn't hurt yet. Nothing else seemed wrong. With clumsy fingers he extracted a syringe from his breast pocket and inserted the needle into the edge of his wound.

He had to rest after discharging the syringe, waiting patiently for relief to lap at his cortex and dissolve sensation. His unfeeling fingers slipped from the syringe, and he forgot about it.

Out past the bay's twin spurs a tip of oleaous ornithopter wing glimmered in the squirming sea. Musgrove's head felt loose. He prodded gently at the padded helmet around his skull. Everything looked misty through the scratched and salt-caked visor. He rubbed at the glass with a dirty mitten, improving nothing. An urge to rip out the glass drew the membranes flickering across his eyes, but he'd been ordered to keep his head warm, so he did half-hearted exercises to help him relax while he rubbed some more at the visor, getting it a little clearer.

It occurred to him that he didn't know what was on the other side of the dyke. He'd seen it from the air – a stretch of flat green, perhaps bright green dulled by skittering sea fret; the steep slopes of the natural bay, the rear heights rising into successive hills – but none of these images were precise. With the syringe still protruding from his leg, he hauled himself to the top of the dyke and across it, then lay on his belly, exhausted.

Knee high grass confronted him. He probed the mud beneath it with a long stick. It was at least waist deep and crusty with cold, but still moist enough below the surface to resist the withdrawal of the stick with slurping irritation. At the far end of this grass, where the ground just began to rise, a box-like ruin stood among ragged trees. To the right and rear of this was a sugarloaf hill. All else was obscured by thick folds of low, advancing cloud.

Musgrove crawled along the dyke's top. A paravane, almost completely rusted through, and a subverted tree stump still spreading a complex aureole of weathered roots, caused his only major detours. The whole journey was at most four hundred metres, but he had to rest frequently and at the end he lay on his face and slept.

The light had almost faded when he began dragging himself up the steep slope of the bay's side. There was roaring in his ears: part sea, part wind, part deep space. All time sense, all conscious memory phased from him. His body occurred to him only as a baffling, ingenious, mobile environment for the encapsulated mind crouched warm within; a mind powered and illuminated by a glowing purpose, an urgent will upwards requiring no articulation.

The dim landscape seemed to slither and change, bulging and splitting, leaping fragmented into showers of sudden brilliant images. Somehow, unacknowledged instincts kept the clawing, meandering carcass safe. Every unconscious decision seemed right. When he slipped and bounded fifty metres back down the slope, that seemed wise too. It was dark long before he reached the top, but feverish lights burned in his eyes.

At high tide, when he'd been on Isle Soay, the sea had foamed an arm's length deep over the knobbly glass roof of Kelpsom's sunk hangars, glinting black-green above the white glare of the arc-lamps. The floor had been cluttered thick with part and whole ornithopter frames, mostly bare, one or two shimmering with the dull polychrome sheen of their membrane skins. Clambering over all, headphones clasped over his pale gold shining skull, his amplified voice clattering from half a hundred wall mounted speakers, the delicate, stick-insect-like Kelpsom moved among his machines; seeming never to stop moving, yet when paused seeming never to have moved or needed to.

In the space among the frames, on a patch of floor only thinly littered with loose parts, Musgrove had lain naked in the heat. Usually Kelpsom's rare visitors were required to sit under a blanket so their presence wouldn't distract him while he worked, but for Musgrove this was waived since he said very little and was usually too distant in dreams to fidget. So he lay on a pile of bleached cushions, a thin sweat filming the semi-permeable plates of his carapace.

Kelpsom came up, shaking out the tangled firelines of the ironware hanging from his working harness.

'This creature,' he tossed Musgrove a thing like a puzzle in the form a small and intricately folded stone crab, 'is a pathor, a space drifter. Quite rare, I believe. They float around the stars, not apparently doing anything. They have silicon based systems which are rather interesting. Inside that shell, they're almost all brain. Thought it might amuse you.'

Musgrove turned the pathor in his hands, glancing at Kelpsom from time to time and nodding vaguely. He was always prepared to be interested in novelties.

'Proportionally,' Kelpsom shed his various burdens, 'their brain centres, of which they have three like the old gods, are enormous. I wired myself into that thing's brain once, but not for long. There are things in there too large for my understanding; a conceptual command of space that I have just no equipment to cope with, many of whose aspects I only dimly perceive and of whose limits I have only the haziest notions.'

Musgrove had no idea of what Kelpsom was trying to say.

'Beyond me,' he said.

Kelpsom expanded as if with the bliss of being understood.

'Whatever there is,' he enunciated slowly, 'there is always something beyond. Wherever I am there is always something beyond me in every direction.'

He trailed into silence again, as though he had once more lost grip of what he wanted to communicate. He frowned dejectedly at the floor.

'Maybe it would be easier to talk about it,' Musgrove offered, 'if you connected me up to this thing, so I had some idea of what it was about. I like new things.'

Kelpsom's usually impassive face changed expression again, admitting a slow ritual smile. His eyes burned dully, like those of one about to quench old fears in blood.

'A peep into deep space?'

'Sounds nice,' said Musgrove.

Kelpsom appeared to think deeply, his right hand fidgetted vaguely with the controls of his running microphone.

'Could be done,' he said eventually. Volumes of sudden distorted sound drowned the original speech but neither seemed to notice. Kelpsom rubbed a chitinous forearm against his jaw, filling the amplified silence with an intolerable screeching. After a minute he ducked away under a half-covered wing, reappearing some time later perched on the top of a section of sleek kestrel fuselage.

Pushing his own microphone away from himself, Musgrove asked, 'When do we do this thing?' Whispered echoes of his voice rippled round the hangar. Without saying anything, Kelpsom came back and began setting up his equipment. Musgrove grinned sleepily as the increasing complex was arranged around him.

Suddenly, snapped wires flying in a stormy halo about his head, Musgrove sprang directionless among the glistening hoard of partial ornithopters. Several jars of cultured organic systems shattered across the floor, spilling inaudible screams. Kelpsom leapt after Musgrove. The pathor, still wired to the ruptured complex, flexed itself imperceptibly in response to the accumulated terror.

Knowing nothing, Musgrove dashed his skull against a steel alloy girder as if to beat out the dismembered brain within. Kelpsom caught up with him and attempted a quick clip with the side of the hand to the base of the neck, but Musgrove stumbled and Kelpsom's forearm buffeted him above the ear. Musgrove veered, sprawling, struck his head on a torc wrench, and finally lay silent. Kelpsom carried him back to the pile of white cushions.

When Musgrove woke he found himself crammed between a sheep's carcass and the overhanging flank of a boulder. A throbbing roar compounded of sea, wind and pain pulsed through him. Pieces of his visor rattled inside his helmet when he moved; it must have shattered at some point during the previous night or day's stumbling, but he could remember nothing.

There was no feeling in his right arm. He did not realise that he was lying on it. Awkwardly, with his left hand, he felt for the pack of loaded syringes in his breast pocket. The pocket was torn; the case was still there but it had broken and the three remaining syringes with it. He shook fragments of sticky plastic from his numb fingers.

He had to get up. A spasm of strenuous wriggling didn't seem to get him very far, but it brought some feeling to his right arm. Sinking his fingers into the sheep's slimy fleece, he tried to pull himself up on to his knees, but only succeeded in disjointing rotten ribs from rotten spine and dislodging a few sleepy grubs. He sank back against the boulder. Beyond the sheep he saw that a light snow had fallen overnight, the prevailing wind having left a ragged semi-circle of clear ground in the lea of the boulder. Deep cloud everywhere threatened heavier falls later in the day.

Sudden pain drew his attention to his leg. With a sense of urgency devoid of desperation he pushed, pulled and squirmed himself on to his knees. Trying to stand, he seized the dead sheep by the horns as if to pull it with him, but the skull came off in his hands and he threw it away disgustedly.

An attack of violent coughing cleared his head somewhat. The sweet smell of impending snow was enticing. He began to crawl away from the shelter of the boulder.

Faces surrounded him when he woke again. Beyond the faces hung still the deep, folding cloud. The faces expressed concern, but he recognised none of them. He wanted to speak but found his mouth bound with mucus. A voice, belonging to someone somewhere behind his head, spoke soothingly, urging him to be calm, to conserve his strength, which seemed sound advice except that he wasn't trying to do anything more than roll his eyes occasionally in a confused attempt to see behind him.

After a while the persistent crooning of soft advice seemed to require an answer. Musgrove tried to swallow some of the phlegm that clogged his mouth, but he only choked and convulsed with helpless gagging coughs until firm hands raised his head and torso and poured an acrid cordial into his gaping throat, forcing him to gulp down the loosened plegm. After that he would gladly have slumped back prone, but a knee against the junction of back and thighs pressed him into more or less sustaining his own weight on his elbows.

For the first time now he noticed a figure stooped over the tear in his thigh, probing with a delicate bladed instrument and a pair of tweezers among the torn muscle and vestigial bone beneath the wound. A hooded sheepskin coat enveloped this person almost completely, showing only his four-jointed fingers, their dainty tools, and the tilting bowl of a long pipe drooping from the shadow of the hood.

Around the central cluster of Musgrove, his supporter and the surgeon, were loosely grouped another half dozen sexless fur-capped figures; perhaps more were behind him. Several disconsolate ponies and a high-sprung snow phaeton with ornate runners stood some distance off. Musgrove's vision of these was blurred. He looked back at his leg. The lips of the wound had turned black. He tried to draw some conclusion from this and from the scene around him, but nothing made any sense.

The figure stooped over the wound turned and nodded. Musgrove was allowed to sink back against some form of cushion. The person who had supported him now appeared above him, looking down through a jewelled snow mask framed in a hood of dark fur; gloves and mask were embroidered with the intricate, impelling vine of Szomas. It had been her mother-gentle tones that had permeated and dispelled his last unconsciousness. His mind flooded with that particular unalloyed gratitude that only the blocking off of true consciousness allows.

Four of the secondary figures moved towards him. His wound, he found, had been bound up. Very gently, wrapped in deep furs, he was carried to the phaeton and lifted in.

Musgrove lived only at the fringe of consciousness. Within this littoral matrix of dreams his recollection of the recent past remained imperfect. Certain images, none in any formal sequence, recurred reassuringly and seemed familiar, but always these dissolved into black holes, vast abysses of dark lit only by the distant elfin lights of endless space.

Some things he recognised: the ornithopter Kelpsom had given him, its fuselage shimmering with the elusive tones of oil on water, the bright bead of its brain gaudy with refracted light; or monstrous blackberry bushes in the woods around Scorched Castle where he had played with lovers in the days before dreams; the tubby wrecks of old floating watchtowers on the reedy wastes of the east coast.

Sometimes whole scenes came to him. Several times he dreamt unseen aspects of his crash: parameters of wind, sea and rock that had escaped him at the time. Twice he was flying over fruit fields, apple bushes whose huge fruit were turning to rot in the rich neglect of autumn. He wished himself below, but as he dropped the bushes became waves and the sea closed overhead while spectral, fluorescent hydra somersaulted around him in the turbid water.

Once, he was awake without knowing it, the woman in the embroidered mask had towered over him, crooning. The enormous jewels on her fingers spiked cold sheer light into his brain, her polychrome hair swirled like enprismed mist in the dim light while she mouthed soft nonsenses, as if in a trance projecting on to his fantastic personae and all the trappings of her own strange dreams.

And always returning, the spring tides of space, the darkness too vast for suns, the sparse crystal fires only betraying the scale of loneliness.

This time it seemed to Musgrove that he was always waking; never awake or sleepy, just waking and always somewhere new. He was sprawled on a fur upholstered bed in a fur room. Black fur lined the walls, grey fur the floor. Darkly variegated furs draped what he imagined to be furniture. There were no windows, and what light there was emanated from a small crucible, white with internal fire, on a spiral stand beside the bed. A rack of boar spears formed the bedhead against which his cushions were piled.

He stretched his left leg, noisily scratching his toes together. His right leg was encased from groin to ankle in splints and bandages. He felt his head, no longer helmeted. It was tender still, but unbandaged now and both cuts seemed to have healed. His left shoulder felt a bit stiff but moved painlessly.

Musgrove became bored, oppressed by the shapeless furriness of the room and the dim light of the crucible.

A flap in the wall bulged open, shaken by a gust of wind. From a night vivid with dry lightning, the woman in the jewelled snowmask swept into the room. Someone unseen drew the flap closed behind her.

The embroidered gloves hovered for a moment at her throat, then as if by sleight of hand the long cape slid to the floor in a succession of freezing ripples. Long plaited hair, shot with strands of many colours, glimmered as she moved. She appeared unaware of Musgrove, but this was caprice.

Musgrove coughed and said, 'I feel rather better today.'

His tone hinted at an apology for his presence, but she turned smiling, the pink point of her tongue playing between the tips of opalescent mandibles.

'Ah, my perky one,' she sang rather than spoke, moulding the words with a curious intonation reminiscent of exotic seabirds, 'my lucky chick, my snow child, welcome to consciousness and to the tent of Lara, Whedon's wife.'

She sat on the edge of the bed and laid a brightly-ringed hand against Musgrove's forehead. The cuffs of her jacket were sewn with tiny bells.

'My surgeon assured me you would wake today.'

Her tone of sensuous maternity disturbed Musgrove. He asked, 'Where are me? Geographically, that is. If it is. Is anything?' He mumbled off into silence, adding suddenly, 'Not that it matters.'

'Above the brook Sligachan, my snow dove, below the bare slopes of Red Forest.'

Lara smiled reassuringly but Musgrove was no wiser. It seemed easier to let her lead any further conversation but she said nothing, just sat gazing at him with a fond, wistful smile until the surgeon appeared with his various tools and a phial of some sweet cordial which he gave to Musgrove.

After drinking this, Musgrove closed his eyes and relaxed, leaving Lara to the pursuit of her enigmatic dreams and the surgeon to his skills.

When Musgrove remembered to look out again he found

Lara gone. Two window flaps in the fur wall had been tied back to let in the early daylight, and through the narrow glass panels set in the tent's side he could see snow-smothered hills cracked by occasional black gulleys, but no part of a camp, no tracks, no sign of life.

Beside the bed the surgeon was rinsing his hands in alcohol. Desiring attention but still unsure of himself, Musgrove muttered inaudibly, his eyes closed to avoid committing himself. The surgeon, holding his hands over the glowing crucible, turned his head to look at Musgrove, but as his pipe was gripped between his lips he said nothing. Brief, pale flames flickered from his wrists to his fingertips. His hands dried, he discovered a chair under the heaped furs and made himself comfortable.

'Interesting wounds you have there,' he spoke hurriedly as if to outrun the natural restraints of a reserved nature. Musgrove didn't reply immediately; he had just wondered whether he could trust this doctor, or Lara, or any of the fur-caked wanderers amongst whom he had fallen.

He was not afraid of them but for them, frightened that he would unwittingly cause them and the trappings of their reality to dissolve through him into the nightmare dark. The questions he wanted to ask, still only vaguely formulated in his confused brain, seemed dangerous and impertinent.

He said finally, 'I don't want to know about anything.'

The surgeon, torn between a choice of solecisms, decided to try once more.

'Perhaps you could tell me how you came to be where we found you. Visitors are rare up here, and we have met no other hunting parties this season. To us your presence is quite a puzzle. This is hardly a populous or hospitable countryside.'

This time it was Musgrove who strove between choices. Ought he to answer or not? Which choice led back to the dark? He tried to think clearly, but his helpless attempts at concentration only confused still further his tenuous notions of reality.

'I was flying,' he spoke haltingly as though trying to outguess the hovering dark. 'Something, a squall or wind recoiling from a cliff, outwitted my machine. I came down in the sea but made land. Then I wandered about a lot. Then you found me.'

Fearing to tempt fate further, Musgrove stopped. His eyes were shut, the dark behind them warm and comforting, and he was afraid to open them, to see the tiny lights that drifted in the other darkness. His breathing became tense and shallow.

The surgeon fidgeted while waiting for Musgrove to continue. He drummed his fingers, one hand against the other, and crossed and re-crossed his legs, flexing ankles and calves inside his long sheepskin boots. After a while, feeling that Musgrove needed prompting, he said, 'I've never been flying . . .'

He broke off. Distantly, through the fluttering silence, he could hear singing. Musgrove shut his eyes tighter. After a few more minutes in which neither spoke, the surgeon left.

One scene in his current wanderings troubled Musgrove particularly in the uneasy hours between the visits of Lara and the doctor. No context occurred for this sequence but it began with two points of light, distant in the roaring darkness, which as they approached cleared into vision through the eye-slits of a snow-mask accompanied by the groaning of the phaeton's runners on the frozen ground.

No fresh snow appeared imminent but it was noticeably less cold. Embedded in a mink bag beside Lara, Musgrove peered out at the gleaming landscape. Escort riders on squat ponies trotted ahead, scuffing feathers of snow behind them. The surgeon on a tall grey rode slightly apart from the two groups, the wind snatching tails of smoke from his pipe. Once he paused to place a fresh pellet in his pipe and coax it alight. Before the phaeton had drawn abreast of him, he resumed his station.

Parallel to their line of march lay a ridge of peaks profiled like a dead giant thrown upon his back, one knee cocked, a severed arm outflung towards the plain, his mouth hanging open in an eroded howl.

For a long time Musgrove stared at this curious configuration. From his extreme youth a memory returned of a long, bifurcated hill said to be the back and thighs of an ancient titan. At the junction of the two spurs stood a small obelisk or menhir, the tale being that that the titan, goaded into a trial of strength by a local sorcerer, had forged a spear of stone with his bare hands and hurled it with such force that it flew right round the world and planted itself in his back. How, Musgrove wondered, had any sorcerer tricked this new giant into parting with his missing arm?

The slits of the snow mask limited Musgrove's peripheral vision, so it was suddenly that he saw the approaching newcomer: someone in ragged blue, bespectacled but otherwise bare mottle-faced against the cold, on a gaunt horse that floundered and stumbled as he flogged it, his arms and legs flailing haste, through the uneven snow. He seemed to be known to some of the escort riders; several of them waved their arms and clutched at their heads in exaggerated gestures of distress, all loud with laughter and mock protests that the wind twisted and distended before sweeping them back to Musgrove and Lara.

The stranger fell in with the fore riders, encouraging their outrage. Several times he looked round at the occupants of the phaeton, and twice made as if to turn his horse and approach them, but both times his bridle was seized and he was held forcibly with his friends.

One fragment of their conversation was carried back almost perfect to Lara and Musgrove. Someone said, 'The trouble with you, Convery, is that you take logic personally,' whereon the newcomer laughed and another cried out, 'Sullied in vain,' then everything became faint and garbled again as the wind veered.

Soon the stranger left them, scrambling his horse into the uncertain snow, and in Musgrove's mind the ubiquitous dark intervened.

Although now sometimes allowed to walk, Musgrove lay as usual on the fur bed in Lara's tent, holding court to Lara and the surgeon and today also to two priestly persons. One of these was tall, one short, each offsetting the other's physique and exaggerating the proportions, but both were heavy-set. They had been brought ostensibly to sense whether any sinister influence attached itself to Lara's pet.

The smaller one, thickly bearded and with a curling, sculptured face and mobile hands, sat on the edge of the bed. His eyes roved constantly towards imagined vistas as though he could not bring himself to listen to the complex stream of his own sinuous conversation.

The tall one said very little, but humphed oppressedly round the tent. Once he pulled his collar over his head and began a strange clumsy dance, flapping his arms and muttering gutterally. Lara looked reproachfully at him, and he subsided into a chair.

Neither of the priests seemed very impressed by Musgrove. They tried to draw him into elaborating on those delirious references to infinity and the dark which Lara had overheard and related to them, but Musgrove, muddled by his own and others' mysteries and the rich cordials pressed on him by the surgeon, could not follow the allusive, intricate periods of their conversation, and would only mumble into dragging silences, his eyes downcast.

Lara was trying to gloss over one of these pauses when yet more people crushed into the tent. There were four of them: the foremost conspicuously enlarged by his bulky coat and with coarse crimson eyes set off by green tattoos intagliated around his scarred mouth; behind him to the left crowded the mottled, still smiling Convery; the last two, hanging back, remained vague smears in the furry shadows.

Lara looked up and smiled, but the tattooed giant glared past her at Musgrove.

'I'm Whedon,' he announced, 'you'll have heard of me.'

The voice was harsh and heavy as the face.

Musgrove, who was adept at ingratiating himself with droll helplessness, gave a winning smile and tried to remember his formulae for amusing brutes, but it was long since anything but dreams had threatened him and Whedon seemed impregnable to the assaults of silent charm.

'Where are you from, Musgrove?'

The tone of command startled Musgrove. He shrugged and put more simper in his smile, doggedly inoffensive.

'I have no reliable memory of my previous existence. Sometimes I seem to have come from nameless autumnal countrysides, sometimes from the sky or the sea, often from far space and the vistas between the stars.'

Whedon, determined to argue, seized on this speech with a poor pretence of annoyance.

'Do you think I'm a fool to be lulled by such elfin gibberish, Musgrove?'

'It's true,' for once, finite consciousness obtruding forcibly upon his habit of dreams, Musgrove was desperate to please, 'I don't know where I'm from. I'm sick. There are gaps in my mind full of immense emptiness, like the fallen angel's fragmentary memories of paradise.'

Whedon was smiling, so Musgrove grinned too.

Whedon said, 'He's determined to insult me,' then to Musgrove, 'We fallen angels must compare hells tomorrow,' then he took his party out, all laughing softly, leaving a bleak silence.

Musgrove felt tainted. Having forsworn his dreams only to compound his humiliation galled him. The scope of his intelligence was still elastic, but some things even the most capricious minds cannot disguise and Whedon's crude hostility was one such. Musgrove wondered how he had insulted Whedon, slowly realising that whatever he'd said it would not have mattered, that there was no logic but the vector of intention in Whedon's four short speeches. Sobriety pressed like mercury through the fatty tissues of Musgrove's brain.

He noticed the two priests, if they were priests, prepare to leave and said petulantly, 'Must I meet Whedon tomorrow?'

They chorused, 'More than meet,' and stepped out of the tent.

'Why "more than meet"?' he asked of Lara and the surgeon. Their silence was heavy with significance.

'He'll kill you,' two tears glistened above the polished ellipses of Lara's cheeks, 'he will prise open your skull with visions and scatter your brains as porridge on the ice. He is a terrible man and very jealous.'

She was obviously deeply moved, the sweep of her emotion soothing Musgrove and stealing the meaning from her words. Musgrove accepted a glass of the surgeon's cordial and asked, 'When will this thing happen?' Reality had already started to recede.

The surgeon said, 'It will be fair.'

Two new tears formed in Lara's liquid eyes. Musgrove drew strength from them. He realised obscurely that he knew more than he admitted to himself, and this dubious hidden faith buoyed him with subliminal elation.

In his gradually lengthening periods of cogency, Musgrove had held in his mind several static images of Kelpsom, poised variously with his bright paraphernalia and his fanciful machines; in each case with a cruel smile that was the obverse of the surgeon's nervous, sympathetic smile; in each case giving the impression of glib, treacherous conversation reciprocal to the surgeon's well-intentioned reticence. The surgeon gave Musgrove no special confidence, but was something, so slight that only subjective distance allowed it to effect a balance, to set against Kelpsom's bland, oblique malevolence.

Frequently the maternal enigma of Lara intervened in these meditations, hovering like an embroidered angel among the jewelled infinities of space with her mother-mistress, moaning silence, smothering him with unspoken intimacies and miasmic space-maternity. She called him her snow bird, her ice child, her crystal waif; and dreamed through him of eternities with the child she could not bear, the child that had here sprung full-grown from the rocks and snow like the sons of the moon that in childhood tales came in winter and were eaten by the sun, from whose bones the seeds burst that brought forth oats.

It had shocked Musgrove at first to find that Lara was actually male. Not shocked in any tabloid moral sense, he was incapable of overt metaphysics, but in some primal nursery way as if his mother had turned out to be a table or his dog a gate. It had been the weight of her maternity that had prompted Musgrove, intent on mild rebellion, to attempt the trivial improprieties, passively discouraged, which led to this discovery.

The shock had not lasted. Very soon he came to feel the squeeze of more profound taboos, as though her male existence was illusory, a punishment to him for offence against her ghostly motherhood. Easily and willingly he slipped again into the matrix of her fantasies: Kelpsom at one horizon, the surgeon at the other, and Musgrove drifting off centre; a solitary line quivering across a private universe.

And now Whedon had come, his bestial presence and stupid jealousy destroying the delicate and indulgent balance of the situation. Now Musgrove remembered Kelpsom fondly, desperately. Kelpsom his friend and wise, Kelpsom so complex, timeless, of such intricate resource. Kelpsom coming to rescue Musgrove, with beaked and taloned ornithopters hunting the killer Whedon across the binding snow. Musgrove sucked relish from these doubtful images of Kelpsom's murderous friendship.

The two priests, he felt sure they were priests, led Musgrove down from the tents to the ice-encrusted bay. They had let him look in a mirror before leaving, and he'd been amazed at how clean his recent experiences had left him. He felt vulnerable. To Musgrove cleanliness was next to nakedness, and he shuffled as he followed through the snow, brooding on his scrubbed, exposed reflection.

An ellipse about twice Musgrove's height in length had been marked with red stain on the ice. A table, fragile and domestic among the wastes of sky and snow, stood beside the ellipse. On the table were three helmets and two short clubs like cropped mattock helves. Musgrove and the two priests stamped clogged snow from their boots and snapped streamers of condensed breath into the wind.

The large priest picked up one of the helmets.

'These helmets are the key. They receive and transmit thought. Each of you will wear one, both of you standing in the marked area, carrying these clubs. Only one blow is allowed; so each combatant tries, through his helmet, to confuse his opponent with novelties of vision and emotion so that the one blow may be placed carefully and unobstructedly. The usual blow in extreme cases like the present is to the heart. Blows to the head are forbidden for fear of damaging the helmets. We have very few of these helmets and they are very precious.'

Musgrove picked up a helmet and examined it. There was a Kelpsom atmosphere about it. Around a skeletal metal frame, varicoloured small systems appeared suspended in cloudy thermoplastic. In one of the organic systems he could see a still undigested fragment of black lichen. A simpler, more packaged design than that which had linked him to the pathor, but essentially the same. He put it down and picked up one of the clubs.

'I'm afraid I'm not in the habit of giving blows to the heart. Do you think . . . a hint . . . ?'

Both priests looked surprised, as if a victim were asking for help in the conduct of sacrifices. Neither of them knew how the blow to the heart was delivered. Whedon knew, and a few others, but these affairs were not common.

Musgrove dropped the subject. He felt safe and wise, as though touching the helmet had infused him with some of Kelpsom's magic.

'Where do these helmets come from?'

The two priests looked quickly and warily at the sky before answering.

'From the snow bird king.'

Kelpsom as demigod, mastering the skies in a giant goose?

Musgrove smiled, burying the last month's artificial fears.

'And the third helmet?'

'For the poet,' both priests were cautious of Musgrove's new, unseemly confidence, 'the poet cannot transmit, only receive. He celebrates the choicest images, afterwards at the feast.'

A large cluster of people had gathered now below the tents, but they remained far off on the slope. Only Whedon and another approached the ellipse.

Musgrove and the poet were introduced. They nodded to each other but said nothing. The poet appeared bored. After each had been installed in his helmet and the clubs distributed, the two priests took away the table. Alone outside the ellipse, the poet briefly repeated the priests' general instructions and triggered the helmets.

In Musgrove's mind the world changed shape. Ruptured pack ice spread where the hills and cloud had been, and the thunder of its breaking filled the sky. He was running helplessly, chasing the spreading cracks, trying to jump and failing, falling and slithering on the shuddering ice. The black gaps of water widened raggedly. To his left three geysers of snow burst upwards screaming as a pressure ridge abruptly formed a new, immediate horizon.

Musgrove, enjoying himself, spread trees across the ice. Whedon changed the ice to lava, crumbling the trees in ashes. Musgrove put a monstrous ornithopter in the sky and gained time to scatter the rent and smouldering carcasses of Whedon's friends between the glowing streams, with a fine, tattered Whedon whimpering behind a bending wall as the lava folded over him.

The rocks reformed: huge boulders on a grained, lifeless mountainside; wind gibbering in narrow tortuous gulleys. Musgrove stooped to examine a sudden orange flower. Brief freak mists manifested Whedon's irritation. Shadowy things wavered unadmitted at the perimeter of the mutual consciousness, the red eyes of a boar flicked elusively among the fluctuating boulders.

Whedon returned the ice. Both in one stared helplessly at the dazzling, searing light. Musgrove placed a prism across their eyes, turning the pain to dim angular spectra, soon doubly refracted through gathering tears.

Lara appeared. Slowly, with lascivious and cruel familiarity, Whedon's scarred hands undressed her. Musgrove revolted. The symbiote that was his and the pathor's combined memories fused. Lara's rainbow hair reversed to the white lattice fires of eight immense crystals that hung burning in the wastes of space. Three in one, Whedon-Musgrove-pathor drifted past, turning gently, basking in the soft tides of gravity. One by one the crystals darkened, imploding casually until their bodies existed only as black gaps in the intolerable dark, windows to a negativity more dreadful than the emptiness of endless space. Two in one, Musgrove-pathor span delicately on.

Coming to, Musgrove found himself still standing on the ice. Whedon lay twisted across the red line of the ellipse, split knuckles clutching the club haft to his constricted chest. The poet stood nearby with closed eyes, his mouth half open and half smiling, amazed and happy.

Musgrove stared at the ice. It seemed dazzled with red and green and very far away. After a while he looked up at the spectators and the tents, only scarves in the wind and the ripple of polychrome furs moved against the trampled snow.

The poet opened his eyes reluctantly. He looked bemused. Even when he saw Whedon, his face showed no emotion. He looked at Whedon for a long time, as one looks without seeing. Then he nodded to Musgrove and they began walking up the slope together, ignoring the silent observers by the tents.

It would be dawn soon.

On the lake, Whedon's pyre sank coughing through the firelit ice.

No one spoke. The poet had just finished his song, and all but one were dazed by its images. Musgrove looked round the feast. There were no women. He liked women around, to admire where men only approved. Lara sat proudly beside him, but that was different. He sipped at his drink, watching the mauve shadows retreat across the snow.

Conversation revived in which Musgrove could take no part, mostly about hunting and other duels. On one side of him was Lara, on the other the surgeon: Lara erect and dignified, only her eyes and smile aflame with her pride in Musgrove; the surgeon silent, a little embarrassed at suddenly becoming so prominent a partisan, but well drunk. Neither had anything to say.

Musgrove looked round the table again. There were many he did not recognise, of those he knew most were quiet among the rattle and laughter. The sculptured, sardonic face of the small priest deigned to smile when the large priest – Musgrove still did not know their names – got up and performed his strangely syncopated leaps with coat over head and arms clapping sides, but neither priest said anything that Musgrove could hear. Occasionally the dry voice of the poet pierced the conversation with aphorisms, to be instantly capped by Convery, who kept surprising Musgrove with displays of lazy independence.

Snow and sky were grey now. Musgrove leant forward in his chair and said, 'Time to go now.'

He stood up unsteadily and walked away, throwing a long, wavering shadow sideways across the snow. Lara made as if to follow, but the surgeon raised his hand to restrain her.

'From the snow he came, perhaps back to the snow he goes.'

Lara sat down again. Everyone at the table had stopped to watch Musgrove. Ofter he stumbled and fell, sometimes crawling for a space, sometimes sitting and playing in the snow. When he was at the bottom of the hill, just above where the divided stream joined the lake, he threw up his arms and shouted with prolonged vowels, 'O-o-o-h, Char-ley, Char-ley . . . '

An immense red-legged crow that had to be an ornithopter hung on the upper wind above the lake, dipping occasionally when the clouds trailed broken streamers. Musgrove was high on the opposite slope, his arms still raised, appearing to touch a sagging patch in the low cloud base.

The clouds lifted slightly and Musgrove fell. The tiny, dark body didn't move. Sharply, the ornithopter curved upwards into the cloud and reappeared on the ridge. Awkwardly the skeletal figure of Kelpsom climbed down and stooped over the body.

Cloud obscured the group. When it cleared, Kelpsom was lifting Musgrove into the machine. Again cloud, then the ridge was bare.

At the long table on the snow, only Lara wept.

TIME MACHINE

by ANNA OSTROWSKA

I TOOK MY friend the Doctor to show him my TIME MACHINE. The Doctor was surprised when he saw my machine. At first he saw the outside and then the inside.

The Doctor asked me 'How do you work this machine?' and I said 'Just use these buttons to go to the past or the future,' and the Doctor was astonished. 'This screen shows my future and yours too, Doctor.' So I asked the Doctor would you like to go to the Future and he said, 'Yes' and I asked what year. '2021' he said.

Soon after the Doctor and I were there already. It was a good landing.

We opened the door to look outside, and then looked around to see if it was all right. We both saw some lights through the woods to get to this wonderful place.

So the Doctor and I went inside to look around the place and then found a large room of controls.

We soon found ourselves trapped by robots, and they told me and the Doctor to stay in this room. The head of the robots told me to get something they want from my Time Machine and so I went to get it.

I was so frightened to be by myself, and then suddenly I saw a man in white, and then he had a gold and silver cloak. And I ran away from him until I came to the Time Machine and went inside. He came in and told me not to be frightened of him. This man told me his name was Aldon and said he was sorry to have frightened me away like that, and I said 'That is all right.'

Aldon said, 'How many of you are there?' and I said 'Just me and the Doctor.' Aldon told me to go back to the Doctor, and to give him the box and also the cloak. So I went back to the robots and told them I never found the box in my

Time Machine. And I told the Doctor about this man named Aldon. Suddenly the Doctor and I got away from the robots, but they came to get us.

We got away from that dreadful place, and so the Doctor and I went back to the Time Machine. So Aldon told me and the Doctor about my people years ago, and how the robots did this to our people.

'So that was it,' said Aldon. I said 'We can help you and your people,' and Aldon said 'Can you?'

'Doctor,' I said, 'how are we going to help them?'

The Doctor said, 'We must.'

'Should I tell Aldon that you and me will help him to fight the robots?' And so Aldon had an idea for us all to fight the robots. Aldon told his people, and the Doctor and myself, to listen.

'I want two of my people to go with the Doctor and Vicky – and the rest of my people wlil come with me.' Suddenly the Doctor and I got away without saying goodbye and Aldon gave the Doctor and myself a cloak each.

So both the Doctor and I went back to our present year 1976.

They all lived happily ever after.

Rosa A
Great
Koen
Ros
Lo
M
Ro
Zé
Ros
R.Pro
Tour d
Ros
A
Jobling75

IN LOVE WITH CENTAUR AND ROSES

by PETER JOBLING

'BRING ME LARGE bunches of roses,' I said, and he brought them to me out of the dusk that hung under the rising moon. He covered his back with roses polythened and wired and basketed, bunches and posies of all the roses grown on earth: golden ones from China, palest pink gossamer-thin roses from the hedgerows of an older England, Bourbon roses like loganberry juice from consulate gardens in the Indian Ocean.

He piled them before me and I picked up a moss rose and scrubbed the resinous moss against my cold cheek. I plucked a damask and smelt the dangerous scent and smiled inwardly, comparing it with the brown shuddering odour of sun-toasted fly-buzzing seaweed.

'Centaur, I love you,' I whispered, stroking his mane and looking deep into his dark brown adoring eyes. He lifted me on his back and took me through forgotten gardens overgrown with briar and rugosa to a huge walled piazza set out before a great lake. Forests stretched away on either side, the dexter black and impenetrable, the sinister a great column of unwavering fire. Between them, on the far shore, ranged a garden planted only with roses.

Centaur swam with little skill, but I placed an arm around his neck and we travelled together over the deep water, and together came up into the rose garden.

He need not pick me roses now. I lay among the roses, I needed no roses in my hands, no roses tucked in my hair, nevertheless I breathed roses and tasted roses, there were roses in my nostrils and roses upon my tongue.

I clapped my hands, calling for sport, and two figures advanced from the forest and the fire, one with skin of silver, the other likely smoothly rusted iron. The moon illuminated one, the other glowed in the flame of the burning wood.

The silver figure reached out as he approached and plucked a pure white rose which dripped a dew that turned to diamond as it fell. The iron plucked a rose so red that all other colours receded from it, it leapt before my eyes, and from its petals spilled blood that glowed like the night eyes of cats.

The figures bowed with a courtly flourish. I flung between them a flawless pink rose and they began to kill each other with long flails of briar and rugosa. With great calligraphic strokes they stripped the silver and iron flesh from each other, until their ribs were hollow cages of ivory and carmine and their faces the blank helmets of forgotten armies.

'Stop them,' Centaur implored, but it was not in my nature to stop them.

'Love me, Centaur,' I said, garlanding his neck and his arms with the pale pink simple roses of June.

The silver warrior, reduced to fine wires and rods, crumpled at last into a heap of candid icicles that melted into the black loam. The red figure, scoured to a fishnet of veins, rippled in the hot wind of the fire and drained like dropped stitches to the same earth; which boiled and tore apart from within, and from it crawled an infant boy clutching a double rose, part red, part white, part golden stamen. 'I am the old king,' he piped, but the language was too new and I could not understand.

The infant, rising to its feet, danced without footfall over the black earth and presented the pied rose to me, slashing the palm of my hand with its comb of thorns.

I dripped cold blood upon the earth, which would not admit it; a ruby grail gathered of itself and became a brief river which bubbled down into the lake, darkening it under the milk light of the moon.

I picked up the child and suckled it and crushed the double rose in my teeth until the nectar spilled over my tongue.

'Carry me, Centaur,' I said softly, and Centaur bore me up and promenaded me under swags of rambling, golden, pink and purple roses. His hooves bruised the drift of petals from fallen blossoms and their deep perfume hung behind my eyes and filled my throat.

The gilded ivory of the moon's shield faded. 'Soon I must again leave you,' I warned, stroking the neck of

Centaur and giving again the cold milk of my breast to the staring child.

Centaur presented me with a black rose, saying: 'We should never part, you and I. Let us never part, ever, my lover of roses.'

The child bit and I tore its mouth from me. I stroked its face and the blood from my hand remodelled its features.

'It is nevertheless time to return,' I insisted, seizing a cloud of yellow roses like stars to wind about my waist and comb into my long trailing hair.

I dived again into the lake, towing Centaur my love and the earth-grown child, past the black trees, past the high pillar of fire. Centaur carried us back to the wind and the cold waves of the sea. On the high cliff strident with gulls he requested again that we never part. I held the child in my right arm and knotted Centaur's mane into my left and instead of kissing him, I dived. Roses scattered in the air like wings.

And so we fell through the dawn and clove the curve of a hollow wave and sank deep, where there are no roses. I descended, as I must descend, to where the light of the sun is a deep blue-black dimness and cold weeds without scent brush against the cold scales of my tail.

Centaur is with me now, time without end, his mane drifting carelessly now, he too drifting carelessly now, his white ribs crumped like the stamens of the oldest rose.

I can taste no roses now, I can breathe no roses now among the spars and anchors of dissolved men. I shall see no more roses, for the child has sucked too thoughtfully my cold milk and now devours me inch by inch, his teeth the blanched rose thorns in the mouths of sharks.

MIRROR MIRROR ON THE WALL

by NICHOLAS EMMETT

STORCHEFT LOOKED THROUGH the scanner, as the ship decelerated. This was a small star and he knew, without understanding why, that small stars usually had small planets in their solar systems. Little more than damn rocks sometimes. Ah well, he supposed it was one of the disadvantages of coming from Skogshorn, for Skogshorn was the biggest planet, circling the biggest star, in Shonnhet galaxy.

He knew he needed a change. He had been too long on microbe-collecting ships. What were they – he, Falk, and Orm, but three messenger boys? And when they brought something interesting back to Skogshorn, who got the praise but the scientist?

Still this rock they were in, nodfart above, was at least several times bigger than the ship. Some of the satellites were so blasted small that putting a little landing cart down on them was enough to put them out of orbit. And the amount of jaw you got for putting something out of orbit – they seemed to think in administration that every lump of dirt in every backward galaxy was important.

Lady Linda gave some last orders before leaving the stables. 'Michael,' she said to her manager. 'Don't give Jock too much feed for a while. He put on too much while on grass. And have you noticed Timothy is a little lame.'

'Yes miss, the ground is hard. Some rain we need. And was there any more word about Tina? The poor kid must have got an awful shock when the tank collapsed on her. It could mean trouble, miss.'

'Not for me. I paid the plane fare for her father and mother to come here, and I have paid the hotel bills, but I won't give a penny more. I hold the firm who inspected the tank last month responsible. She can take action against them.'

'I must go now. I am speaking to the Save the Georgian House Society. It is disgraceful, Michael, how they are spoiling Stephen's Green. Putting up monstrous office buildings. Dublin will become a second-class American desert.'

She jumped into her Jensen grand tourer, and let the automatic six litre take her out the gate of the estate, and into the Phoenix Park. The blue projectile passed the speed limit with a derisive cough from its motor. She liked this stretch, eighty an hour and not yet surrounded by all those idiots driving vans and such.

Suddenly her ears were hammered by a terrible noise, and a dark shadow fell over the city. In terror, young, good-looking Lady Linda, let her arms fall to the side, while her Jensen mounted the grass and jumped elegantly towards some trees.

Storcheft landed his cart, got out, and turned the microbe detector on. Yes there was life here. The metallic whine had begun, and the blue, small light jumped around looking for the heaviest concentration. It stopped a short distance away, and he thought; this place is packed with microbes. Still one sample was all he had room for. He was not going to do what young Kaltsne had done. Overloading his ship, trying to earn extra lyds, he had strained his raskdrive and had his ship sucked into a black space, sucked right out the universe.

Carrying his sample cutter he shook the morbid thoughts from his mind, and went to where the blue light shone. Then he pressed the button, and the sample cutter chopped a neat hole in the rock. In a bored fashion he put the sample into a box and wrote, *Sample third satellite/Svart system/Melkebann galaxy*, then trudged back to his landing cart.

Mr Burke closed the door of his flat carefully and turned the key in the double lock. The way things were these days in Dublin, he thought, even a pensioner's few things were not safe. Pity the owl knee was getting so stiff. What would he do if he could not get up to Harrington's for a drink? Sit in the cursed flat all the time? Still, as long as he could get up to Harrington's for a few pints, and a bit of a chat.

At the small shop just before the pub he bought his dinner, a package of soap, and some bread and butter. But before he could get in to the pub a dark shadow fell on the street and a brutal noise smote his ears. He stood there with the calmness of old age, wondering if a new world war had begun. Then he heard great thumping sounds, as though a giant walked the earth, and the houses began to fall. A pity I could not get some Guinness into me before I start on whatever strange thing this is, he thought, with amusement just before the building fell on him.

Storcheft got back, drove his landing cart into the ship and Falk set out a direction searcher, while Orm prepared to put the ship into raskfart drive.

They left the Melkebann galaxy and spent a boring month playing lexspil. Chinasjakk, and looking through the scanner, before they arrived at Skogshorn, and landed beside the analysis building. Then Falk and Orm wished him goodbye, and went to find a gatebil to take them to the brothels in Gamlebyem. Storcheft purposely headed towards the administration block to give in his notice. He was going to tell them to get another boy to go microbe hunting in the outback. He would study, get a planet job, find a steady mate –

Nobby Clark stood beside his taxi. Above his head a board proclaimed,

TAXIS FOR HIRE
TOURS OF DUBLIN
BY THE HOUR
OR HALF DAY

Across the street under Cleary's clock stood three men and a girl. They smelled of drink, and looked dirty.

'What didde say te ye? Tell us again,' asked the husband, shaking her by the shoulders. 'What didde say te ye, when he took ye home?'

'First he said Wall Street was a dump te live in,' she said. 'Then he tried te get the hand under me skirt.'

'And didde ye let him?' asked the bigger of the husband's brothers. 'We're not going te claim him if ye let him.'

'I swear te the mother of Jesus. I didn't let him touch me.'

'Come on, we'll get the bastard,' said the husband.

Purposefully they crossed the road, the younger brother

fingering the broken bottle in his pocket.

Nobby Clark saw them, and knew he could not get into the car and get away in time. Maybe if he ran –

The broken bottle was raised in the air when the shadow fell across Dublin. They stopped moving, all four, as a brainsmashing noise came, followed by an awful thumping, and the buildings began to fall.

Flink the scientist looked again through his microscope. This was going to cause a stir on Skogshorn. That is if he was right. But first he must get somebody with better eyesight to look into the microscope.

'Come here,' he shouted to his assistant, Ikkedumb. I think I have something odd here. These microbes seem to have an organised life, rough buildings, even if I am not mistaken, some form of writing. 'Can you make that out?'

Ikkedumb looked and wrote down what he saw,

TAXIS FOR HIRE
TOURS OF DUBLIN
BY THE HOUR
OR HALF DAY

MISSA PRIVATA

by KEITH ROBERTS

'The earthquake is not satisfied at once.'

– Wordsworth, arr. Britten

1

SHE WONDERED HOW the coffin would be made to move, on what rails or tracks, and likewise if that movement would be silent, as silent as the rest of this now-quiet building. Move it must, and the square plain doors behind it part, and surely there would be light. She fumbled with a memory from farthest childhood, of a neighbour standing nodding and smiling, dry-eyed and funeral-dressed, it was as if he was going into the sun.

She held her gloves crushed in her hand, she had no memory of taking them off, they were plain gloves, black and soft. She lowered her head, seeing with arbitrary clearness how the dark fabric reflected back a bluish sheen. The light from the tall windows, summer light, the trees outside were green, yet seemed diffused. It lay flat across the bare cream walls, a silent light she decided, silent as the building that took the priest's words, soaked them into its fabric so that though he stood scarce ten feet from her he was not audible. Her mind made for itself in contrast the light of a cathedral window, some great tall place of glass, rich, silent, Omega and Alpha he, let the organ thunder. She sat cross-legged then singing with the other children and the globes were alight in the big hall, old-fashioned globes that reminded her in forgotten summers of fossil moons. And we are quite sure, we are positive, she has a definite Talent.

Though silence itself could thunder, as this place of cream walls and blue drapes had roared at her with a deadly, caressing quiet, its voice a hidden gramophone. The mouse-like notes appalled though she had not broken her step, To a Wild Rose, Farnon, Robert J. her mind hazarded; and some joke momentarily obsessed her so that Jack had touched her arm, turned her into the pew where she must stand. She wondered if he might grasp now the other silence that had assaulted her, the enormity of the Tavener Whale, an old piece, outmoded, maybe disgraced, a battered record picked up on a Portobello stall. At first its banalities had failed to grip then the old dreams had come of crushing forces, rocks that moved with immeasurable stealth, and she understood how a storm might be so vast it could only be tinkled on sanctus bells, tapped out by a little drum. Sound, the sensation of sound, could be reversed, as now perhaps, a telly screen flicking to its own negative. Though Jack had remained unconvinced, he grinned at her and pushed back the little sweep of hair and said it's more like half a pilchard.

A shelf before her held slim booklets, cream-bound, bland as the place itself, to pick one up and open, part now merely of a group, seemed strange. And there again was the coffin, the casket she supposed it should be called, glimpsed briefly during the slow drive, reappeared like a bulky conjuring trick under the tall arch before the plain grey doors. She was startled by it, and startled too by her unpreparedness for what was after all a performance. She wondered for the first time, why had they not mentioned it, they seemed not wholly efficient, if it was fitting to cover the hair in a place such as this. She put a hand half up, there were women in the congregation, her mind had registered them but not retained, she wondered if they were bareheaded too and could not turn to see.

The priest, was he a priest, had all but finished now, we know the sacrifices he made, happy to have given to his daughter, and to us, so short when he had sat for an hour, she felt it must have been an hour, on the sofa in what had been her father's flat, the sofa with its floral grease-marked cover, behind it radio gear stacked and dusty, grey facias looped with frayed wire, two years now since licences had been withdrawn, she wondered why the transmitters had not been taken away. It had been the final blow of course, what had been the others, they had all known what had killed him, losing his last interest. The young man, the priest, seemed ill at ease; apologetic, nail-examining. Yes of course he knew of her career, he must have been very proud; though he himself had never in fact, there was so little time, so very little time, now if you could give me, a few details, the little things, it all helped. To, say something, make something up, just a few words, a very simple service. While she wondered, part-bemused, how he could be so fitted to his station, thin face and thinning sandy hair, old tweed jacket leather-bound, his cloth dusty and a little frayed. No music, the old man had ordered, no music, we will remove him now, Miss Welles, to a Chapel of Rest, sexton bettles in anxious scurrying black.

And there was to be no sunset glow, no movement, the curtains had closed, behind them Michael Douglas Welles, full of the stiff pomposity of death, was being bundled towards his last indignity. Obscurely she felt cheated; she had been taken by surprise, it was as if some final act – word, gesture, lingering glance – remained to be committed, would be for ever uncompleted now. She took a half step forward, irresolute, and once more felt Jack's hand on her arm. As always the Korean touched, when he must touch, delicately, nearly apologetically, like a flower she thought and surprised herself with the thought, a wiry brown flower.

The celebrant had passed her; must have passed, because he stood now at the door. He was waiting as the other folk were waiting, eyes averted, expressionless, uncomfortable in their little wooden stalls. She had fluffed her entrance now she was spoiling her exit, her mind laughed, inward, at how Paul would have raged then she wiped at her face, the streak of water that had made itself there. She thought how hard it would be to explain that the tear was not for *him*, for the tawdry box behind her, but for another; then that the tear was not a tear but water merely, a secretion of the body embarrassingly made public. Her mother's death so many years ago was a pain she had not retained so once more she was a tyro, a beginner. She thought how strange it was not to have understood before it was thrust on her the salient fact of death, its absurdity. Death was pinstripe trousers and green carbon forms, florid faces professionally composed, the pudgy white powerful hands; and next-door shufflings, hissed instructions, the stealthy thumps with which they bore the distorted departed away. Then the sun was hot on her face, trees like green shocks of light, tulips beside the porch growing from asphalt wounds; and a last thought came, disconnected, that if the place behind her was indeed a Whale, full of cavernous, consuming quiet, then it had cast her up, a woman Jonah, on to desert sand.

Paul was too much with her still, closer than she would

have desired. The last time she had ridden in a private car had been with him; his image still seemed strongly imprinted on her mind, silver waving hair, young-old face harsh-lit, the white silk scarf, *comme d'habitude*, impeccable overcoat. No engine sound from behind the glass then bushes slid past, they were circling a little roundabout, she hadn't understood that that would happen. Then she was passing the place again, the smokestained walls, Car Park for West Chapel, tower under the May-fresh trees. Absence and presence like death and life seemed invested with arbitrariness, a mere perversity of space and time; so that it seemed her father must step forward now and flag to be taken home. Jack smiled at her and she half-turned to squeeze his wrist. Her purse lay on the seat; she opened it, took out a two inch square of tissue. The car turned left, away from the trees; she wiped her eyes and the sides of her nose, feeling the lemony tang, flicked at her hair, nape length since the police had started carrying scissors again, makeup would have been a mercy and a blessing.

Jack said, 'I don't think I ever told you how I got to Britain first time.' She didn't answer and he carried on regardless. 'Dad was a tutor at Seoul University,' he said. 'We'd got a pretty good life. Then when the takeover came, my mother was half European. Dad got us on a banana boat. All the best people arrive by banana boat.'

The Finchley Road looked deserted, the shopping precint on the left with the big Abbey National sign, all yellow-stained by the vehicle's tinted glass. She thought, 'This is what Paul would have done.' She said, 'Your mother went back though, didn't she?'

He grinned and nodded. 'Yes,' he said, 'when I was sixteen. She couldn't stand my practising any more.'

It was a long-standing joke of course. He'd always promised one day he'd take up the birdcage and toasting fork. She said, 'What happened to her?'

He shook his head. 'Nothing much. Dad knew it was safe, things had quietened down a lot. It had been six years of course, most of the Embassies were open again.'

The windows of John Barnes were boarded over, and the paint can people had been active. 'PSYCHEDELIC WARLORDS' sprawled in yard-high letters; beyond, inscrutably, were the words 'ST MICHAEL' and a slender, well-drawn cross. She said, 'Do you ever hear from them?' and

Jack said, 'I got a card at Christmas. They don't write all that much.'

He'd said nothing really of course. Nothing of the napalm bombing, the maimed refugee ships, the corpse-choked sea. And there would have been screaming; she heard the screams, silent as the chapel. She said, 'Jack, what would you do? If . . . ' She let the question hang in air, unwilling to finish the thought.

He clouded momentarily, then he smiled again. Not a flower she thought a bird, a gentle, flashing bird. He said, 'Oh, you can't keep a good accompanist down. We always crop up somewhere.' But she had seen the worry at the back of the dark eyes. She thought as she had thought before, 'How can they be like this? They teach us to be human.'

Despite all, London was still a city of trees. They lined the great swoop into Maida Vale, hazy, vibrant-green against vistas of red brick, bright cream stone. Jack said, 'We had relations here of course. My granny married an Englishman. That was after the first war, the big one. He was in the Gloucesters. He kept me going till I got a start. He was pretty good to me.'

They had skirted Little Venice, passed beneath the gaunt sweep of the Westway. Towards Notting Hill the streets were busier, she saw folk turn and stare. As they had stared an hour ago, or was it two, at the little *cortège*; and an old man, white-haired, had doffed his cap at sight of the hearse, stood uncovered at the kerbside till a Militiaman jostled him, shoved him back with the butt of his automatic. She felt the tears sting again at that, tears for the stranger, and shook her head, half-angry. She said, 'What's your granny like?'

Jack considered. 'She makes saki,' he said. 'She's very ugly.' He grinned again. 'All Korean grannies are very ugly.'

She said, 'She sounds great.'

Jack said, 'When I first got here, my English was pretty ropey. The first time I met Tony I called him "honourable grandfather". He didn't get over it for months.'

Save the official Army and Government limousines there were few cars in London now; or anywhere else for that matter. There were of course buses in plenty, grey-painted; she mourned with others the passing of the old gay red. They rattled and shook, overloaded, wheezing clouds of diesel. The drabness was universal; she saw more shop windows boarded over, others half empty of goods. The commonest article of dress now was a boilersuit-like unisex garment of blue denim, even office workers had succumbed to it; while Mao sandals were the thing among the younger set. You cut them from car tyres, when they could be found, threaded them with cord to keep them on. She had been told they were very comfortable. She stared at the crowds jostling along the Bayswater Road, disinterested. A holdup at an unattended roadworks, streamers flapping forlornly from their ropes, a hand-scrawled message BEWARE DEFECTIVE LIGHTS; and the car began to wind through the wilderness that had been North Kensington.

Jack had fallen silent, frowning slightly, touching his lip, staring ahead at the driver; his stiff back and unresponsive neck. Despite herself her thoughts drifted to the morning a week ago, to the sudden pounding on the downstairs door; her alarmed descent, the pang as she saw through the spy-hole the grey of the People's Militia. The message had been curt, stilted; she found herself nodding, thanking the man even, wanting nothing but that he go away, leave her alone with the new thought. She closed the door of the flat, stood leaning on it, hands behind her on the knob. Her lips moved; but assimilation, it seemed, was not immediately possible. She became confused; so that plans for the clothes she must wear, the appointments she must cancel and the letters she must write ran together in a bright jumble from which she could make no sense. Then as now she had needed Paul, her thoughts had run to him, but Paul was . . . not available. Instead she put on a coat and took her purse and sat on a bus, noisy and stinking and as ever slow, and stared out at the bright, strange world, the world that for the first time didn't contain her father. Then there was the remembered street, children and a dog watching as she climbed the tenement steps, rapped the door. She was admitted; and there were the stairs, dark as ever and fusty-smelling, graffiti hacked and savage against brown paint, red aerosol smear on the landing wall; and policemen and a doctor and faces of neighbours, some prurient, some hostile, the tired, watchful beetles of the Burial Service. And it had all been arranged, the instructions had been clear, a model if we may say Miss Welles of prudence and foresight, the money had been paid, a simple service, no music, a cardio-vascular accident, we will be removing him now Miss Welles to a

Chapel of Rest. And if she would take the card, we have marked the viewing times, see, just here, we would ask you to observe them, a certain strictness, unfortunate but . . . a very crowded schedule, we were sure you would understand. Then she was left holding the card, wondering that they thought she might anger him by further visiting, the old grey man in his box, hearing the roars as Villa played at home, unable to understand, to make his clay feet move. A confusion between death and life while she opened cupboards, laid papers and bric-a-brac in stacks and moved the stacks, why had he stored so many bars of soap, wrapped between yellowed underclothes, where could they go now the Salvation Army was closed, found bread coupons and his ration book, his pension hadn't been drawn, an army passbook and out-of-date coins, there were tins with jagged edges in the kitchen alcove, she found a plastic bucket, its side had been burned, she took them to the dustbin in the area but it was overflowing and a woman was watching from a window with grubby muslin curtains so she brought the bucket back upstairs, no music, there was the *Requiem aeternam* and the *Kyrie*, *Dies Irae* and the *Domine Jesu Christe*, *Sanctus*, *Agnus Dei*, *Lux aeterna*, *Libera me*, then the door opened, she had left it on the latch, it seemed to open apologetically, Jack stood looking round saying Jesus what a dump. She started crying then, an Englishman would have looked alarmed or taken her in his arms maybe, the Korean did neither, stood, fingers touching her shoulder, bird-like, a shadow as the day began to fade. The sobs were hard and racking, bringing no relief, sobs not for death but for squalor and disorder and inadequacy, Pamina torn from her world of snakes and stars.

Jack said gently, 'There was nothing you could do, you know. It was the way he wanted. And he'd signed the forms.'

She looked up. They were passing the gigantic frontages of Queen's Gate Terrace; tenements now to their garrets, stucco peeling, dilapidated as the rest. She closed her eyes, felt the car swing, accelerate, swing again and stop.

The driver opened her door. She got out, stood feeling the pavement heave a little, like getting off a ship. The steps of the house were like those of the place she had quitted. She gripped the railing and the car moved away; she thought Jack tipped the driver, but didn't see. She found the downstairs key, turned to see the Korean standing worried on the cracked flags and nearly laughed at a wild thought that crossed her mind, that if she ordered him to take her to bed and love her he might obey from politeness. She said, 'It's all right, Jack. I'm all right now.'

The little flat seemed nearly unfamiliar. She carried jeans and a sweater to the loo to change. It seemed she might put away with her other clothes the cream walls, the whispering gramophone. Jack had put the kettle on; she got out a packet of Earl Grey tea, she had sealed it against a special occasion, she supposed this qualified. She watched as he drank, sipping the delicate, the Oriental flavour. He curved his hands round the cup, making the drinking a little ceremony of his own. Later, the china washed in the diminutive sink, he said, 'What are you going to do?'

She said, 'What about?'

He said, 'Tomorrow.'

She said, 'Go on with it, I suppose.' Her mind, dulled, shied away from the problems the question posed.

He looked away, ill at ease for the first time. He said, 'Under the circumstances . . . It wouldn't be expected, after all.'

She stared at him. She thought, 'Not you too' and of course he understood the thought. He said, 'I didn't mean . . .'

She said, 'It's all right. I know what you meant.' She rose to stand arms folded, staring out across rooftops. The sun was westering now; somewhere in the golden haze, closed away behind terraces and trees, the Royal Albert Hall was still the biggest jelly mould in Europe. It was due for renaming, or so the press had rumoured; the Tchaikovsky Hall seemed likely now Shostakovich was out of favour again, though Balakiref was a strong contender.

He still looked undecided; and she turned back to him. She said, 'After all, nothing's been banned. I couldn't sing if it was banned.'

He made a little gesture, of resignation. He said, 'That's true.' He half-glanced at her, and to the window; and she nearly smiled. There were such things as unofficial bans; equally, there were unofficial curfews. She said, 'You'd best get on, Jack. It's getting late.'

He rose; and there was the pain again. He said, 'Are you . . .'

'I'm fine. Honestly. I shall be all right.'

He said, 'I did think, maybe . . . what he did . . . ' He stopped; but she had already finished the thought. *To help me. One last thing. A Worker's funeral.*

He said unhappily, 'I'd best go anyway. I'm not being much use.'

She kissed him, lightly. It seemed to confuse him. She said, 'I couldn't have managed without you. You know that.'

He smiled, a little wanly. He said, 'I'll pick you up.'

She shook her head. She said, 'I'll be all right. *Go on*, Jack. I'll see you tomorrow.'

She watched him walk away, from the high window of the flat; a small figure, almost doll-like, shoulders hunched and hands in pockets. He looked back briefly, once; then he was gone, and the great white street was empty.

She lay on the bed, limply, hands at her sides. His absence filled the room already. She thought, 'I couldn't ask more. More than he could give.' She knew, and he had known, that she would be safer alone. This was a London where the common man walked free; as long as he was white, and a card-carrying Member.

She let her eyes move round the room. Elderly lino, a rug that had seen better days; big old wardrobe, dress on a hanger, kitchen alcove with its twin-ring burner, Ascot over the sink. The alcove was partly screened by a plastic curtain on a rail, patterns of weed and crudely-drawn fish. She loathed the material, but it was all she had been able to find. At least the flatlet had a private loo and shower; she'd done well for herself, really.

Paul's picture stood on the dressing table. It was a good one of him, her favourite, the face quirky, nearly grinning. She remembered how seeing it there had angered him; afterwards when he visited she had hidden it in a drawer. She tried to understand what she had felt for him. She thought, 'Other people can have a father in God.' The thought led on to the old man she had burned. Like refuse really. But the body was refuse, when the spirit had fled. So Church and State agreed.

By the dresser a polythene sack held all she had brought from her father's flat. Old photographs, herself as a child, her mother in a garden with roses and a pond; and records she had once owned, the first she had bought, unplayable now; some schoolbooks, the army things, an out of date diary with housekeeping details in her father's hand. Lastly a scrapbook she had been startled to find, cheap and brown-paged, the Tower scrapbook it called itself, a drawing on the cover of the Tower of London in black and red, dotted and splashed so it looked as if the building was sprinkled with blood. Inside, badly-gummed press clippings, some from years back; recitals she had forgotten, others that were still fresh in her mind. Made her public debut at, singing for the first time in, the up-and-coming Stella Welles, triumph for new young team. Confirmed her position as, vivacity with fullness of tone, Korean Young Soo Kim, will be remembered, will perform. Congratulations, Stella Welles. In Memoriam, Stella Welles.

She looked up with a start. She must have dozed; for it had seemed she was standing in the wings of an enormous stage. She heard the orchestra, rattle and rising whisper of the curtain, stepped forward smiling; then had come the shock, the terrible realisation that no bar of the music was familiar, that she had somehow omitted to learn or even read her part. Her heart had seemed to stop; and the lurch had woken her.

The room was shadowy now, the western sky darkening to dusk. She let her eyes drift half closed again. She was remembering her father's glee when the first massive aid had started to arrive; and Paul Eulenstein's rage, as he stamped white-faced from rehearsal. *'Now they will have their New Britain! Let them eat it! Let them sleep it! Let them breathe it!'* Then the slam of the dressing-room door, the sudden silence; and little sounds, tinkles and scrapes, as the orchestra began to pack itself away. She had quarrelled with old Michael that night and again the following week; perhaps it was from that the bitterness had flowed, how futile it all seemed now. She remembered scurrying home breathless, half across London, after that first interview with Paul, They're taking me she had said, *They're taking me*; and Michael had swung her round laughing, his noisy chit of a girl, and later marched her out to candlelight and good food and Beaujolais Nouveau, the old campaigner, twinkling at the waitresses, cheeky and suave. Yet so soon it seemed he was an old man in a tiny room, the room too cold, could it all have been her fault, could it have been anybody's, hunched over the radios, filling in his QSL cards, nodding surly at the cupboard for her to make him tea; and later when the hobby was denied him there was the tranny blaring its perpetual rock, not to be turned down. Though rock was silenced now, with many other things.

Her record player stood on a table beside the bed; she reached to it, clicked the main switch for the comfort of the little green and red beacons. They were like cue lights, illuminating a tiny stage. She wondered why she had not seen before that music itself could be a little death, a death repeated daily, the proud fierce masks of makeup washed down sinks, Queen of the Night banished with Tytania's train. It was a lesson clear enough to be learned, in a hundred hotel bedrooms with telly and pizza and *vin du pays.* From that she thought of the great stage a mile away behind its shuttered doors and wondered if Pamina still danced in blackness, if something of her could be said to remain; and Philodel the Airy Shape, and all the rest. It seemed strange now, ever to call a memory happy; for memories by definition were surely ghosts. What had Paul said? She remembered him at a Master Class, Paul at seventy, looking forty-five in high-necked white jumper, elegant slacks. *'The memory is like a room. The room has walls, and on them are many hooks. But there is no floor. So if we throw things inside they will fall through and be lost. We must place what we need, carefully; to be ready for us, when we shall want it again.'* She wished she could reach into herself, into the room, and detach memories; let them float away, one by one, into a peaceful void.

She had summoned, unwitting, a grimy tower set amongst brilliant trees; to drive it away she thought again of Jack, nonexistent because not here. Jack stamping out the Passacaglia and Fugue on a pedal Feldberg, Jack prodding at the manuals of a Neupert saying I think this one double declutches, Jack misreading a key signature in practice, starting her two tones too high; and when she stopped, aggrieved, grinning at her over the harpsichord and saying, 'You can never trust these bloody Orientals.' She was crying again, though it didn't matter with nobody there to see.

She had undressed; now she stood barefooted before a very tall music stool. The stool was tall, she realised, because she was a child. She opened the funny plush-topped lid, propped it with its thin brass stay. The music sheets were yellow and shiny and old-fashioned, the notes like mice and little scurrying birds, trapped behind the long bars of a zoo. She buried her nose in the sheets. Music to her already had a scent of its own, dusty and sharp together; like lavender, the polish her mother used in the chilly little room. The floorboards of the room shone, the piano that stood there loomed bear-brown and friendly. Its keys intrigued her with their alternations of white and black, even, odd, even; she would press the curved pedals down, legs at fullest stretch, listen to hear the struck notes die a thousand miles away. She played wild *études*, at the age of five; and Michael would come grumbling or her mother, she would be borne out struggling and the high door firmly closed.

The years seemed crowded in on her. She was nine, taking lessons from Miss Watson, waiting her turn in the front room of the big old house, the room that smelled of cooking and cream paint; fourteen, dreaming her days away in a hot, clattering school; seventeen and in love, Debussy the only Fact in the world. Then twenty, standing in the big grey room she knew so well, with the single upright piano and the bare board floor, the tall windows that looked out on to traffic. Paul was playing, Paul whom she had not seen for most of a season; frowning up at her, narrowing his eyes while she sang and let the pride come, conscious of new control, knowing she had worked and studied hard. Till finally he raised his hands for quiet. He waited, seeming lost in thought, before he spoke; then he said, 'What is the voice?' She began to speak, hesitantly, of larynx, pharynx and wind supply; and the hands fell with a crash, he raged at her, *'I teach singing, not surgery!'* Then as she recoiled, shocked, 'The voice is a flute. A lovely flute, here, in the throat. Power is nothing, nothing, nothing. And this tremolo, this sempiternal shake . . . *Gehen Sie, ver schwinden Sie! Raus . . . !'* So she ran from him, humiliated and furious, knowing as she had known before that the years were wasted, that the hoping and failing, hoping and failing would be endless because his demands were monstrous. She lay sleepless that night too, squeezing bitter tears; because the end of all struggle was death, the spirit failing and the voice. She was one, it seemed, with the lost and lonely of three hundred years; the crippled Delius, the blinded, patient Händel, Beethoven raging and suppurating, Mozart sketching his own dancing Requiem. She saw the face of Music clear at last; and Music watched back, with maggots for its eyes.

She was nearly laughing, because it was all so long ago.

And Paul's rages never lasted, least of all with her. She remembered a story once current, of him flinging down his baton and storming from rehearsal, but muttering 'Ten minutes' to the last desk of violins. She remembered too a little public concert, when would it have been, a fortnight later, three weeks of bitter application, of abasement; and Paul sitting with the audience, impassive, leaning back, his long legs neatly crossed. His voice was silent; but his eyes were on her face and his hands moved, making a gentle downward shape. *'You are young,'* they said, *'you are a flute. Gently, gently, the power will come. Remember, you are a flute.'*

So four years passed; and all he had said at the end of them was, 'Good. Now go and sing with the broadcasting people.' So she had applied, to the State Radio Chorus, and a place had been found, perhaps the way was smoothed; and she thought she was forgotten till he had sent for her. To walk into the remembered room was strange; but nothing was changed, the sunlight lay in patches on the floor, the traffic roared while he sat as ever, gravely, at the battered upright. He raised his hands, lowered them, opened his mouth as if to speak, changed his mind and for the first time she could remember, grinned at her. He said, 'You are looking well, Stella, give me the D above C,' and she stared back blankly, she knew his programme for the season, she understood what he proposed but could not believe. So she came to sit in a great Hall, orchestra and chorus ranged up in their tiers and the music falling like a wall of sound, *O Fortuna* and the *Ecce Gratum*, the Abbot and the Roasted Swan, nobody, he had said, writes tunes quite like a Municher. She remembered the curious detachment that had gripped her as she waited for her part, not apprehension but a strangeness of awareness, a part of her mind counting automatic and cool while with the rest she wondered that men should come together to put metal tubes to their mouths and saw at cords, beat on the skins of animals tightly stretched; while she and the others waited to vibrate membranes a half inch long, in turn and to command. All, she saw, had led to this, to her sitting in a bright red dress, Blanziflor and Helena; the songbooks and the music stool, the scurrying notes, records bought with shillings scraped and saved, the red glass lillies in Miss Watson's porch. Then she was caught away, locked within herself while the power flowed like the woman touching Jesus, through and beyond the tall man on the podium, *Dulcissime*, I give my all to you. And it was over, unbelievably, the thunder was applause, the lamps brightening like coloured eyes, Paul bringing the orchestra to its feet and the streamers falling in their drifts across the stage, bouquets crackling and huge. Then as now she seemed hypersensitised so that the tears stung as she bowed and laughed, so many flowers killed for her. And later, in wondering quiet, roses from Paul and the card she still kept tucked away, the *beau geste*, Porpora's words, every singer surely had them by heart, *Go, I can teach you nothing more.* While the lights cooled in their lines, almost she heard the wiry snaps as the banks of switches were thrown, in the hall where mysteriously shrubs and flowers bloomed, the Garden of Remembrance, a living, a growing Memorial, the plaque will be discreet; famous for our azaleas, I myself prefer the yellow azalea, the original wild azalea of Japan, the car too hot, Park for West Chapel, Miss Welles you would be well advised.

There were too many people in the room, she could no longer cope. Paul was talking to her certainly, his face intent and sad, but she couldn't hear the words. The Burials man was there, with his invisible soap; and Jack again, alarm on his face, shouting a warning. She tried to start up, to turn, but it was too late, no time even for the full sting of terror. Footsteps thundered on the landing, the door burst open and Michael ran at her, livid-faced. He would have reached her, but he was nine feet tall. His head struck the lintel with a ringing crash; he fell back raging, and she sat up. She was panting, she thought she had cried out, perhaps for Paul. But that was useless; for Paul was . . . ridden hence, her mind supplied, cloppingly. *Geritten Hinnen, hinnen,* shirted but with air.

It was enough. She pushed herself from the bed, leaned a hand to the wall, felt for the light switch, it was five to three. She walked to the loo, ran the tap in the hand basin, rinsed her face and wrists. Her hands were shaking a little; she opened the tin-fronted cabinet over the basin, uncapped the bottle, shook the little red, blue and brown torpedoes into her palm. Two only remaining, from years ago; a searing pain, a friendly doctor. She returned one to the bottle, filled a tumbler, drank and swallowed. She walked back to the bed, twitched the covers straight, remembered the light, the drugged can snore, the thought was abhorrent to her, she remembered to turn on her side. The red and green facia lamps glowed unheeded while the Tuinal, last resort of a decadent *bourgeoisie*, drew her swiftly into unconsciousness.

2

THE CAR HAD been the only moving object in the long, concrete-fronted street, warehouses to either side and empty office blocks; and garbage sacks piled head-high, nobody seemed to collect rubbish any more. The old man had appeared from nowhere, raging and purple-faced, to fling the empty dustbin with a clang. The Moskovitch screeched to a halt, wing-dented, she remembered the shouts, the uniformed figures stark against the light; the old drunk running and the rattle of shots, huge in the confining space. And the black sacks bursting as she cowered and a thin cat bolting, three-legged and squalling. She turned her face away as the bus approached the death spot but nothing stirred, the sun lay empty on the building fronts. The vehicle turned left with a grating of gears, headed down towards the river.

She had woken early, with the curious thought that for Michael this was D-day plus eight in Heaven. She showered, made herself coffee, listened to the radio news. She dressed, jeans and a jacket, tied a 'kerchief through her hair; she had not yet brought herself to accept the headscarf, badge of the new respectability. Then she took her voice down to the shops. It was a curious idea of Paul's, that she was not its owner but its guardian. Curious, but persuasive; the notion had grown till her voice had acquired all but a discrete existence. For its sake she eschewed late nights and over-tiredness; spirits were *verboten*, while Paul had even shown a tendency to supervise her wines. Though that of course had been in the days when wines were still readily purchasable.

She headed first for the local Commissariat. She ate little or no meat, and usually had a surplus of coupons. She traded half a month's supply for egg and cheese vouchers, and set out on the hunt. She enjoyed shopping, the anonymity it gave. She was a small girl, rounded and neat. No raving beauty, she had long ago decided; but there was a certain something, a *je ne sais crois*. Or perhaps she was merely a peg on which to hang personae; Pamina, Philodel, Vaughan Williams's wordless Siren. Her speaking voice was deeper, and she had allowed a certain huskiness to remain. By habit, she spoke softly; two tenths of power, Paul would have said. Five to six tenths for chorus work, no more than eight for solo; though for the D above C she had given him nine. Always the reserve, he had insisted, over and over; there must be a reserve, a pool of power from which to draw. Though in that as in all things he had taught by seeming contradictions; for every muscle, head to toes, must go to make the voice. The whole body in the voice, and the whole singer in the tone. She balanced irreconcilables, year by year; and her technique improved. *'Technique must be perfection; only then can it be forgotten, and we begin to learn . . .'* As with technique, so with herself; she had become more contained, assured. That too, she supposed, was a gift from him.

She kept an appointment at eleven with Madame Baudrier. The title was a hollow enough courtesy these days; but the old lady enjoyed it. She seemed surprised to see her. She sat stiff-backed at the piano, in the high gaunt room with its north-facing mansard lights, tomb-cold in winter and ruinously expensive to maintain. On the mantel over the blocked-in fireplace a wide-mouthed vase held a delicate arrangement of buttercups and a thin-stemmed, pinkish-white flower she didn't know. There had been a time when the shelf had trailed with roses; now the wild flowers sufficed, forget-me-nots and oxeye daisies, cerise spikes of the willow herb once more invading London. Madame Baudrier's elegance had a steely quality that largely defied poverty.

She worked through, swiftly, what she wished to revise; and the old tutor made no comment. She compressed her lips finally and closed the music, shook her head and laid it aside. She said dryly, '*Excellent.* Now we will think about the Verstovski songs again.' But she had shaken her head. She said, 'Not this morning, Madame, I am tired. I must go soon, and rest.'

The other glanced at her, bird-bright. She said, 'So, you

will not sing for me. Then, . . . sit, there, sit. And *I* will sing for *you.*'

Her voice, an old woman's voice, was clear still and precise. 'Here, you see, we have the difficulty of the broad *O*, we have spoken of it many times. And again, *Oooo.* Here, we must *place* to the head, we must be *sfogato*, high, light, unburdened. This the poet intends, do you not agree? And here, it is a lullaby, the children are asleep, they are in the next room, they must not wake . . . ' She played the last bars of accompaniment, the little postlude like a tinkling nursery clock; then suddenly, '*Why* will you do this thing, why? *Ma petite, tu es stupide* . . . Despite you, they will have their way. First it was the music of Germany; and you were his pupil, they will be watching. Now because some silly people make a trouble, and shoot with guns . . . Oh this country, this country, it is too much . . . '

She said slowly, 'I haven't been forbidden.'

Madame Baudrier made a gesture in which was all of France. She rose stiffly, crossed the room to rattle, back turned, with cups. She said, 'The churches remain. And their doors are open. But only the unwise enter. They close their grip, little by little. Can you not see? Can you not understand?'

She filled two cups, set the percolator back on the little stove. The cups were bone china; the coffee would be black and bitter. She walked back to the sofa. She said, 'This you have not realised. That they do what they must; and they are tired.' She sipped at the coffee, and sighed. 'They did not want your country,' she said. 'Not with their great Land. It was you who willed it, your own people. It was an *embarrassment.* But the fist must close. Like an old mechanical man.' She set the cup aside, laid a hand on her knee. 'It will change,' she said. 'In one week, or two, you will see. They are unsure, and so very silly. Have patience, just a little patience; and all will be as before.'

But the coffin was gliding again, on its silent tracks, while the trees stood round in living green. She stared, eyes moist, at nothing; and Madame Baudrier sighed once more. '*Ma pauvre,*' she said gently. 'Such a pretty head; and such a hard, hard wall . . . '

The bus grumbled to a halt; and she stepped down uncertainly. She had slept in the afternoon, a full three hours; but it seemed the floating sensation, nearly of lightheadedness, had not left her. She wondered if the drug she had taken had a long term after-effect. The vehicle moved away; and she began to walk, carrying her holdall, purse gripped from habit in her other hand. And there was the long bridge ahead, stretching empty to the Waterloo Road, the slow broad flowing of the Thames; across the water the stained complex of concrete she had come to know so well.

She leaned on the bridge parapet, stared up towards Westminster, half lost in hazy sunlight. She was trying to remember how to hate. She must hate them, surely, for what they had done. But there was nothing; just coldness, and the memory of Paul. She was like the woman in the play, was it by Shaw, who didn't know why she had chosen the arena. At the end, it was going to be the same. She thought, 'I have forgotten.'

The river was low, the bare black banks of mud sour-smelling. A tug moved upstream towards the rail bridge, drawing a string of empty barges; the rumble of its engines just reached her. She started to walk, across the bridge. She had never cared for politics; so now, as ever, she failed to understand. Music of the Left, music of the Right, fascist, reactionary, capitalist, bourgeois; how could such notions be contained within a stave? It seemed impossible; as it had seemed impossible, to the child's mind, that the sounds of an orchestra, the notes of a piano, could all be trapped within that narrow wire cage. She swung the grip, wondering with part of her mind if Jack would have arrived. She was conscious, it seemed for the first time, of the great breadth of the river, the massiveness of the buildings that clustered its banks, her own tiny insignificance in contrast. The whole thing, at the last, seemed absurd. She thought. 'They won't even notice.'

The big metal abstract that had dominated the terrace beside the QE Hall – the Scanlon Hall, she remembered she must call it now – had long since been removed, condemned as decadent. She remembered walking beside it once with Paul. He had christened it, in a rare moment of levity, the Colossophone; and she had wondered, giggling, at the effect could it be blown. But he had turned to her, once more with perfect gravity. 'The end would fall out of the Festival Hall, of course . . . ' She glanced across, swiftly, to where the sculpture had stood; but the terracing, like the bridge, was deserted.

Outside the place she hesitated again. It still seemed somehow faintly shocking to see her name in print; and these posters were big and bold. STELLA WELLES: AN ENGLISH SONG RECITAL. She pressed on by them, now with the drying of the throat, the little wave of tension that must always come, and pass. Too early as yet for an audience; and the stage door, mercifully, was unbolted. She stepped through, into comparative gloom; the gloom of a building that, like the rest of Britain, had dispensed with one third of its electric power.

Unisex she abhorred; but the puritanism of the new order must nonetheless be respected. She had chosen a high-necked dress, black-bodiced and with white satiny sleeves. It would look as if she was wearing a sweater. She unwrapped it quickly, shook it from its creases; then she paused. There had been another time, long ago now, when she had worn it; a time when the magic of *Die Zauberflöte* had seemed to permeate the night itself, so that a car ride back to London from a Hall best not remembered had seemed a fairy progress. She remembered the chirring of insects, blue rush of the night air, up and away over the long bonnet; and honeysuckle fragrance on the lawns where she had walked, the hands gripping the car's wheel, a face warm-lit by dash lights that had seemed wild and strong and keen. Champagne then and dancing and later, much, much later, the long, slow slide to sleep. She thought, 'Was *that* when it happened, when I fell away? When Michael began to hate?'

She covered her hair, sat at the mirror. She had understood, it seemed, a basic truth; that she had wept so bitterly because she could feel no grief.

Some makeup was permitted now, for stage performances; and she knew how to get the best from limited means. She worked swiftly, while the hall rustled and filled, became by degrees alive; a half hour later, when they tapped the door and she stooped a last time to the mirror, it was the delicious face of Pamina that watched back.

Round the hall the banks of lamps looked brownish. Always, now, they seemed somehow too dull. The boards of the rostrum gleamed, empty and broad, and the show pipes of the organ in their plain wood frame. Angled to one side, the big Neupert; and Jack dress-suited, impassive and neat. To stage left, beyond the lights, the motley of a modern audience, to her right the blocks of unisex blue; between them a straggling river, narrow but significant, of empty seats. From the blue, a silence; from the rest a scattering of applause, rising and richening as she walked to stage centre, bowed. She knew, or Paul had taught, the drama of simplicity; she stood still, head down and hands at her sides, and waited for quiet. The brown eyes dimmed; and she turned to Jack, and smiled.

Her palms were sweaty, where she gripped the briefcase; and she wished the journey, jerking and slow though it was, could be indefinitely prolonged. She knew now, why had she not realised before, that she could not go through with what had been proposed, that she would sit the bus all day, till it finished its grinding circle at the place from which she had come. This she knew with certainty; yet when her stop was called her feet found the steps, she dropped down, stood blinking in sunlight at the strange folk, the strange pavement, the strange buildings to either side. The bus moved off; and she walked again, mechanical, heart pounding, past the great cream frontages. She found the place she sought, impossible that it could stand here and be real, a weed growing from beside the step and paint peeling under the high stone porch. The hall beyond was cooler, institutional, brown linoleum darkly polished, grey-painted walls. Somewhere a piano playing and a voice chanting, irritable and loud, *one*-two-three-four, *one*-two-three-four; and a bust in an alcove, like a joke.

The staircase was broad and uncarpeted, wrought iron banisters topped by rails of shiny wood; and a tall window at the landing, like the dentists she had used while at school, and nearly with the same faint smell; tingling, antiseptic. She heard, not one instrument now, but many; a jangling confusion, all round about. On the landing a girl scurried past, hornrimmed glasses and flying hair, arms loaded with books; so busy, so self-assured, she all but shrank away. She turned right, walking in a dream, dry-throated; tapped the big door, received no answer, tapped again and opened. The room beyond, the tall, bare room, was empty; grey-painted again, an old piano, varnish chipped, standing in one corner, windows letting in a dusty flood of light, traffic hum from the road below. She crossed to stand staring down, not seeing. A clock ticked, steady; she hugged the briefcase, and the door behind her closed.

He was tall, taller than she had realised, and older too perhaps; the blue eyes faded a little, mouth tortoise-wrinkled at the corners. But there was no mistaking. She caught her breath, trapped; and he smiled. He said, 'Miss Welles, good afternoon. I am Paul Eulenstein.'

He crossed to the piano, laid the notes he carried on its top, sat hands on knees and raised his brows. He said, 'Come closer, please. I do not eat young ladies.'

She did as she was told.

Her raised his hands, dropped them again. He said, 'I am twenty minutes late. I apologise. I have been talking, on the telephone. Always, when I am on the telephone, people make me talk and talk, and will not let me go. Do you know why?'

She shook her head. She feared she couldn't speak.

He said, 'It is because I am old. And they are patient. They think, if they wait, that perhaps I will die. Then they will say, 'I, and I only, was the last! The last to speak to Paul Eulenstein!' Do you see? But I am stubborn! I do not die!'

She smiled; and he rose, began to pace the floor. He said, 'Now I will tell you a secret. To conduct music, for me, is like telling a joke. You do not understand? Then I will explain.'

He tapped his pocket. He said, 'I have many friends. Very many friends. But I do not know many jokes. So I keep a little book. In it I write what jokes I have told to whom. Do you see? In this way, when I tell a story, I know it is never to the same person twice. If the story is new to everyone, then it is new to me. Over and over. And all my friends think, "What a clever man he is!" '

He sat back at the piano, spread his hands as if to encompass the keys. 'Also with music,' he said. 'When I am touring, I will not conduct the same piece twice in any town. They come to me and say, "The subscribers will be different tomorrow, everyone in the hall. Everyone!" But I am cunning, I do not believe. I think, "Perhaps one, just one, has come again! He has slipped in past the door!" He will hear me again, and the music will not be new. And he will think, "He is not a clever man at all but rather a silly one, who wears too-bright bow ties." '

He smiled again. He said, 'That is why the music is always new. One hundred times, two hundred, five hundred times and it is still new, every night. Because the people who listen are new. Do you see now? Good! Then already we have made great progress!'

He took a pair of glasses from his pocket, opened them with a little flourish, consulted for the first time the sheaf of notes. He said, 'You have studied the piano. That is excellent. For the young singer, this is most important. You have chosen your voice for an instrument, this is purely melodic, the piano not so. You will learn another literature, other than your own. And you will not become over-tired. Also there is a book I shall want you to read, by Ffrangcon-Davies, I will give you its title in a moment and you can find it in a library. The way is hard, all ways are hard, but faith can move the largest mountains. There will be much to do . . . ' And on and on, while she wondered at his energy. She thought, 'But to talk like this, to tell me all these things, he hasn't heard me yet. I might not be any good!' But by the time he finally held out his hand and said, 'Now, what have you brought for me?' the fear had gone, she could smile at him in return. Later, when she at last realised the point of the performance, she thought, 'That is why he is great. Because he understands what is happening inside other people.'

The corridors, the maze of passages beyond the great stage, seemed full and buzzing. She pushed and jostled, desperate, seeing the Militia uniforms, hearing the scurrying footsteps, shouted commands; and the way was barred. She drew herself up, knowing her eyes were blazing. She said, 'Where is he, what is happening? *Let me pass* . . . '

He was sitting in his dressing-room, the dark coat round his shoulders and the scarf. For the first time, he looked old; old and incredibly tired. She ran to him; she would have spoken, but he took her hands. 'No, my dear,' he said, 'no words. For you, I no longer exist. I can bring you no more luck.'

He shook his head. 'It is not the music,' he said. 'They hate me two times over. First, because I am a German; then, because my name is Owlcup. Mr Owlcup. Some others of us they called Wood Devils. Perhaps it was just . . . ' He rose, supporting himself momentarily by the arms of the chair; and she was thrust aside. He said to the grey uniforms that flanked him, 'Gentlemen, if you are ready . . . '

The death took place last night in a London nursing home of the pianist and conductor Paul Eulenstein. Charged six weeks ago with doctrinal non-alignment, Eulenstein was awaiting trial by a People's Tribunal for crimes against the British state.

The lamps were brightening in their lines. She dropped her head and waited; and the applause was starting, first here and there, deepening into a footstamp from the students bulked round the stage and spreading still, to the blocks of blue, they were on their feet, she saw hands raised clapping above heads, heard the calls. She ran off and back, hearing the volume rise again and steady; then the third time, bowing low, taking Jack's hand, pulling him forward. Her hair had tousled; she flung it back laughing, flushed a little, turned to peck his cheek; and they wouldn't let her go, she took a fourth call on her own, a fifth. And it was over at last, tension draining, rattle of the handclaps dying back, turning to the buzz of talk, shuffle and scrape of feet as the hall began to empty. She ran for her dressing-room, full of the hollowness she had felt before, sat face in hands, she was shaking, she made herself be calm, it was over now, please God don't let the memories come back, not any more. She brushed at her hair, mechanically, began to dab her face. The knock came then, muffled, almost hesitant; she sat a moment quite still, Paul she thought, what should I have done. She said, 'Come in.'

He was a biggish man, running to stoutness. He seemed uncomfortable in the coarse grey uniform, fingers easing at the collar, eyes shifting. He hemmed and coughed, a most unfortunate demonstration, as Sector Commissar it was of course his duty to report, representative of the People, she must surely have been aware. Yes yes she knew and did not blame, but he was not yet done. The need for vigilance, the endless need, doctrinal solidarity, a clear enough direction though of course not *stated*; while for his own part . . .

She stopped what she was doing. She said, 'What? What did you say?'

The collar again, fumbling; and moistening his lips. A pity really, he quite liked her stuff himself.

And she was white flame, trembling head to foot. She screamed at him, *'Get out! You fucking traffic warden, GET OUT . . . !'* And he was backing for the door, alarmed, hand behind him rattling at the latch. He said, 'You'll never sing in public again.' The door slammed shut; she heard the flustered footsteps hurry away.

She looked down. She was holding a solvent bottle gripped in her fist, she had no memory of snatching it up. She supposed there had been a moment when she could have smashed it into his face.

She put it down, sat back at the mirror and began, slowly, to peel Pamina's great lashes. It was after all of little significance. Soon, her husband would return; and she would bear him other, fleshly children.

THE ETERNAL INVALID:

A Celebration of Life with the Author of RASH

by THOMAS M. DISCH

WHEN I CALLED on G. G. Allbard at his flat in Ealing on the afternoon of March 13, 1975, the celebrated author of THE WOUNDED WORLD and DAY OF THE DIABETIC greeted me warmly from his sickbed, offered me an aromatic cup of motherwort tea, and at once began, with that anguished enthusiasm for which he is so well-known, to discuss the present state of his health:

Allbard: No, I really can't say I've been feeling quite tip-top lately. Been laid out since last Friday with the flu. Terrible flu. But I've only got myself to blame. Should have been vaccinated. Strange, I wouldn't have thought that I'd have gone from herpes to a simple case of influenza, but that's life, isn't it? Always imitating art. Seriously though: what else is RASH about? This tea by the by, is *very* good for renal disorders, I understand.

Interviewer: About RASH, Mr Allbard, I wonder if it wouldn't be fair to say –

Allbard: As to that, I think the clearest way for you to begin to see what RASH is about is to look at the photographs I used as the basis for the plot. Rather in the way a pathologist would use x-rays, I suppose. They're right here, as chance would have it, under the sheets. This one – never mind the Vaseline – Is this her armpit? Yes, her left armpit, and these three boils: look, it's quite incredible, but if you superimpose them over a map of London, this one – let's call it A – corresponds to my flat here in Ealing, and then this one, B, goes over the nursing agency where Edna was working at the time I met her, and C is smack on top of Paddington General Hospital. Where I had those polyps taken out! Incredible, isn't it? Almost as if some lingering viruses were guiding my hand as I wrote. I can't account for it. I've tried with the map of Weymouth too, where we went to recover after I'd finished the cholera stories, but so far I can't get a fit. Though possibly, if I had the picture blown up . . . ?'

Interviewer: Mr Allbard, you wrote in RASH that –

Allbard: Oh, here's another! My, I don't know if I should be showing you this, but after all we're grown men and we've all had it at some time or other, haven't we? Edna took this with my Instamatic, while she was changing the dressing on it. That green, here along the vein, puts me in mind of the most beautiful Soutine that I saw once at the Tate. I *think* it was the Tate: I never get round to the galleries any more, though as you know I've had some extraordinary insights into Expressionist art. And I know many famous artists personally. And in a manner of speaking I could be said to be an artist myself. Did you see my show at the Boorman Gallery?

Interviewer: Oh yes, and I thought it was a –

Allbard: Smashing, wasn't it? I don't think anyone till now has ever appreciated the sympathy card for *what it is.* Or you Americans call them Get Well cards, don't you?

Interviewer: Actually, Mr Allbard, I'm not an Am –

Allbard: (Reading from sympathy card)

> Here's hoping that a Special Guy
> Will be up and swinging by and by.

That's rather arousing, I should say. 'Up and swinging' can be taken in so many other ways, though, that the mind gets quite lost. It's like one of those Tibetan mandalas .Or what about this one? Edna's mother sent it to me, would you believe, but too late, unfortunately, for the exhibition.

> There are days when dark clouds gather
> And times when Life gets tough.
> If you're brave, it doesn't matter –
> Just smile and show your stuff!

Do you know what I did when I got that? Within five minutes I was having a bowel movement in rhymed couplets! An endless procession of hard small greyish marbles, one pair after another. As if my body were answering Mrs Davison's message at the most primordial level of response.

It's all part of the big picture. Think of how Ossian appeared right at the end of the so-called Enlightenment. Think of Virchow's work in histology. I haven't done anything but draw the line between the numbered dots, so to speak. In any case, there I was on the toilet for quite two hours and thirty-one minutes, writing at white heat the whole while.

Interviewer: What –

Allbard: – story would that have been, you ask? In fact, it was the chapter in RASH in which Dr Porteus assists at the false mastectomy of Happy Rockefeller. That passage, which surely is one of the brilliant in the book, so offended poor old Bludgeon in *The Times* that he very nearly gave me grounds for libel, bless his murmurous heart. He practically accused me of being responsible for Edna's present condition, as though the character who goes by my name in the book were *me* and 'Edna' were Edna! Of course, I can't deny that I'm *interested* in radical mastectomy, but so are millions of newspaper readers. I'm equally interested in cancer, in emphysema, in hypnotherapy, in Victorian surgical instruments, and in the experiments performed at Ravensbruck, but I daresay that doesn't make me *responsible* for such things. As a writer I simply state what I see. Naturally, I *am* sorry for what happened to Edna – who more so than I? – but all of us who go into surgery know that we're taking a calculated risk. It's true, as Bludgeon says, that I was allowed to be present at the operation, like the 'Allbard' in the novel, but as to actually taking a hand in it, as 'Allbard' does – it's a preposterous and indecent suggestion.

Interviewer: I would never have supposed that –

Allbard: What they refuse to understand, you see, is that a literature of extremity, like mine, is therapeutic. By revealing the hidden significance of our ailments it allows us to live in harmony with them. Illness opens up *larger* realms of being. It is the quintessentially modern experience. Hospitals are the cathedrals of the twentieth century. Take a simple thing like vaccination. Only a culture that could produce Strauss's SALOME could conceive of *resisting* the lure of disease by yielding to it. That yielding must be held within limits, needless to say. It won't do to go out and be vaccinated for typhoid six times in an afternoon, as 'Allbard' does at the end of RASH. But you can't deny that that represents the secret longing of the vaccinee. Would you mind:

that box of Kleenex there on the paperback of Gray's *Anatomy*? And if you could readjust the blinds. And then if you would take the rubber bottle on the mantelpiece and fill it with warm soapy water, I'd be much obliged.

A DATE WITH THE HYDRA

by ROBERT MEADLEY

FOR SOME OF us who tread loudly on the cosmic stairs, striking at shadows to discourage the dragon-hordes of Time, there is danger afoot – a mouse is trying to stab us in the ankle. A well-meaning mouse, desirous only of a little attention, a saucer of bread and milk and perhaps to soothe his toothless age; even a kick in the gums would be better than nothing. His name is Clarke Kent, the ancient space-mariner. If you let him he'll turn from one to three or six or any number of avatars, all dismally similar, but it isn't your pennies he's busking for, the old bugger has a warehouse full of loot-stuffed mattresses; what he wants is to feel your strong young arm under his bony claw and to re-embody his dreams with the boldness in your blue eyes.

'I was a single child, always solitary and bookish, reading constantly from some tender age. *Loneliness* is a word that has deepfelt meaning to me. Until the age of twelve I did not have a single friend among my classmates, nor did I belong to any gang or pack. Totally without companions I was absorbed in reading.'

That's Harry Harrison, one of the more robust contributors to *Hell's Cartographers* (Weidenfeld & Nicolson, £3.50). Some Personal Histories of Science Fiction Writers, ed. Brian W. Aldiss and Harry Harrison. There are six histories in this book, but the plots, as if dictated by the gods of Genre, are horribly alike. The solitary child escapes through science fiction to the derelict toytown of Fandom, learns guile and swordplay at the court of John W. Campbell, defeats and enfriends the tentacular but genial monster Jamesjoyce, and ascends to heaven in a chariot of papier-mache. Brian Aldiss almost disgraced himself with a happy childhood, but at the age of eight was entombed in that castle of horrors, the English Public School, so all turned out for the best.

'My parents were remote figures . . . so that I was raised mainly by Lottie, our mulatto housekeeper, and by my loving and amiable maternal grandmother. It was a painful time, lonely and embittering; I did make friends but, growing up in isolation and learning none of the social graces, I usually managed to alienate them quickly, striking at them with my sharp tongue if not my feeble fists.'

That's Robert Silverberg inviting seven stone weaklings to kick sand in his face, but it could have been almost any of them. Devouring whole libraries – Proust while being weaned, Tolstoy during a skipped football match – they stumble, or are tripped into the world of Pulps, and then . . .

'I discovered I was not alone in the world, when I joined a magazine's circulation-promotion scheme called The Science Fiction League, attended meetings of its Brooklyn chapter and met people like Donald Wollheim, John Michel and others. Fandom was born.'

That's Frederick Pohl emptying the strangled cat out of the bag. If there is any interest in this book besides its trivial moral (I was small and puny but *now* I'm small and FAT), it lies in the portraits of this strange world of Fandom, a tiny alternate universe where the maimed and hysterical are transformed into galactic bullies, defending the true faith at sword point against elusive infidels. Human beings are contemptible, but Science Fiction will zap them into shape soon enough. There is a reason why much science fiction is so restricted, it's strapped together in surgical hardware. And if you think I'm exaggerating, look into this gallery of fright:

'The Futurians, when I met them later, were an odd-looking group. Wollheim was the oldest and least beautiful (Kornbluth once introduced him as "this gargoyle on my right"). He was, I learned later, almost pathologically shy, but he was the unquestioned leader of the group, and John Michel, who worshipped him, later informed me that Donald's personality was such that he could have any woman he wanted. Lowndes was ungainly and flat-footed; he had buck teeth which made him lisp and splutter, and a hectice glare like a cockatoo's. Michel was slender and looked so much more normal than the rest that he seemed handsome by contrast, although he was pockmarked and balding...'

That's Damon Knight, himself a major contender in the hospitalisation stakes, willing the world into a deformity from which sf can rescue it. No wonder science fiction needed the props of microcosmic fandom to keep it going. It's a miracle that any of them found sufficient co-ordination to move a pen.

Other genres have produced good writers (Raymond Chandler, Will Henry, Iris Murdoch) but we don't take any notice of *them*. Science fiction is more than a genre, more than a publishers' category or a vehicle for literature, it's an act of faith, a Mystery. And in case the authors meant to be present can't persuade us of this, others are dragged in. Science fiction is 'the most significant literature one can write' (Isaac Asimov); 'most other literature isn't concerned with reality' (Arthur C. Clarke). Amazing stuff. We aren't told which has the wooden leg and which the sadistic aunty, but guesses are encouraged. Any trick is fair in the great crusade. If they can't convert us with a smile or a hatchet, they'll try it with a sob:

'I discovered that much of what I was writing in 1971 was barely sf at all or was a kind of parody of science fiction or borrowed a genuine science fiction theme for use in an otherwise 'straight' mainstream novel. This realisation inspired flickers of guilt in me. I no longer had to apologise, certainly not, for shortcomings of literary quality; but was this new Silverberg really serving the needs of the hard-core science fiction audience? Was he providing the kind of sincerely felt fiction about the future that readers still seemed to prefer, or was he doing fancy dancing for his own amusement and that of a jaded elite?'

This man isn't worried about his grocery bills, he thinks he's got a serious moral problem. But what is his problem? Where, apart from theme, is the difference between science fiction and the 'straight' novel? Does he mean he's letting 'life' into Arthur C. Clarke's 'reality'? There are lots of cues – 'guilt', 'sincerely felt', 'jaded elite' – and we're all ready for the lynching party, but who are we hanging and why? It's the Mystery again. In his vatic trance the priest doesn't feel impelled to explain himself, the mob only needs to know he's said something that sounds right.

Still, I'm glad he doesn't have to apologise for shortcomings of literary quality. He might if he left the closed ranks of Fandom, but there's no need for that. Fandom has limped into the twentieth century and gone international.

'How we meet! In Tokyo and Trieste, Montreal and Moscow, London and LA. The streets outside the hotel windows look different, but inside there are the same familiar faces. If I ever find myself marooned on an Alp or lost in the Sahara I have an infallible system of getting help. I will simply announce the existence of a science fiction symposium, and in half an hour Brian Aldiss and Arthur Clarke will be there.'

How's that for a Sartrean map of Hell?

Of course there is a world outside Fandom. Alfred Bester and the majority of sf readers live there. But is isn't a real world. The Alfred Bester in this book seems to have been normal as child, naturally gregarious, oblivious of Fandom – obviously Brian Aldiss made him up as a foil for the others.

Stop! While I wade on with my failing power-axe, someone has sneaked in and nailed up a happy ending. Everyone is golden now, looking at the world from four-roomed writing suites and all married to the world's most wonderful woman. They weren't really a phalanx of cripples, they were raunchy individualists who just happened to have their hands up the skirts of the same muse and been smacked for it. The ugly duckling pose was just a plot device assumed by these masters of disguise (how many have been present is no longer certain), the truckling to editors and fans just part of sf's master plan.

In a million-roomed writing suite overlooking the Vatican the sf orgy is under way. Caricatures move in pairs. Self-deprecation couples with conceit while sympathy aborts applause. Nemesis and hubris simper together under a Venusian palm. God and Mammon are the masks of Janus. All is forgiven. Pats on the head beat the reader down until the midget dervishes of Fandom loom like giant moths, desperate for warmth.

Well, since they're impregnable now behind their barriers of riches, let's take a last look at the dirty boarding house they came from. Fandom in Pulp Street, a cosy place with grubby chintz mantraps and fringed oubliettes, a tomb from tomb where you could rise to minor fame over the votive corpses of idiot admirers.

'It was rather easy for an amateur to get published and

thus become an instant professional in the thirties. Especially in the latter part of that time, just before World War II, there were dozens of magazines hungry for material, and only a handful of editors had enough taste and wisdom to distinguish good from bad. Some of us – I was one – found an end-run around even that obstacle by becoming editors ourselves.'

Discounting the smirk of modesty (and it's easy after the first few, there are ten on every page), it's evident that you didn't have to be much of a writer to get on in the pulps, perhaps even the less of a writer you were the better. Formula and speed were the slave-drivers. But these writers have come a long way since then.

Brian Aldiss contributes the final, romantic death-rattle:

'What we see today is the too easy acceptance of sf. The sharp idiom we created has blurred to become one of the bland flavourings of mass media; the unembarrassed muse we espoused is one of the jades of television.'

Who cares about meaning so long as you hit the right cues? The road signed 'Inferno' ends with the literature of porridge, blopping over a little stove.

ARTHUR C. CLARKE'S CLONE

by JOHN CLUTE

ONCE UPON A time, long ago in the exciting 60s, darkbearded saturnine fatfaced Stanley Kubrick happened to read a story by the engaging bespectacled Arthur C. Clarke. This story, which was called 'The Sentinel', caused Stanley Kubrick to think many ambitious, worldly thoughts. If only I could get Arthur's monicker on the dotted line, I could very nearly laugh (thought Stanley Kubrick) Western civilisation to death. Later that night in Ceylon Mr Clarke, often referred to as the colossus of sf, awoke from fretful slumber to find standing over his bed a darkbearded saturnine fatfaced Mephistophelean figure clutching a copy of 'The Sentinel' in pallid early-Yeatsian hands.

– Good evening, Arthur, said Stanley, for it was he; I want to offer you the world. Sign here.

He thrust the contract forward, and the knife.

– Offer me the world? said Arthur, obscurely attracted to the plump charismatic leprechaun-like figure by his bed. But I already love the world and all its intricate doings, and I am happy explaining it to my friends all over. Here, look at this transparent plastic man with all his nerves and organs showing which I keep by my writing desk for easy reference. He's my friend, Stanley! You can see that in his hand he holds a copy of *Men Like Gods* by H. G. Wells. 'The jewel on the reptile's head that had brought Utopia out of the confusions of human life,' says H. G. Wells in that very same book, Stanley, 'was curiosity, the play impulse, prolonged and expanded in adult life into an insatiable appetite for knowledge and an habitual creative agency. All Utopians had become as little children, learners and makers.' So let that be my answer, Stanley, H.G.'s and mine. I am as a child, and play with my transparent man. What need have I for riches?

– Christ, Arthur, that was moving, expostulated the insistent, mesmeric Stanley. But please lend me an ear for just a moment, will you? Friend? Teacher? Did you know you're a kind of guru to me, Arthur? No kidding. But I've got something to tell you. Listen. Last week I was chewing the fat with one of the Washington consiglieri, and as he was showing some signs of fatigue, rational-hope-for-the-future-wise, I mentioned your name, and he said: Stanley my boy, would that Arthur C. Clarke were with me at this very moment as I face the problems of our burgeoning technology, not to speak of the death of Lake Erie, nor of the return-of-soured-vets-from-Nam-perplex, and so forth. Shit, Arthur, don't it start to penetrate, baby? I mean you've gotta help us get on with the job, guide us in the direction of tomorrow. You've gotta point the way. We're all stuck down here in the cesspool without ya.

– Cesspool, Stanley? chided the redoubtable sf writer.

– Just a figure of speech, smiled the sinister *auteur terrible*, crossing his fingers. But don't it kinda show what a lousy mess we're in, when words like Shitsville and cesspool and abattoir and nada nada come so easy to the lips of cultural apex folk like myself? You gotta help us, Arthur. You gotta show us the high-road outa Shitsville where it sometimes looks like we're for the dark like, you know, like maybe we shoulda deepsixed Newton and all those other sleepwalker fruitcakes back when before they had a chance to dump us here in Shitsville, Arthur, where the centre don't hold, and you sleep rough and your lungs rot and you get warts off the kindly zephyr from the chemical plant here in Shitsville, baby. O my God the strain, the anguish. It's like Rectumsville, Arthur baby. It's the hole in the bottom of the sink.

– Hush, soothed the sf colossus, hush now. Don't worry about a thing. I'll write you a nice script. It may just help to save this dear world of ours. And Arthur C. Clarke took the triplicate form, and signed it in his own pleasant blood, and dropped back to sleep thinking, What a good boy am I, to merit such a treat.

But Stanley had other thoughts as he buzzed back into the dark industrial West. So it's a dear world, Arthur, is it (he thought), and it's peopled with nice transparent plastic men, is it? Do you know what I'm going to do, Arthur? I'm going to take the script you give me, full of expansive bland technological and humanist optimism as I'm sure it will be, and out of your dreams for the future I'm going to make *2001, A Space Odyssey.* Ha ha ha. Where your heroes are makers and doers transparent to the light of reason within them defining their natures, mine will be stale hollow puppets, victims of the technology or special effects *your* heroes integrate with smiling. Where your story models the *connectedness* of things and the clear entailments of reason calling the tune of the deep-structure of the world, my story will plummet sickeningly into a caesura between the discovery of the fathomless rectangle on the Moon and the Jupiter mission that inexplicably follows. Where your superman will 'think' of something to do with himself, mine will stare through us, chillingly, as I try to in my art. I'll take your script, Arthur, and will hardly change a word. I won't have to. I'll just work a sign-change, a semiotic nudge, Arthur, and everyone will be able to see that beneath your dreams of immanent reason squats Shitsville, where we live.

And he did.

And Arthur gazed – possibly in bewilderment – at what Stanley had done to his daydreams of enhancement, and wrote a novelisation of *2001* full of connectedness and transparency and goodwill, though no one seemed to listen, so then he wrote RENDEZVOUS AT RAMA (1973) chockfull of c and t and gw, and won awards and kudos, and now he's done it again, published another novel, IMPERIAL EARTH (Gollancz: £3.5), but redolent of the same sustaining value-system, so that the moral of the fable of the midnight gabfest of Stanley and Arthur still holds true: Do not sell your dreams of c and t and gw to the movies, for they will signchange those dreams into nightmares,

IMPERIAL EARTH could not be called a good novel, but to dismiss it as a failed fiction – because its characters are cardboard, its storyline exiguous, and so forth – would be to deny by omission the translucent, effortless epiphanousness of the book, which resides less in its nature as a novel than in the fact that it reads as a kind of elated *prophecy* of a time to come beyond our time of troubles when population will be controlled, conflicts among nations stilled, sexual dimorphism soothed of those rough edges and coulisses we all skirt these days, and the world itself – the green Earth – returned to its natural state. Men Like Gods Ville.

Duncan Makenzie is a third generation clone, grandson and son of the Chief Executives of Titan, Saturn's vast moon. He experiences no traumas at being identikit; his relations with Pop and Grandpop Clone benignly reverse the scarifying descent into age of the protagonist at the end of *2001*. Duncan knows where his next meal is coming from, as Titan supplies the inner planets with hydrogen to fuel commerce. Invited to visit Earth to help celebrate the 500th anniversary of the American Revolution, Duncan accepts with clear-skinned boyish enthusiasm; in any case, it's time for him to go to Earth to clone off a fourth Makenzie. Only fly in the ointment is Duncan's childhood pal, the brilliant, unbalanced Karl, a blond Adonis and creative research scientist who envies Duncan because he's a Makenzie.

Duncan flies to Earth; Duncan sees what Earth is like in 2276: like any protagonist in a juvenile (though he's over 30), he is sort of surprised by the joy of things. Later Karl dies pathetically, and Duncan clones the corpse and returns with a blond baby to Titan, to upset the apple cart *just a little*. So not very much happens: the book's heart lies in the lengthy, exhilarated description of the flight to Earth and of Duncan's expanding perceptions when he gets there. IMPERIAL EARTH is a travelogue of the kind of future Arthur C. Clarke may well actually believe we're going to get. The effect is soothing, pathos-ridden, uplifting; a sort of pastoral high. The occasional sombre note does no more to make Clarke into Barry Malzberg than 'Recessional' turned Kipling into George Gissing.

Filmed, IMPERIAL EARTH would be a vision of decerebrate zombies roaming Alphaville. So what is truth? Maybe we don't really need the bloody movie.

SOME OF THE CONTRIBUTORS TO NEW WORLDS 10

MICHAEL MOORCOCK was from 1964 editor (and later publisher) of NW and NWQ. His first story in NW was in 1958, *Going Home*, a collaboration with B. J. Bayley. He is the author of some forty books, most of which he terms 'Fantastic Romances' (Elric, Hawkmoon, Corum, etc.), including the Jerry Cornelius novels and *Behold the Man*, which won the Nebula with the short version published in NW in 1966. He occasionally performs with the rock band Hawkwind (for whom he writes) and has made an album with his own band The Deep Fix (*New Worlds Fair*). *Constant Five* is the last of a series of novellas for NWQ about 'The Dancers at the End of Time' (itself the overall title of a trilogy comprising *An Alien Heat*, *The Hollow Lands* and *The End of All Songs*). He has recently completed the final volume of his Jerry Cornelius tetralogy, *The Condition of Muzak.*

MICHAEL BUTTERWORTH is 28, editor and publisher of *Corridor* and *Wordworks*, magazines of new writing. His many short stories, which have appeared in *New Worlds*, *Ambit* and *SF Monthly*, have been anthologised. He has just completed a novel, *Time of the Hawklords*, ('Hawkwind rocking at the end of time',) in collaboration with Michael Moorcock. Born in Yorkshire, he now lives in Manchester, a single parent with two young children.

BARRY BAYLEY is a regular contributor to NW. His novel, *Soul of the Robot*, is published by Allison and Busby.

ADRIAN ECKERSLEY is 28. After a career as a student and car mechanic he now teaches English at a polytechnic near London. 'My ambition is to write a rock opera that is neither plastic nor decadent.' *Con* is his first published story.

WILLIAM JON WATKINS is 34 and lives in the USA with his wife, Sandra, and three children. He has published three novels, *Ecodeath, The God Machine* and *Clickwhistle* and many short stories, poems and reviews. He is an Associate Professor in Humanities at Brookdale Community College in New Jersey. He works at night, often writing from 11 to 5 a.m.

ROBERT CALVERT is a poet and musician, singer with the heavy rock group, *Hawkwind*. His latest album is called *Lucky Leif and the Longships* (with Michael Moorcock on banjo).

ROBERT MEADLEY is 28, was born in Yorkshire and now lives in London. 'Expelled public school,' he says, 'dispelled university, one-time anarchist, pamphleteer and itinerant layabout, lapsed dabbler in educational research, refuse disposal and the crating of sculptures – now at a loose end.' He has published stories in *New Worlds* and *Frendz* and is currently working on a novel.

ANNA OSTROWSKA lives in Bicester, Oxfordshire. She left school recently and *Time Machine* is her first story.

PETER JOBLING heads the Art Department of a large comprehensive school in the North East. His first story appeared in *New Worlds 8.*

NICHOLAS EMMETT, an Irishman, lives in Norway with his Norwegian wife. As a young man he had fifty jobs – in a tobacco factory, as a newspaper seller and as a platelayer on the railway in a gang mainly consisting of tough ex-convicts. He has lived all over Europe, was owner driver of a taxi in Dublin for six years and has published many short stories and articles in newspapers and magazines and had a one-act play done at the Abbey Theatre, Dublin.

KEITH ROBERTS was born in Northamptonshire in 1935. An ex-editor of *SF Impulse*, in which his *Pavane* story cycle first appeared, he produced many cover paintings for both *Impulse* and *New Worlds* and still earns his living partly as an artist. More recent publications include his short story collection, *Machines and Men*, an historical novel, *The Boat of Fate*/and *The Chalk Giants*, sections of which first appeared in the *New Worlds Quarterly* series. Another collection, *The Grain Kings*, is due shortly from Hutchinson's.

He lives at present a few yards from the end of the Regatta course at Henley-on-Thames. Rowing is one of the few things in which he is not interested.

THOMAS M. DISCH has published many short stories in *New Worlds*. He is the author of the sf novels *The Genocides*, *Camp Concentration*, and *334* and wrote the mystery novel, *Black Alice*, in collaboration with John Sladek. He has edited many anthologies, including the much-praised *Bad Moon Rising*. He lives in New York.

JOHN CLUTE has been associated with *New Worlds* and *New Worlds Quarterly* since 1966, when one of his few short stories, *A Man Must Die*, was published. He has written criticism for *New Worlds* and *Fantasy and Science Fiction*. His novel, *The Disinheriting Party*, (an early version of part of which appeared in NWQ 5) is published by Allison and Busby.

GEOFF RYMAN is a young Canadian living in Britain. He has published two articles on Andy Warhol in *Photon*, a US magazine, and is currently working on a series of children's books, to be published by Stainer and Bell. *Diary of a Translator* is his first published story.

THE SHIP WHO SANG by ANNE McCAFFREY

The brain was perfect, the tiny, crippled body useless. So technology rescued the brain and put it in an environment that conditioned it to live in a different kind of body – a spaceship. Here the human mind, more subtle, infinitely more complex than any computer ever devised, could be linked to the massive and delicate strengths, the total recall, and the incredible speeds of space. But the brain behind the ship was entirely feminine – a complex, loving, strong, weak, gentle, savage – a personality, all-woman, called Helva. . . .

0 552 10163 X – 65p

RESTOREE by ANNE McCAFFREY

There was a sudden stench of a dead sea creature. . . .

There was the horror of a huge black shape closing over her. . . .

There was nothing. . . .

Then there were pieces of memory . . . isolated fragments that were so horrible her mind refused to accept them . . . intense heat and shivering cold . . . excruciating pain . . . dismembered pieces of the human body . . . sawn bones and searing screams. . . .

And when she awoke she found she was in a world that was not earth, and with a face and body that were not her face and body.

She had become a Restoree. . . .

0 552 10161 3 – 65p

A SELECTED LIST OF CORGI SCIENCE FICTION FOR YOUR READING PLEASURE

☐ 10022 6	NEW WORLDS NINE	*ed. Hilary Bailey*	50p
☐ 10182 6	NEW WORLDS TEN	*ed. Hilary Bailey*	50p
☐ 09824 8	NEQ THE SWORD	*Piers Anthony*	40p
☐ 09731 4	SOS THE ROPE	*Piers Anthony*	40p
☐ 09736 5	VAR THE STICK	*Piers Anthony*	40p
☐ 09081 6	STAR TREK 2	*James Blish*	25p
☐ 09082 4	STAR TREK 3	*James Blish*	25p
☐ 09445 5	STAR TREK 4	*James Blish*	30p
☐ 09446 3	STAR TREK 5	*James Blish*	30p
☐ 09447 1	STAR TREK 6	*James Blish*	30p
☐ 09765 9	THE HALLOWEEN TREE	*Ray Bradbury*	60p
☐ 09492 7	NEW WRITINGS IN SF 22	*ed. Kenneth Bulmer*	35p
☐ 09681 4	NEW WRITINGS IN SF 23	*ed. Kenneth Bulmer*	40p
☐ 09554 0	NINE PRINCES IN AMBER	*Roger Zelazny*	35p
☐ 09608 3	JACK OF SHADOWS	*Roger Zelazny*	35p
☐ 09906 6	THE GUNS OF AVALON	*Roger Zelazny*	45p
☐ 10021 8	THE DOORS OF HIS FACE	*Roger Zelazny*	50p
☐ 10161 3	RESTOREE	*Anne McCaffrey*	65p
☐ 10162 1	DECISION AT DOONA	*Anne McCaffrey*	65p
☐ 10163 X	THE SHIP WHO SANG	*Anne McCaffrey*	65p

CORGI SF COLLECTOR'S LIBRARY

☐ 09237 1	FANTASTIC VOYAGE	*Isaac Asimov*	50p
☐ 09784 5	THE SILVER LOCUSTS	*Ray Bradbury*	40p
☐ 09238 X	FAHRENHEIT 451	*Ray Bradbury*	35p
☐ 09706 3	I SING THE BODY ELECTRIC	*Ray Bradbury*	45p
☐ 09333 5	THE GOLDEN APPLES OF THE SUN	*Ray Bradbury*	40p
☐ 09413 7	REPORT ON PLANET THREE	*Arthur C. Clarke*	40p
☐ 09473 0	THE CITY AND THE STARS	*Arthur C. Clarke*	40p
☐ 09236 3	DRAGONFLIGHT	*Anne McCaffrey*	65p
☐ 09474 9	A CANTICLE FOR LEIBOWITZ	*Walter M. Miller Jr.*	45p
☐ 09414 5	EARTH ABIDES	*George R. Stewart*	35p
☐ 09239 8	MORE THAN HUMAN	*Theodore Sturgeon*	35p
☐ 10213 X	STAR SURGEON	*James White*	50p
☐ 10214 8	HOSPITAL STATION	*James White*	50p

All these books are available at your bookshop or newsagent; or can be ordered direct from the publisher. Just tick the titles you want and fill in the form below.

CORGI BOOKS, Cash Sales Department, P.O. Box 11, Falmouth, Cornwall.

Please send cheque or postal order, no currency.

U.K. send 18p for first book plus 8p per copy for each additional book ordered to a maximum charge of 66p to cover the cost of postage and packing.

B.F.P.O. and Eire allow 18p for first book plus 8p per copy for the next 6 books, thereafter 3p per book.

NAME (block letters)..

ADDRESS ....

(AUGUST 76)..

While every effort is made to keep prices low, it is sometimes necessary to increase prices at short notice. Corgi Books reserve the right to show new retail prices on covers which may differ from those previously advertised in the text or elsewhere.